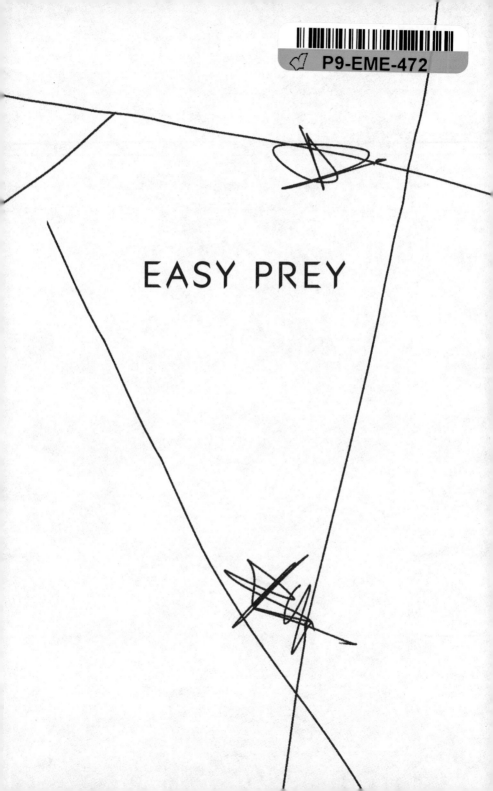

EASY PREY

EASY PREY

by Catherine Lo

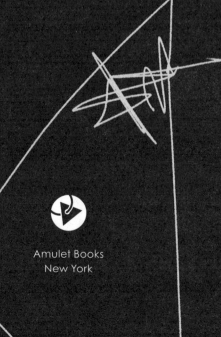

Amulet Books
New York

PUBLISHER'S NOTE: This is a work of fiction. Names, characters, places, and incidents are either the product of the author's imagination or used fictitiously, and any resemblance to actual persons, living or dead, business establishments, events, or locales is entirely coincidental.

Library of Congress Cataloging-in-Publication Data

Names: Lo, Catherine, author.
Title: Easy prey / by Catherine Lo.
Description: New York: Amulet Books, 2018. | Summary: Told in three voices, Edgewood High School students Mouse, Drew, and Jenna not only had access to a teacher's racy photographs before they went viral, each had a motive for using them.
Identifiers: LCCN 2018001780 | ISBN 978-1-4197-3190-7 (hardcover with jacket)
Subjects: | CYAC: Sexting—Fiction. | Gossip—Fiction. | Social media—Fiction. | Conduct of life—Fiction. | High schools—Fiction. | Schools—Fiction. | Mystery and detective stories.
Classification: LCC PZ7.1.L6 Eas 2018 | DDC [Fic] —dc23

ISBN 978-1-4197-3190-7

Text copyright © 2018 Catherine Lo
Cover art copyright © 2018 June Park
Top photo © David Zach/Getty Images; middle photo © Studio Paolo NYC; bottom photo by Timothy Paul Smith on Unsplash
Book design by Siobhán Gallagher

Printed and bound in U.S.A.
10 9 8 7 6 5 4 3 2 1

Amulet Books® is a registered trademark of Harry N. Abrams, Inc.

Amulet Books are available at special discounts when purchased in quantity for premiums and promotions as well as fundraising or educational use. Special editions can also be created to specification. For details, contact specialsales@abramsbooks.com or the address below.

ABRAMS The Art of Books
195 Broadway, New York, NY 10007
abramsbooks.com

For Ernie, Ethan, and Mackenzie.
Always and forever.

TODAY . . . .

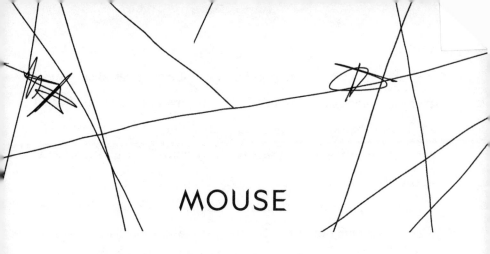

MOUSE

PARKING LOT. Edgewood High School. 7:34 a.m.

"I said seven o'clock, right?" Drew asks for the fifth time, checking his enormous watch. "I should have just told her six thirty, so she'd make it on time."

He glares at me like it's my fault. Like I have any control over what Jenna does.

"She'll be here," I mutter. I pull out my phone to text her again just as she comes into view across the parking lot. She's walking deliberately slowly, refusing to rush just because Drew summoned us here. That's how I know she hasn't seen it yet.

"Nice of you to join us," Drew calls, leaning back against his car with his arms crossed over his chest. "We've only been standing out here for forty minutes waiting for you."

I take an involuntary step back as Jenna's eyes snap onto Drew from across the parking lot. Her spine stiffens and she picks up her pace, homing in on us like a torpedo.

"Good morning to you, too, Drew," she says, batting her

eyelashes in a very un-Jenna-like way. "Such a great idea to meet at the ass-crack of dawn. I do so love paying to take public transit a full hour before my school bus runs." She grips a cup of cheap gas-station coffee so hard that her fingernails leave little crescents in the Styrofoam.

I am forever watching Jenna's hands. There's something mesmerizing about how graceful they are. She took ballet right up until last year, when she suddenly abandoned all her old interests. And though she tries her hardest to look tough, her hands give her away every time.

"I see you both have cars today," she says pointedly, looking between my mother's Corolla and Drew's BMW Roadster. "How very gentlemanly of you to offer me a ride."

I look down to avoid her eyes. Drew can be a jerk, so she won't be surprised he didn't drive her, but I know she'll find it suspicious that I didn't offer. Jenna and I have been friends since sixth grade—back when everyone called me Matthew instead of Mouse and back when Jenna still trusted people.

The truth is, Drew and I made a pact in the middle of the night that we'd all come in separately this morning. Neither of us wanted the other to get to Jenna first with the news.

She walks over and sets her coffee on the hood of Drew's BMW, making his fingers twitch. That car is Drew's life. He polishes it every day and parks it out here at the far edges of the parking lot so that no one will bump or scrape it.

Drew swallows hard, a muscle in his jaw jumping. When he finally speaks, I can tell the effort it's taking to keep his voice light. "I'd have offered you a ride, but I'm pretty sure your mother would shoot me on sight if I showed up at your door at seven o'clock in the morning."

The corner of Jenna's mouth twitches as she tries to hold back a smile. "I *knew* you were afraid of my mom."

I grit my teeth as a moment passes between them. It's like I'm invisible. Jenna's eyes are crinkled up in a way that makes my knees weak, and Drew is flashing his dimples at her. They probably wouldn't even notice if I walked away right now, and if we weren't on the verge of a crisis of epic proportions, I probably would.

"If the two of you are done," I interrupt, "can we please talk about @yrwrstnitemare now?"

Jenna startles, like she's just realizing I'm here. *Fantastic.* "Morning, Mouse," she says. "What the hell's *at your worst nightmare?*"

"You seriously don't know?" Drew asks, stepping between us.

Jenna throws her hands in the air. "Jesus Christ, you two. Someone just tell me what the hell is going on."

"It's a Twitter handle," I tell her, fishing my phone out of my back pocket. "@yrwrstnitemare. Someone posted a tweet from it just after midnight."

I hand my phone to her, and she barely glances at it. "So what? You called me here because some idiot tweeted in the middle of the night?"

"Open the link, Jen," Drew tells her, his voice unnervingly flat.

She rolls her eyes and touches her finger to my phone screen. "Holy shit."

"Now you get it?" Drew asks.

"Holy shit! Holy shit . . . holy shit . . . holy shit . . ." Jenna scrolls to the bottom of the Web page and then walks over to the curb and sits down, her head between her knees. Either she really didn't see it till now, or she should seriously consider a career in acting.

"Why?" she moans, lifting her head and glaring at us. "We made a deal. You guys promised to erase those."

"We did! This wasn't us," I tell her, looking over at Drew to back me up. "Jen, you have to know that I'd . . . *we'd* never do this."

She scrolls through the photos on my phone again. "What is this? A blog?"

"Totally anonymous," Drew says. "I checked it out this morning. Anyone could have set that up."

Jenna looks back and forth between us, and I have to work hard not to shrink under the intensity of her stare. "I want to believe you guys, but *come on*. This is every single photo we had. No one but us even knew about these pictures. The only explanation that makes any sense is that it was one—or more—of us, and I know it wasn't *me*."

"Well, it wasn't me," Drew says, meeting her gaze and holding it. Jen stands up and walks over till they're almost nose-to-nose.

"Say it again," she says.

"It wasn't me."

She searches his eyes and then nods her head before turning to me.

"You can't be serious!" I squeak out.

"Say it."

"You *know* me, Jen. I'd never do something like this."

"Then say it."

I swallow hard and meet her gaze, my heart breaking into a million pieces. "It wasn't me."

We stare at each other for what feels like an eternity before Drew interrupts. "Listen. How easy was it for us to get ahold of those pictures? For all we know, Bailey was sending them to tons of people."

Jenna breaks my stare and blinks at Drew. "You think so?"

"Absolutely. There's no saying it was even a student. Anyone could have tweeted that link. Right, Mouse?" He looks over at me with eyebrows raised.

"Of course," I choke out, even though it seems incredibly unlikely. No one but a student would have created a blog called *Miss Bailey Exposed*, and the original tweet included the athletic council's Twitter account as a mention, which explains how it went viral so fast. Someone on the council retweeted it within the hour, and then every student athlete in school went nuts. By the time I checked Twitter at six o'clock this morning, it had already been retweeted sixteen hundred times. I don't tell Jenna any of this, though. I'm still reeling over the fact that she doesn't trust me.

"We have to stick together on this," Drew says, taking Jenna's hands. "We didn't do anything wrong, but it wouldn't look good if any of us talked about the photos." He stops to look at me. "I need to know right now if either one of you told *anyone*."

I shake my head. "Who would I tell?"

Drew smirks. "Jen?"

She rolls her eyes. "Yeah, Drew. I bragged about the fact that I'd seen my law teacher naked."

"OK then," Drew says, shrugging his shoulders like this is all a nonissue. "We're golden. There's nothing tying us to those pictures. No one knows we had them, and we had Mouse's big brain covering our tracks the whole time. We officially know nothing about anything."

Jenna bites her lip. "You really think it's that easy?" she asks, looking at me.

"Sure," I say, nodding way too fast to be convincing. "We're totally fine."

FOUR WEEKS AGO . . .

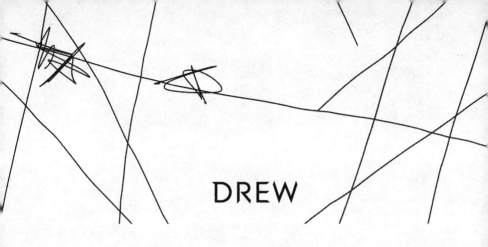

DREW

"EYES ON YOUR OWN PAPERS!" Miss Bailey snaps, patrolling up and down the rows of desks like a prison guard on the lookout for contraband.

I wait till she passes and then slide the blank test off my desk and into my backpack, replacing it with the copy I'd filled out earlier. This class is a joke.

My buddy Kevin snickers to my right. I smile at him and then hunch over my paper as Bailey heads back down my row. You'd think, with how carefully she watches us during tests, that it would be hard to cheat in her class. You'd be wrong.

This is the fifth year Miss Bailey has taught senior law, and she has never, not once, changed up her tests or lessons. Back a few years ago, when my older brother, Harrison, took this class, people used to sell their notebooks at the end of the semester. These days, everything is posted online. Most people memorize the answers the night before, but I can't be bothered with that shit. I download the tests, Photoshop out the old answers, and then print them off and fill them in. The only challenge is making enough "mistakes" that I don't raise any red flags.

Technology is a beautiful thing.

By the time Bailey collects the tests and begins droning on about how our Canadian judicial system differs from the United States', I'm bored out of my mind. I flip to the calendar in the back of my binder to see what other thrilling topics she has in store for us.

I'm not going to lie. I took this course for the easy A, just like everyone else. Who wants to spend their last year of high school stressing about college cutoffs? Senior year is for partying. It's for making memories and going out with a bang. Which explains why this class is stacked with almost every senior on the basketball and football teams, as well as the entire cheerleading squad. The only exceptions are Jenna Bradley, who recently abandoned her goody-two-shoes persona and joined the rest of us in slackerdom, and Mouse Maguire, genius extraordinaire. Kids like Mouse don't take joke courses like senior law. Unless they're in love with Jenna Bradley, of course. I don't need a mega-brain like Mouse's to see why he's in this class.

According to the calendar, Bailey'll be announcing the group project today. That project is the one thing we can't fake in this pathetic class. Bailey chooses the groups herself and picks a new topic each year from current events.

I let my eyes rove over my classmates, wondering who I'll be working with. I'm hoping for either Candace Murphy or Keisha Clarke, but any of the girls in class will do. Except Jenna. Jesus.

My phone vibrates in my back pocket, but I know better than to check it with Bailey in the room. She has a strict "No Devices" policy and has been known to confiscate phones for days. She's probably afraid we'll take video of her god-awful teaching practices. If I sucked this badly at my job, I wouldn't risk anyone recording me, either.

"All right, class," Miss Bailey says, shuffling the notes on her desk. "I want to discuss your next assignment, and I'll need everyone's full attention."

Kevin leans across the aisle and kicks at my shoe. "Solid three today."

"You're high," I say, scoping out Bailey. "Five. At least."

"What are you guys talking about?" Ella Martins purrs from behind me. She's leaning forward over her desk with her arms pressed to her sides to show off maximum cleavage.

Kevin raises his eyebrows at me, but I shake my head in response. Ella wouldn't see the humor in our rating scale.

She pouts and flutters her eyelashes, so Kevin leans in for a better view. "I'm just deciding what time I should pick you up tonight," he tells her.

"Dream on, Kevin," she says, before giving me a long look. Poor Kev. Ella's been throwing herself at me for months, but she's too sweet for my tastes. I like my girls with a little more bite to them.

"If you're all done with social hour back there," Bailey interrupts, "I'd love to get on with my class."

Kevin looks from Bailey to me and shakes his head sadly. "You're right, man," he mutters. "Definite five."

We started the rating scale a few months ago, after Miss Bailey started wearing low-cut, skintight tops and short skirts to class. Every day before practice, we rate each day's outfit by how many beers we'd have to drink before getting freaky with her.

"Now that I have your attention, this next assignment is a group project that will be worth 15 percent of your final grade." Bailey puts her hands on her hips and glares around the room, waiting for us to complain. It's too bad she's such a bitch. She does have sort of a banging body, if you don't mind that she's kinda short and has a nose that's too big for her face. Still, from the neck down . . .

"I know this won't be popular, but I don't believe in letting students choose their own groups. I've had far too much experience with people making poor choices about group members, so several years ago I decided that it was better all around for me to assign the groups for you." This is a lie and we all know it. Bailey has chosen the groups since she first started teaching this course. She's so full of shit.

"I'll be handing out the assignment sheets to group leaders, who will be in charge of coordinating all work. Leaders, you've been selected because you are responsible and because I feel you possess the skills necessary to keep your group on track. Your assignment sheet lists the names of your fellow group members. As soon as I've finished handing out the papers, please find your group and begin with step one."

I catch Keisha looking over at me and give her a wink. She licks her lips and then mouths, *I hope we're in the same group.*

Me too, Keisha. Me too.

Chairs scrape against the floor as group leaders scurry around trying to coordinate their groups. I keep my eyes on Keisha, but the pout that transforms her face as Ella sits beside her and shows her their assignment sheet lets me know that I didn't score a spot with them. That's a shame. Between Ella and Keisha, I wouldn't have to lift a finger the whole project.

"Um . . . Drew?"

My heart sinks a little at the sound of a guy's voice but absolutely plummets when I look up to find Mouse standing over me. This has got to be a joke.

"Yeah?" I'm praying that he just needs to get past me to whatever unfortunate soul Bailey paired up with him.

"We're . . . um . . . we're in the same group." He steps aside and motions behind him, where I see Jenna standing. "The three of us."

What. The. Fuck.

I look up at Bailey to see if this is some kind of sick joke. This class is full of my best friends, and I end up working with Mouse Maguire and Boobs Bradley?

"You're kidding," I say, before I can stop myself.

Mouse looks miserable. And well he should. This has to be the most awkward grouping in the history of high school.

Jenna narrows her eyes at me but then pastes a wide smile on so fast that I wonder if I imagined the bitter look. "Are you saying you're not excited to be working with me?"

I blink at her, confused. Jenna hates me. Me and everyone else on the basketball team. So why do I detect a hint of flirtatiousness in her tone?

She grabs a chair and pulls it up beside me so that our legs are touching, before turning hooded eyes on Mouse. "So, fill us in, group leader. What's our bullshit topic?"

"Shh!" Mouse hisses, craning his neck to make sure Bailey isn't listening.

"Oh, don't be such a hypocrite," Jenna says, making him squirm. "You hate this class. You've filed at least five complaints about Bailey since the beginning of semester."

"Whoa," I say, leaning forward. "You filed complaints about Bailey?"

"Shhh!" Mouse hisses again, sinking down into his seat and ducking his head. "I complained *confidentially*. I need this grade high enough that it doesn't pull down my average, and Miss Bailey will destroy me if she finds out."

"*I'll* destroy you if you mess this up," I tell him. "This class is a gift. It's practically an Edgewood institution."

"It's a mockery of education."

"Give me a break. This class lets me stay on the basketball team and get into college without busting my ass. Besides, you knew what you were getting into when you signed up. What's to complain about?"

Mouse looks to Jenna for help, but she shrugs her shoulders and turns to me. "I've been telling him this same shit all semester."

"Forget it," Mouse mumbles, looking down at our assignment sheet. "Let's just get to work."

Jenna sighs. "He's upset because people who are cheating are getting better grades than him. Mouse isn't used to being anything other than the top student in a class."

"So why not cheat like the rest of us?" I ask.

"That's what *I* told him," Jenna says, shooting a pointed look at Mouse. "The whole reason I convinced you to take this class was to lower your stress levels. Not raise them."

"*Begged* me to take this class, you mean. And what a brilliant idea that was."

Jenna's eyes flash. "If you'd take the stick out of your ass, it would be. All you have to do is a quick Google search and you'd have all the answers to every test. You waste so much time on unnecessary shit."

Mouse sighs and pulls his laptop out of his bag. "What's the point of taking a class if you're not going to learn anything?"

"Is he serious?" I ask Jenna, before turning on Mouse. "Are you being serious right now?"

Mouse starts to say something in response, but his face freezes as he catches sight of his laptop screen.

"Like it?" Jenna asks, snapping her gum. "It's my way of saying thanks for saving my ass last night."

I slide my chair sideways and catch a glimpse of his screen before he snaps the laptop closed. "My Little Pony?"

"See? Even star athletes like Drew are Bronies."

"I am *not* a Brony," Mouse says through clenched teeth. "Stop saying that."

"What the hell is a Brony?" I ask, unable to keep the smile off my face. It's fun watching Jenna torture Mouse.

"Bronies are a fandom composed mainly of adult males who have a deep appreciation for the My Little Pony franchise," Jenna deadpans.

"That's not a thing," I say.

"Everything's a thing," Jenna responds, just as Miss Bailey walks up.

"It doesn't seem like there's a lot of productive work going on here," Bailey says. She turns to Mouse with arms crossed. "I wondered whether it was wise to put you in charge of your own group, but I took you seriously when you said you wanted the chance to develop some leadership skills. Do I need to reassign this role to Andrew?"

Mouse squints his eyes at her, obviously confused. "I never—"

"Hey, Miss Bailey," Jenna interrupts, popping her gum loudly. "How come you didn't make *me* group leader?"

Bailey sighs and shakes her head. "No gum in my class, Jenna. You know that."

"Oh, right!" Jenna takes the gum out of her mouth and smiles sweetly at Bailey before sticking it to the underside of her desk.

Then three things happen simultaneously: Miss Bailey goes apeshit, Mouse groans and buries his face in his hands, and I fall in love.

"Get. Out," Bailey shouts, her voice cracking. "And don't come back until you are ready to apologize for your behavior."

Jenna salutes her and picks up her bag, blowing a kiss at me and Mouse before walking out of the room.

Bailey takes a step after her and then stops, seeming to falter. She turns and takes in the shocked faces of my classmates, and her face flames red. "Back to work everyone," she says with forced cheerfulness. "The show's over." She smooths her skirt and tucks her hair behind her ears before squaring her shoulders and walking over to Mouse's desk. "I will never understand your friendship with her," she says with quiet rage. "And I have no idea why you'd ever want to work with her."

Mouse blinks hard behind his Coke-bottle glasses as Bailey walks away. "I'm so screwed," he groans. "She's going to fail me just for being friends with Jenna, isn't she?" He rubs his forehead and looks to me for reassurance. "How does she know I wanted to work with Jenna, anyway?"

"*Everyone* knows you want to work with her," I tell him. "You practically drool every time you look at her."

His eyes go wide and he starts sputtering at me, falling over himself to deny what anyone with eyes can see. Poor kid. He's friend-zoned and doesn't even realize it. Of course, if you ask me, he's lucky to even be friends with a girl like Jenna. She's hot and dangerous and . . .

. . . And I really need to stop thinking about her or risk getting my ass kicked. Because she's my best friend Troy's ex-girlfriend. Troy, who also happens to be Mouse's cousin. This little study group of ours couldn't be more awkward.

Mouse opens his laptop and cringes again at the sight of the desktop background.

"How'd Jenna get ahold of that thing, anyway?" I ask him. Mouse guards his laptop like state secrets are buried in there.

"Long story," he mumbles, angling the screen away from the class so he can change the background without anyone noticing. "Hers broke last night and she had a paper to finish. She called me in a panic and I had to run mine over to her house."

"You're so whipped," I tease him, slapping him on the shoulder and nearly knocking him out of his chair. "I hope you password-protected your porn."

"Very funny."

Bailey walks past our desks again, so I muster up some fake enthusiasm. "What's our project topic, group leader?"

Mouse looks down and groans.

"What?"

"It's . . . *Privacy laws and the Internet.*"

I was wrong. Things just officially became more awkward.

The sound of the bell rescues me from the torture that is working with Mouse. Bailey wanted a detailed timeline of when we'd be meeting to work on the project, and Mouse was terrified to put anything down on paper without Jenna's approval.

"Jesus Christ," I said, ripping the page away from him. "Just write shit down. It's not like Bailey's going to show up at your house to make sure we're sticking to the schedule." I wrote down a bunch of random dates and handed it in just as the bell rang.

Out in the hall, Kevin falls into step beside me, gloating over the fact that he's in Keisha and Ella's group.

"Maybe you'll finally get some play," I joke. Kevin's not known for his luck with the ladies. The trouble is, he tries way too hard, and it freaks girls out.

"Aw, don't be jealous," he mocks me, pulling me into a headlock and kicking open the door to the locker room. "Maybe you'll manage to bag J—"

Kevin catches sight of Troy across the locker room and shuts the hell up.

Troy is one of those guys who rival teams ask to see the paperwork for, to confirm that he's not some college kid we smuggled onto our team. He's six-and-a-half feet tall, with arm muscles that are bigger than my thighs, which isn't easy to take. Walking down the hall with Troy makes me look like I'm thirteen years old. He's my best friend in the world, though. Troy's what my dad calls a *stand-up guy*. He keeps his word, he never betrays a confidence, and he values friendship in a way that most guys don't. So I put up with looking like his wimpy white friend, because I can't imagine my life without him.

"Hey, asshole," Troy shouts across the room. "I hear you're working with Jenna."

"Thanks a lot," I mutter to Kevin. I'd been hoping to tell Troy myself. Preferably when he was fall-down drunk on Friday night, so he wouldn't be able to get in a good swing at me.

Kevin shakes his head and holds his hands up in the air. "Wasn't me, man. I had my hands too full with Keisha and Ella. No time for texting Troy when I'm surrounded by luscious cheerleaders."

"Luscious?" I ask, trying to keep a straight face. "No wonder you can't get laid."

I laugh at the look on Kevin's face and then make my way over to Troy.

"Dude," I say, fist-bumping him. "It's a fucking nightmare of a group project. Bailey's class. I'd switch groups if I could, but Bailey's a bitch. I'm stuck with both Jenna and your cousin, if you can believe that shit."

Troy laughs and shakes his head. "I told you not to take that bullshit class."

"I still can't believe you *didn't* take it," I say, pulling off my shirt and reaching into my locker for my gym uniform. "It's an Edgewood tradition. All the jocks take it."

"All the *dumb* jocks take it. Besides, you couldn't pay me to sit through Bailey's class. She's insane."

"Can't argue with you there—about Bailey, not about me being a dumb jock."

"You're the exception," he laughs, sitting down on the bench to tie his shoes.

"Holy shit! Are those the new Jordans?"

"Pretty sweet, huh?"

"You know I have to hate you now, right?" Troy is our town hero. If any of us will go on to play college ball—and maybe even in the NBA—it's Troy. It's the kind of story people love: star player from the poor end of town rising up to become famous. Everyone competes for Troy's attention, including local businesses. So even though he couldn't afford a pair of no-name shoes from Walmart on his own dime, he's always decked out in the latest gear. His old Jordans were hardly even broken in yet, and here he is with a brand-new pair that won't hit the shelves till next month.

"I'd give you my old ones, but I don't think they'd fit your dainty little feet," he says, sliding off the bench as I take a swing at him. Troy loves making fun of my size, and while I'm not exactly a small guy, my size-eleven shoes can't really stack up against his size fourteens.

"You're getting faster," I say, getting in my own dig. Troy might outshoot me on the court, but I always outrun him on the track.

"You know it," he says, bobbing and weaving. "C'mon. Just try and land one."

Everyone stops what they're doing and watches us go at it. We're just fooling around, but everyone starts cheering and yelling like it's a real fight.

I take a couple of halfhearted swings, just to keep him moving. The more defensive he's being, the less likely he is to land anything.

"I thought you were working out?" he jeers, sidestepping me and landing a hit on my left side. It hurts, but I can tell he pulled the punch, which pisses me off.

I hop up and down on the balls of my feet, shaking out my arms to distract myself from the pain. "That's all you got? You're getting soft, Maguire."

"Yeah, right," he says, coming at me again.

I feint left and then swing around, landing a hard punch to his belly. It's like hitting a brick wall, and the impact zings all the way up my arm.

I surprise us both with the hit. I didn't pull that punch at all. In fact, I pretty much gave it all I had.

"Shit," Troy laughs, bending over and rubbing his stomach. "That one hurt!"

I suspect he's playing things up to make me look good, but I feel a swell of pride anyways. "Sorry, bro. Got carried away." I reach out to pat him on the shoulder and he pulls me into a headlock.

"One question," he says, low so only I can hear. "You planning on making moves on Jenna?"

"Never," I tell him.

"Good man," Troy says, letting me go and nudging my shoulder. The guys around us start bitching, disappointed our fight trailed off.

I finish changing slowly, waiting for the crowd to disperse.

"Let's go, already." Troy prods, standing by the locker-room door. He can't stand being the last one into the gym. Everything is a competition to Troy.

"How'd you hear Jenna was in my group?" I ask, curious about who the gossip was. I know it wasn't Jenna—she hasn't spoken to Troy since the day her topless photos made the rounds at school thanks to his Twitter account. He's only now just started to get over the heartache of losing her. He tried convincing her it wasn't him, but she wouldn't listen to anything he had to say. She cut him off completely. Just like that.

Troy barks out a laugh and flashes me a smile. "I hear everything, Drew. Remember that."

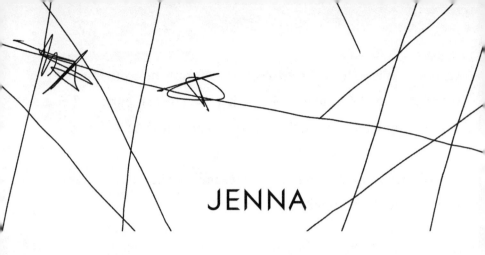

JENNA

"JENNA BRADLEY TO THE OFFICE, PLEASE. Jenna Bradley to the office."

I pick up my phone to check the time. 9:35. Isaacs is early today, which means I'm busted. I should be in English class right now, not camped out in a stairwell avoiding human contact.

Mrs. Isaacs is my vice principal, and Tuesdays are our check-in days. I'm to report to the office before my first-period class for one of her pep talks about *getting back on track* and *not letting the actions of others determine the course of my future*. But I never report before first period. And it usually takes her until she's finished her second cup of coffee around ten o'clock to bother tracking me down.

I flip my notebook shut and shove it in my bag. She'll want to know why I'm skipping second period. I smile to myself, wondering how she'd take the truth: I used up all my patience in Bailey's class this morning and decided I needed a break from the bullshit. I doubt she'd appreciate the honesty, though. Isaacs isn't particularly interested in the truth.

I take the long way to the office, stopping by my locker to drop off my books and the vending machines to pick up an iced tea. When I figure just enough time has elapsed that Isaacs is irritated but not so mad that she's tempted to phone home, I stroll into the office and give a little salute to Miss Singh, the head secretary. She's a riot, Miss Singh. I can usually count on a few minutes of shooting the shit with her before Isaacs calls me back. No one knows more about what goes on in a school than the secretaries.

"Good morning, Trouble," she greets me. "You should know that Mrs. Isaacs got a call from your law teacher before paging you to the office."

I lean against the wall beside her desk. "Level of irritation?"

"Miss Bailey's or Mrs. Isaacs's?"

"Isaacs's. I already know Bailey was flipping her shit."

"Language, please, Miss Bradley. My sensitive ears cannot handle your swearing."

"You sound like my grandma," I tease her. Miss Singh is in her mid-thirties, and she's forever freaking out about her age.

"Your *grandmother*," she sputters, with fake irritation. "You listen here, you little whippersnapper!"

Whippersnapper. It sounds hilarious in her accent, and I laugh so hard I snort.

"I didn't expect to find you in such high spirits, Jenna," Mrs. Isaacs interrupts. "Particularly after hearing from your first-period teacher."

Damn that woman and her silent shoes. Why can't she wear heels?

I turn and wink at Miss Singh and then rearrange my face into the look of aggressive disinterest that I've perfected over the last year. "First period . . . ?" I ask, like I can't remember what happened.

"Apparently, the only period you've attended so far today." She turns and walks toward her office. I'm tempted to stay where I am, but I'm not in the mood for the fallout. Instead, I pop open my can of iced tea and take a long sip as I follow her back to her jail cell of an office.

"How long has it been since our last check-in, Jenna," Mrs. Isaacs asks, settling into her chair and eyeing my drink. Her No Food or Beverages rule won't hold today.

I shrug. "Sometime last week."

She opens the notebook on her desk and flips through the pages. "Last Tuesday. Do you remember what we talked about?"

"Same as always. My attendance, grades, classes . . ." I let my voice trail off. The check-ins are a sore spot with me because they're total bullshit. They're all about Isaacs feeling better about what happened and have nothing to do with me.

"And do you remember what I asked you?"

I shake my head and study the contents of the corkboard mounted to the wall beside me. Isaacs chooses a new theme each month and plasters the board with pamphlets. This month is Internet Safety. I smirk.

"Jenna?"

"Yes."

"Yes, you remember what I asked you?"

"No."

She sighs, flipping forward in her book and making a note under today's date. I lean forward to read it. *Uncooperative.* Sounds about right.

She raises her eyes and catches me reading, then moves the book to the far corner of her desk.

"Let's start again," she says in a buttery voice. "I want to help you. I always want to help you. But you tie my hands." She holds her hands out in front of her, as though they're in handcuffs. "It's hard to help someone who pushes me away at every turn."

I've heard a version of this talk a million times before. "I'm really doing fine, Mrs. Isaacs," I tell her. "Everything is great."

"Is that so?" She pulls a business card out of her top drawer and slides it across the desk toward me.

Lynda Donovan, Probation Officer

Oh holy hell.

"Ms. Donovan stopped by to check on your progress before closing your file."

My ears perk up at *closing your file.*

"I ask you every week about what's happening in your life, and yet somehow you've never thought to mention that you had charges pending or that you were on probation."

29

I shrug. "It was for something that happened outside of school."

"So I gather," she says wryly. "Ms. Donovan couldn't discuss the details without your consent. She did, however, mention that you've been attending court-mandated anger-management sessions and asked if I'd seen evidence of your *growth*."

According to Jillian, my court-appointed counselor, I have an anger-management problem that manifests itself in "acting out" behavior. She says that I have a tendency to react impulsively and that I need to channel my emotions in more constructive ways.

Whatever.

The very fact that I even *have* a court-appointed counselor is complete bullshit.

Ex-boyfriend posts pictures of girl's boobs on the Internet, he gets a slap on the wrist.

Ex-girlfriend lights a *tiny* fire inside his truck, she gets fifty hours of community service and court-mandated counseling.

Is there no justice in the world?

Of course, all that happened last year. I finished my community-service requirement last weekend, and if my probation officer is thinking of closing my file . . .

"What did you tell her?" I ask, making a special effort to sound casual.

"I said I would speak to a few of your teachers and get back to her. But then I got a phone call from Miss Bailey, and when I called your English classroom to find you, you weren't there.

What exactly am I supposed to tell your probation officer, Jenna?"

I shrug my shoulders and look away.

"You understand, don't you, that I can't lie? I would love to tell Ms. Donovan about the positive changes you've made, but from where I'm sitting, there aren't any improvements to report." She shuffles some papers on her desk and then reads from one. "Your grades have dropped 20 percent since this time last year. *Twenty percent.* Your attendance is atrocious, you show no regard for the rules of the school, you're rude and uncooperative in law class—"

"Bailey's a bitch," I interrupt. "It's not my fault that she's decided I'm worthless. You should see the way she treats me."

Mrs. Isaacs buries her face in her hands. "This is what I'm talking about," she mumbles through her fingers.

"Talk to my other teachers. Like Jones or Williams. They love me."

"Yes, they do. But they also all say the same thing—that you're smart and capable but don't work to your full potential. They love having you in class, but you're frequently absent—"

"It's not like I'm failing," I interrupt. "My grades are all in the seventies."

"Down from grades in the nineties last year. You've gone from being one of the most promising students at this school to being a juvenile delinquent." She waves Ms. Donovan's card in the air for emphasis. "It's not too late to turn things around, you know. Everyone around you wants to see you succeed. Especially me."

I level my gaze at her, taking deep breaths just like Jillian taught me.

"We've met every week since last year, Jenna, but you still won't open up to me. You sit in that chair and glare at me but give me absolutely nothing. If you'd at least *talk* to me . . . if you'd let me in just a little bit, then I'd have something to report back to Ms. Donovan."

"I don't want to talk to you," I say through clenched teeth. "I have my counselor and Ms. Donovan to talk to. These check-ins are a waste of time."

She stands up and wheels her chair around the edge of her desk, then sits down with her knees practically touching mine. I feel my back and neck stiffen, and the walls of the room start to close in.

"I'm not the enemy, Jenna. I know you're disappointed that we weren't able to decisively uncover whoever was responsible for posting those pictures of you last year, but you need to know that we did our best."

I count backward from ten to one and then imagine a wave of calm washing over me, but it's like trying to block a tsunami with a sandbag. Why is it Jillian never taught me anything *useful*?

"Bullshit!" I explode. "You had all the evidence in the world. It's not like the photos were posted from an anonymous account—you had Troy's tweet and every single person who retweeted it right there in black and white."

"It was more complicated than that—"

"No. You *chose* to ignore the evidence because without Troy and his friends, our basketball team would never have made it to the championships."

"You're simplifying what happened. You have to understand that those were very serious allegations that could have ruined a boy's life and destroyed a very promising career before it even got started. The sad fact is that students have access to each other's accounts, and there was a strong possibility that someone else could have tweeted the pictures other than Troy."

What about my life? I don't even bother to ask the question out loud.

"So, you could have investigated *that*," I say. "If this happened to someone else—like a teacher, or you, or your own daughter, you wouldn't quit trying to find out the truth at the first obstacle. You would make sure that everyone involved was punished. Tell me one person who got consequences. Just one. Because from where I'm sitting, the only person who got punished in all this was me."

"You know I can't discuss what happened to the other students,

Jenna, but I *am* glad that you're talking about this. It's good to get these feelings out."

I feel tears of frustration prickling my eyes, and I have to get out of here before they spill over. "This conversation is over," I tell her. "And so are the check-ins. Tell my probation officer whatever you want."

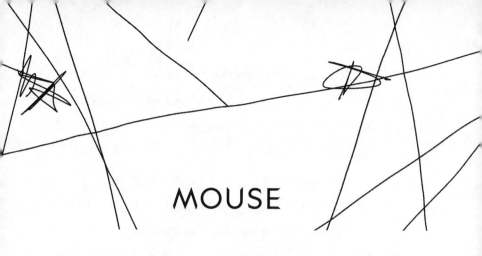

MOUSE

"MATTHEW," MY MOTHER SAYS SOFTLY, CHECKING THE HALLWAY BEHIND HER BEFORE SLIPPING INTO MY ROOM. "Your father loves you very much. You know that, don't you?"

This is what she always says.

I nod my head and open my Chemistry textbook, hoping she'll leave me alone. By my calculations, this is the twenty-seventh time we've had this conversation, and I'm painfully aware that nothing I say will ever change her mind.

"My darling boy," she says, sitting on the edge of the bed and cupping my face in her cool hands. "I wish you wouldn't take things to heart so much. Your father's bark is worse than his bite. It's just his way."

"I know," I force out, twisting away so that she's no longer touching me.

"He just worries about you, that's all. That girl caused a lot of trouble for your cousin and his family. And the things she did . . ." She gives a little shudder.

"*That girl* is Jenna, Mom. You know her."

She shakes her head and runs her hand over my hair. "I know the girl she used to be. People change, Matthew. And not always for the better."

I can't even swallow, my throat is so full of all the things I want to say but can't. All this because my dad decided to play the involved parent for an evening and spot-check my phone.

"Hand it over, son," he commanded when it chimed with an incoming text in the middle of dinner. I felt my stomach drop to the floor. My father does not allow devices at the dinner table, and I'd been a fool to leave it in the pocket of my blazer.

I stood up on shaky legs and took a step toward him. "I'm sorry, sir. I didn't realize my phone was in here." I patted the pocket of my jacket, hoping he'd accept the apology and move on.

"Obviously. But carelessness has consequences. It's been a while since I checked your phone, and this seems as good a time as ever."

I felt my heart throb in my chest. I hadn't erased Jenna's texts for days.

"I wish you'd trust me," I said, my stomach jumping around inside me. "I'm almost eighteen now, and I've never been in trouble for anything." It's true. The only time I've ever been called to the office was when they presented me with a merit award. Even with everything I did for Troy and his teammates last year, I've never had so much as a detention. But I knew my father wouldn't listen to that argument. If Golden Boy Troy could mess up, then anyone could.

"Almost eighteen isn't eighteen. And a boy isn't grown until he leaves his parents' house. Don't leave me waiting." He held out his hand and leveled me with his most intimidating stare.

I hesitated, wondering for a wild moment if I'd be able to unlock the phone and erase my messages before he could wrestle it from my hands. Given that my dad runs five miles a day and I need my inhaler just to climb the stairs, the odds were not good. Plus, even if I managed it, I'd get a beating for insubordination.

I took a deep breath and handed over my phone. My pulse pounded in my ears as I watched him swipe his finger across the screen and enter the passcode. The old passcode.

"Are you messing with me, son?"

"N-no sir. I'm sorry. The passcode is 8249."

He grunted and punched in the numbers, then slipped on his glasses and poked away at the screen. I looked over at my mother, who was fiddling with the napkin in her lap and avoiding my gaze.

I clasped my hands behind my back and tried to swallow down my panic. There wasn't anything incriminating in there except Jenna's texts. But that would be enough. That would be the worst, actually. If he'd found a photo of me snorting drugs, he wouldn't be as disappointed as seeing that I'm still talking to—

"Jenna Bradley," he said in a terrifyingly quiet voice.

I closed my eyes and wished I could disappear. I knew I should have saved her number with fake contact information a long time ago, but I could never bring myself to give up the thrill I got from seeing her name pop up on my screen every time she texted.

I heard the clatter of my phone dropping onto the table and eased open my eyes.

"You're still communicating with the girl who dragged your cousin's name through the mud."

I bit down on the insides of my cheeks to keep from arguing. If anyone's name got dragged through the mud, it was Jenna's. Troy's a hero in our high school and a star in this town. He got off scot-free, just like he always does, and Jenna became the slut who tried to ruin his life. Try telling that to my father, though. As far as he's concerned, Troy is perfect, and anyone who would dare question that perfection deserves whatever they have coming to them.

"We have a class together, and—"

"That was a yes or no question!" Dad shouted, slamming his fist down on the table and making my mother jump.

If I was a more self-destructive person, I'd have pointed out that it wasn't a question at all, but I preferred not to be reduced to a grease spot on the floor, so I just nodded my head and looked down.

"You have no loyalty. No honor. How many times have I told you that the only thing worth having in this world is your honor?"

I felt heat rushing into my face, and I wished I was brave

enough to turn the tables on my dad. To ask him how much honor is involved in bullying your own son.

"Your uncle and I grew up with nothing. We lived in a cramped apartment in a dangerous neighborhood, and we swore our own kids would never have to live like that. We've worked our butts off so that we could provide for you boys. So, tell me where I went wrong."

"You didn't—"

"You're goddamn right I didn't. My brother and I raised our boys the exact same way. So explain to me how his son is captain of the basketball team and my son is . . ." He waved his hand in my direction.

I blinked back tears and looked down at the table, knowing there was nothing I could say or do to make any difference.

My father sat back heavily in his chair. "I've been wondering why Troy doesn't come around here anymore . . . why you two stopped being friendly. And now I know. That boy has been nothing but good to you, and this is how you repay him."

Nothing but good to me. I'd have agreed to that up until last year, when he deserted me as soon as I was no longer useful to him.

"All of this is a mistake. I spent my life making sure you never had to struggle like I did, but it's the struggle that made me. Your mother and I have been too soft on you, and it's made you weak and entitled." He picked up my phone. "This is mine now. You need to *earn* your privileges from here on out, and you can start by apologizing to Troy for your disloyalty and telling *Jenna Bradley* that you want nothing to do with her. Am I understood?"

"Yes, sir," I said, even though what I wanted to say was, *she's a better person than you'll ever be.*

I think that's what's bothering me the most right now, as I sit here stewing in my room. Even more than my father's insults and my mother's excuses. What really bothers me is that I didn't defend Jenna. That I let my father spit out her name like something foul when she's the best thing that's ever happened to me.

I rub my eyes under my glasses as a wave of tiredness washes over me. It's useless to argue with my mother. She sees what she wants to see. "It's fine, Mom."

"So, you'll do what your father asks?" The hope in her eyes squeezes all the air out of my lungs. That's why she's really here.

"I said I would."

"I know that you're fond of her, but I think—"

"I said I would!" I snap.

She reels back like I hit her. "I'm just looking out for your best interests."

"Then get me my phone back," I mutter, looking away from her.

"You know I can't do that," she says, holding her hand up to my cheek again. "But it's just a phone. You'll do what your father asks and then everything can go back to normal."

I watch her slip out of my room and wonder why she works so hard to keep a peace that never lasts. There's always another argument around the corner with my dad. Always another way to let him down. You'd think she'd be tired of it by now. I know I am.

I slide out of bed and ease my door shut, turning the lock on the doorknob. Then I pull out the top drawer of my dresser and reach underneath for the envelope I've taped there. Between the five hundred dollars that Troy's teammates paid me for the database I designed and the sales from the apps I wrote to protect their photos and messaging programs, I've made well over a thousand dollars. And after paying the application fees for the schools I want to attend, I've got $945 left. I re-count the bills and then place them back in the envelope. It's nowhere near how much I'll need to move out, but it's a start.

Last year, when I told my father I wanted to go to either MIT or Cornell after graduation, he looked at me like I'd lost my mind. "What makes you think you could get into schools like those?"

I was shocked. "I've maintained an A average all through school," I reminded him. "I have perfect grades in both chemistry and physics right now. I'm smart, Dad. I can do this."

"It takes more than smarts to get into those American schools. Maybe if you were an athlete, like Troy, you'd have a hope of getting in. But just getting good grades doesn't make you special, son. You need to be well-rounded. And you are not a well-rounded person."

41

I blinked at him, trying to process his words. I'd always known my father looked down on me for not being more athletic, but I'd honestly thought he respected my intelligence. It had never occurred to me before that he saw me as anything less than brilliant.

Dad's face softened a bit at the look on my face. "Now don't feel bad. Your mother and I have never expected you to get into a school like Cornell. We'll be very proud of you if you get accepted to the University of Toronto or McMaster."

If.

"The University of Toronto or McMaster," I echoed dully. That was the extent of their dreams for me. A lifetime of near-perfect grades, spotless attendance, and countless awards of excellence, and the most they saw me achieving was getting into a school that I could commute to from home.

"Those are both excellent schools," he reminded me sharply. "The kind of schools I wish I'd been able to go to at your age."

"They are good schools," I agreed, his tone sending prickles of fear down my spine. "And I'll apply to them both, of course. But I'd still like to fill out applications to MIT and Cornell. You never know unless you try. Right?"

He pressed his lips into a line and shook his head. "I've been saving money for your education since the day you were born. You know that. Every spare dollar I had. Your mother and I have sacrificed a lot over the years to build up those savings. And we didn't make all those sacrifices just to watch you throw our money away applying to schools that will never accept you."

I knew I should let the subject drop for a while. I knew not to push him too far. But I saw my dreams for the future evaporating in front of me, and I couldn't give up without a fight. "What if I paid the application fees for MIT and Cornell myself?"

His brow furrowed and he looked almost . . . hurt, for a moment. "What if *you* paid the fees?" he asked, as though testing out how the words felt. A muscle jumped in his jaw and his eyes went hard. "Of all the ungrateful things . . ." He stood up so that he towered over me. "Do you think I had a father who saved to send me to university?" he thundered. "Do you think that was ever an option for me? No. I'm giving you better than I ever had in my own life, and it's still not enough for you."

He gave a hard, little laugh. "*What if I paid the application fees myself?*" he mocked. "Give me a goddamn break. You've never worked a day in your life. We are done talking about this. Your mother and I will pay for you to apply to schools within commuting distance and that's it. Be thankful for what you have for once, instead of being resentful you can't have more."

The minute he stormed out of the room, I made a decision. My days of being at the mercy of my father's whims were over.

So I started making my own money. I showed Troy the apps I'd designed for hiding and password-protecting folders on phones, and he introduced me to his teammates, who bought every new program I came up with. And then, when their competition to collect photos of girls at school began, they asked me to design a way to store the pictures that couldn't be traced back to any of them. My hands were shaking when I told them it would cost five hundred dollars, but they agreed so fast that I wished I'd asked for more.

I've spent the last year prepping for my SATs and ACTs, perfecting my applications to MIT and Cornell, saving my money, and researching financial aid and scholarships. I'm *going* to make this happen—with or without my father's help.

I re-tape the envelope to the bottom of the drawer and close it. I'm going to prove to my dad that he's wrong about me. And when I'm far away, living out my dreams and becoming the success that he never thought I'd be, my father will regret the way he underestimated me. I can just see him bragging to his friends about his brilliant son who's studying computer science and engineering at MIT. He'll say it like he had something to do with it, but in his heart, he'll know that it was all me—that I made it farther than he ever thought I could and that I did it all on my own.

I'll do anything to make that happen.

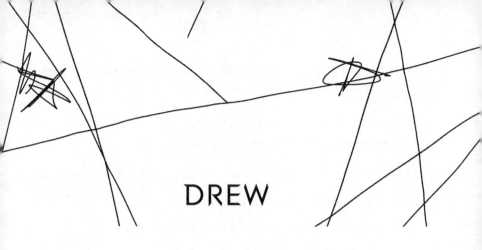

DREW

"WHOA," JENNA SAYS, LOOKING OVER MY SHOULDER AS SHE COMES TO SIT BESIDE ME IN BAILEY'S CLASS. "That's not good."

I shrug like it's no big deal, but I can't stop staring at the big red F at the top of my English test. *Macbeth*.

"I studied for this," I tell her, even though I'm not really in the mood to talk about it. Coach will bench me if I don't pull up my grade.

"Studied how?" she asks, as Mouse sits down beside her.

"I read plot summaries online and watched a ton of YouTube clips. I spent like two hours preparing. But the test was all about identifying quotations and explaining their significance." I crumple the test into a ball so I no longer have to look at it. "Why do we have to study Shakespeare anyways? This play is like a million years old."

"But still relevant today," Jenna says with a crooked smile. "You should read it. It's about a guy who kills the king because of his own ambition and then goes into a downward spiral of guilt and paranoia."

"Yeah, that sounds like a real party. I'll get right on that."

"You seriously didn't read the play?" Mouse asks.

I shoot him a murderous look. I texted him all last night asking for copies of his notes, but he never responded. "No, I didn't read the play. Which you would have known if you'd bothered to check your messages even once."

Jenna laughs. "Mouse? Not check his phone?" She reaches out and rests her hand against his forehead. "Are you running a fever? Should we get you to a hospital?"

"Very funny," he mutters. "My father confiscated my phone."

"What'd you do, get less than 90 percent on a test?" I don't even bother trying to keep the bitterness out of my voice.

"Something like that."

Jenna looks shocked. "What the hell? How long till you get it back?"

"Not any time soon," Mouse says miserably. "It's been confiscated indefinitely. Apparently, I have to earn it back, whatever that means."

Jenna slumps back in her chair and bites her thumbnail, looking almost as upset as Mouse.

"Why are *you* tripping out over this?" I ask her. I haven't seen Jenna express emotion about anything since last year, so it's kinda freaky to see her lose it over Mouse getting grounded from his phone.

"I'm not," she says defensively. "It's just . . . how are we supposed to keep in touch? . . . For the project, I mean . . ."

"Don't text me," Mouse says. "I'm serious. Don't forget and send me a message by accident, OK?"

Jenna cocks her head to the side. "What's the big deal?"

"My father will be checking my phone."

"So what?" she asks, narrowing her eyes at him. "What are you afraid of?"

Mouse scoffs. "Nothing. I just don't like my dad knowing any-thing about my life at school. You know that."

"Then how come you told *me* not to text? How come you didn't tell Drew?"

Mouse turns to me. "Don't text me until I get my phone back." He looks at Jenna. "Happy?"

She slowly crosses her arms over her chest and shoots him an evil-looking stare.

"There's only one explanation for this weirdness," I interrupt. "You two are exchanging freaky texts, aren't you?"

Jenna flicks her gaze over to me and arches an eyebrow. "Jealous?"

I would be, if I really believed that Jenna and Mouse could ever be a couple. But this is Mouse Maguire we're talking about. He wouldn't know what to do with a girl if his life depended on it.

"Maybe," I drawl, winking at her. "If you're looking for someone to message while our friend here is out of commission, I'd be happy to give you my number."

Jenna mimes throwing up and then gives me the finger right as Miss Bailey walks over.

"In the interests of seeing this group actually get some work done, I'll pretend I didn't see that," Bailey says, smiling at Jenna before heading to the front of the class.

Jenna's mouth drops open in surprise, and for an instant she looks so much like the old Jenna that my breath hitches in my chest. I'd forgotten what she was like before last year—how unguarded she used to be.

I tear my eyes away from her and see that Mouse is watching me intently.

"She must've gotten laid last night," I joke, my voice coming out hollow.

Mouse looks at me like I've lost my mind. "What?"

Jenna snorts out a laugh. "Because she *smiled* at me," she explains. "It's like a miracle or something."

"Or one of the seven signs of the apocalypse," I joke, wanting to hear her laugh again.

Mouse fidgets in his seat and then clears his throat. "Anyway, Jenna . . ." he begins, but Miss Bailey starts talking before he can say anything more.

"I need your attention up here, please," she says, clapping her hands. "By now you should have discussed this year's topic as a group and put some thought into possible case studies." I sneak a look at Mouse. We haven't told Jenna about the topic yet. "I want to remind you that this project is worth 15 percent of your final grade, so there's no time to waste." She folds her hands in front of her and smiles at us, sending a chill down my spine. It's creepy when bitchy teachers act nice.

"I expect each group to find a different case study from current events. Once you've chosen yours, you can claim it on the sign-up sheet on my desk. For today only, you may use your devices to browse for ideas. I'll give you the rest of this class period to come to a consensus within your group. After today, though, you'll need to meet outside of class to get the work completed."

"Whoa," Jenna whispers, when Miss Bailey stops talking. "Devices permitted? She *definitely* got laid." She reaches for Mouse's binder. "Let's take a look at that assignment sheet."

Poor Mouse looks like he's about to throw up. "Hang on," he says, grabbing his binder out of her hands. "We have something to tell you." He turns to me and I feel the corner of my mouth twitch up in a smile.

"Go for it," I tell him, wondering whether he'll pass out before he can get the words out.

He takes a deep breath and lets it out in a rush. "We haven't . . . I mean, last class you got kicked out before . . . I wanted to tell you what our . . ."

Jesus Christ. He's sweating so much that he's going to leave a puddle on the chair. "What Mouse is too scared to tell you is that this year's topic is Privacy and the Internet."

Jenna frowns at me. "So?"

I shrug. "He thought you might lose your shit."

"No, I didn't," he protests weakly. "Not exactly."

She rolls her eyes. "What makes me lose my shit is everyone always expecting me to lose my shit." She snatches the binder out of Mouse's hands, making him flinch.

I settle back into my chair and watch Jenna flip through Mouse's notes, looking for the assignment. She seems pretty chill, all things considered, so I decide to press my luck. "So . . ." I say, as casually as I can, " . . . about what Bailey just said about meeting outside of school to do this project—are we gonna do that?"

Jenna keeps flipping through the binder and lets Mouse field the question.

"What do you mean?" Mouse asks, adjusting his glasses. "How else will we get the work done if Miss Bailey isn't going to give us class time?"

"We could divide up the work and each do our own part. That way we'd just have to meet to put everything together at the end."

"In other words," Jenna interrupts, "Drew wants us to do all the work."

"That would be great, but that's not what I was getting at," I insist. "Look, we're all busy, right? It'll be easier for all of us if we work on our own parts independently. It'll save us the trouble of trying to coordinate meeting times."

Jenna shoots me a look that says she's not falling for my bullshit.

Mouse shakes his head. "I don't think that's a good idea. Miss Bailey expects us to work together, so I think we should do that."

"Of course you do," I say pointedly. "Because you always do what people expect you to."

Mouse's eyes widen and he shifts in his seat.

"Oh, leave him alone," Jenna says. "Don't get all pissy just because you're not working with a bunch of bimbo cheerleaders who'll do all the work for you."

She's got me there. I let my eyes wander over to Ella's group, where Kevin is looking down Keisha's shirt while she bends over their assignment sheet. "Fine. When should we meet?"

Mouse opens his laptop and peers at the screen. "I'm busy tonight and for an hour after school on Thursday. How about Friday?"

I laugh, thinking he's joking. Mouse just blinks at me.

"You're serious?" I ask. "You have nothing better to do on a Friday night than work on a bullshit project?"

Mouse bristles, and I notice Jenna's eyes crinkle up with a smile that she hides behind the assignment page.

"The weekend, then?" Mouse tries.

Jenna tosses the paper onto the desk. "Let's do Thursday night. After you finish tutoring and Drew's practice is over."

"How'd you know I had practice?"

"It's basketball season. Of course you have practice."

I shrug. "Thursday's fine with me. Just text me the time and place."

"I can't text, remember?" Mouse says. "Let's say six o'clock at the public library. You guys can email if anything comes up. It's not as fast as texting, but it'll have to do."

I take a deep breath and debate whether to help the little dweeb out. I don't exactly want him knowing about my side business, but he's so pathetic lugging around that laptop like it's a giant phone.

"Do you want a burner phone?" I finally ask him.

"A what?"

"A burner phone. A pay-as-you-go phone that's not on contract. For fifty bucks, I can get you a new smartphone with voice, texting, and unlimited data for one month. Clock starts ticking the first time you use it."

Jenna raises an eyebrow. "Sounds shady."

I roll my eyes. "The phone will work, you'll have a number your parents know nothing about, and you can do whatever you want on there without anyone knowing."

"You have one?" Jenna asks, looking interested.

"Of course. When my parents check my phone, they find the

boring one I use for school stuff. Everything personal is on the burner. Before my month is up I just put more money on it."

"Huh. So, if we text you?"

"Depends. Which number do you want?" I flash her a flirtatious smile and she looks away.

"I'll take one," Mouse jumps in excitedly.

"Hold up, little Mouse," Jenna says. "How do you know the phone isn't stolen? And how do you know he's giving you a good price?"

"I don't care." He looks like a kid on Christmas morning. "It's worth it to have something my father can't take away."

"Hang on a second," I say to Jenna. "What makes you think my phones are stolen?"

She laughs. "C'mon, Drew. People don't usually sell legit merchandise out of their lockers."

I shouldn't care what she thinks, but it bugs me that she assumes I'm a criminal. "I know a guy who used to play football here with my brother, and he has an in with his dad's company, that's all. He gets the phones at a discount and sells them to me, then I resell them here. There's nothing illegal about it."

She holds up her hands in mock surrender. "You don't have to explain yourself to me. I'm just saying that the whole thing sounds shady. Why deal in secret, untraceable phones unless shit's going on that people could get in trouble for?"

"You don't have to be a drug dealer or a criminal to have secrets,

Jen. Everyone in this school has stuff they don't want their parents knowing. That's just part of life. I give people the chance to maintain their privacy and have something of their own that they don't need to depend on their parents for."

"Oh," she says, her voice dripping with sarcasm. "Now I get it! You're performing a community service—"

"That's *exactly* what he's doing," Mouse cuts in. "And I am desperately in need of that service."

"So why not just go into a provider and sign up for your own phone, Mouse? Why buy one from Al Capone here?"

"I can't just walk into a store and sign up for a new plan, Jenna. You need a credit card for that, and it's not like I can ask my dad to borrow his." He looks over at me nervously. "I don't need a credit card to refill one of your phones, do I?"

"Nope," I assure him. "You can buy refill vouchers just about anywhere, but I get them at a discount from my buddy. If you've got the cash, I can hook you up whenever you need one."

"Perfect. How soon can I get a phone?" Mouse asks.

"How soon can you get me fifty dollars?"

"By the end of fourth period?"

"You got it. Meet me by my locker before the bell and I'll take care of you."

By the time the bell rings, we still haven't chosen a case study or figured out anything to do with the project, but I have fifty dollars coming to me, Mouse has a new phone, and we have a meeting set up for Thursday. Not too shabby.

"Later," Jenna says, slinging her bag over her shoulder and sliding a pair of aviator sunglasses onto her face.

"Wait," I say as she turns to leave. "You know . . . I can hook you up with a phone, too, if you want. Nothing shady. I promise." The words feel heavy in my mouth and I'm stunned by how much I want her to accept my offer.

She turns around and purses her lips. I try to imagine the look in her eyes, but all I can see is my reflection in her aviators.

"Me?" she asks, a tiny smile tugging at the corner of her mouth. "Why would I need one of your phones? I've got nothing to hide."

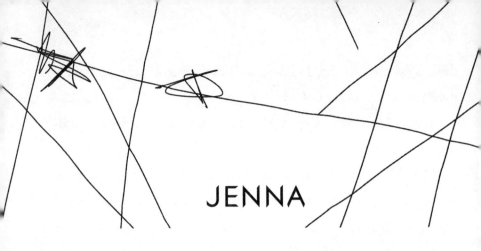

JENNA

"JESUS, J.J.," MY MOM SHOUTS OVER THE KATY PERRY I HAVE BLASTING. "Turn the goddamn music down!"

I throw my book aside and lunge for my iPod, knocking it out of the dock in my rush to silence the music. My mom's not supposed to be home for another hour.

"You are so busted," she laughs, snatching it up before I can get to it. "To think . . . I could destroy your whole tough-girl reputation with this."

I'm not amused. At school, I crank the Black Veil Brides and Bring Me the Horizon. Loud, angry music that confuses the hell out of my former friends.

I make a grab for my iPod, but my mom swivels and scrolls through my playlist. "Dear God," she moans. "I thought I raised you better than this."

It's my old iPod. The one that never leaves the house. The guilty-pleasure iPod stocked with humiliatingly great pop songs. I have everything from Katy Perry and One Direction to old-school Britney Spears and Backstreet Boys. There's even a little preteen Justin Bieber on there. It's disgusting, I know.

My little brother, Jonah, marches into my room, looking pointedly at his watch. "We are going to be late," he informs my mother. "We have exactly twelve minutes until my appointment and the drive will take seventeen point five minutes." He looks up, taking in the sight of Mom dancing around with my iPod while I seethe. "Hello, Jenna. You look displeased."

I suck in my lips and bite down on them in an attempt to keep from smiling. It's hard to stay angry with Jonah around. "I *am* displeased, Joe. Tell Mom to give me back my iPod."

"It's Jonah," he says, just like I knew he would. He turns to my mom. "Jenna requires her iPod, and I require a ride to the dentist. Oral hygiene is very important." Jonah looks at his watch again and sighs. "I'll be waiting in the car."

"I have weird children," my mother declares, handing me back my iPod and turning to the door just as Jonah's head pops back around the corner.

"Jenna?" he says.

"Yeah, bro?"

"I think Katy Perry is great."

"Thanks, big guy," I say, sticking my tongue out at our mother.

"Weird," she laments, shaking her head and following my brother down the hallway.

My mother sucks. And by sucks, I mean she's fabulous in

a very inconvenient way. Do you know how hard it is to be a rebellious teenager when your mom is a tattoo artist? And not just any old tattoo artist, but one with a fine arts degree who divides her time between the local tattoo studio and a posh gallery downtown.

My mother basically *invented* rebellion, so she thinks everything I do is amusing. Bright pink streak in my hair in fifth grade? "Adorable." Belly button pierced in seventh grade? "Cute!" Stumbling home drunk and puking on the kitchen floor? "Best way to learn your limits."

So, the day I went off the rails last year, I knew she wouldn't freak out like a regular mom, but I did expect her to . . . I don't know, pick up the pieces, maybe? Take charge. Fix me.

It was three days after my topless photos went live and I was done with everything and everyone. Ella had just dumped me as her best friend, my vice principal had blamed me for being dumb enough to send Troy photos, and some asshole had made color copies of my pictures and tacked them up all over school. I lost it.

That afternoon is a complete blur, but the gist of it is, I hacked off my waist-length blond hair and dyed it black, attacked my wardrobe with scissors and safety pins, and threw out everything pink and girly in my room—including eight years' worth of ballet paraphernalia and my prized pointe shoes. My mom found me sitting in a pile of ripped-up clothing with dark streaks down my face from the hair coloring. She didn't even skip a beat. She walked right into my bathroom and came back with a warm washcloth.

"I like the black hair," she said, wiping my face and tilting my head up so I'd meet her gaze. "It really makes your eyes pop."

I pulled away and blinked back tears. "Don't pretend I'm OK, because I'm not. I'm a mess."

"Of course you are. But you won't be forever."

I shook my head and gestured at the chaos surrounding me. "Aren't you even mad? You should be yelling at me for the mess I've made of everything . . . my hair, my clothes, my *life*."

Ella's mother would have kicked her ass for a stunt like this. She would have yanked her up off the floor and marched her to the salon to have her hair fixed, then filled garbage bags with the ruined clothing and taken her shopping for new outfits to cover up her shame. She would have painted over Ella's mistakes with pretty colors and rebuilt her from the ground up.

Mom balled up the blackened washcloth and tossed it into my hamper. "I think it's about time I told you the secret of life. Get ready."

I snorted out a bitter laugh. "You've had the secret of life all this time and you're just telling me now? Don't you think that info would have been useful *before*?"

"It doesn't work like that, J.J. Shitty things happen no matter lat you do. But it's not the shitty stuff that defines you—it's what you do after."

"That's your big secret?"

"Nope. My secret is the 24-Hour Rule."

I rolled my eyes and moved to get up. I knew it was going to be something stupid.

"The 24-Hour Rule is something your grandmother taught me. Actually, the only useful thing she *ever* taught me."

I sat back down at the mention of my grandmother. I've never met her. She disowned my mother when my mom got pregnant with me at seventeen.

"When something goes wrong—when life knocks you down and everything falls apart—you have exactly twenty-four hours to fall to pieces. Rage, break things, eat buckets of ice cream, hide in your bed and cry . . ." She looked around my room and smiled. " . . . Or chop off all your hair and set fire to your pointe shoes. Anything you want. But when your twenty-four hours is up, you need to stand up, dust yourself off, and take control of your life."

I blinked at her. "Is that what you did? When my father left?"

She startled at the mention of my father. "I've never told you that story, have I?"

I held my breath and shook my head.

She drew her knees up and rested her chin on them. "When I found out I was pregnant, I thought my life was over. Your father

60

skipped town, your grandparents kicked me out of the house, and my friends treated me like I was diseased. I . . . did something like this," she said, gesturing around my room. "But add in getting my first tattoo and pawning your grandmother's engagement ring to buy a bus ticket to Toronto and pay my first and last months' rent on a basement apartment."

"You didn't."

"I sure did. I stole her jewelry the night she kicked me out. It took me fifteen years to pay her back for it. I mailed her the cash with photos of my gorgeous family and my artwork hanging in the gallery downtown a few summers ago. No return address."

"Whoa."

"The point is, my life wasn't over. It was just beginning. Without all that mess, I wouldn't have had you. I wouldn't have moved to Toronto and studied art, and I would never have met your stepfather or had Jonah. I made those things happen by not giving in. By taking control and fighting every step of the way. So, you can have this time to rage, my little butterfly, but then you need to pick yourself up off this floor and be the woman I know you can be."

"Don't call me that," I reminded her. Mom dubbed me Butterfly back in sixth grade, when she came up with Mouse's nickname. His name stuck, but mine didn't. Largely because I had a habit of punching anyone who dared call me that.

"You'll always be my Butterfly," she teased me, running her fingers through my choppy hair. "Even when you try to disguise yourself as a vampire bat."

"How can you even say that after your big *Be strong and take control* speech? Butterflies are weak and fragile. They can be crushed way too easily."

She shook her head. "I've never thought of butterflies as weak. To me, they're about transformation and survival. Did you know that monarch butterflies are toxic to predators? They can fly around bright and beautiful because anything that tries to eat them will get sick. Their coloring is actually a warning that scares off anything that would prey on them." She got up and planted a kiss on the top of my head. "I'd never name you after something weak. I know you're made of stronger stuff than that. You're my iron butterfly."

I watched her walk out of my room. *Iron butterfly.* That was the perfect description for her. She's tiny and dainty looking at five feet tall, with raven-black hair she wears in a pixie cut and humongous blue eyes that make her look like Betty Boop—a comparison she despises. My stepdad, Gary, calls her "ten pounds of crazy in a five-pound bag," but I like her description better. It's the very first tattoo she ever got, back when she first found out she was pregnant and alone—a Shakespearean quote on her left shoulder blade that says, *Though she be but little, she is fierce.* That's my mom.

And even though I look like her complete opposite, towering over her at five feet, seven inches, with the fair coloring I got from my dad, that day was the first day I allowed myself to hope that maybe I was more like her than I'd thought.

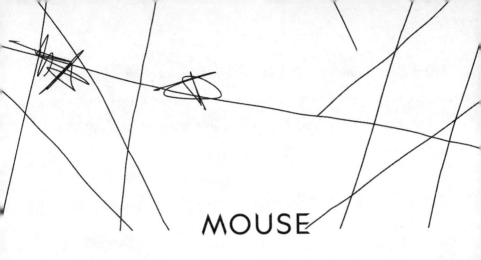

MOUSE

I CHECK MY WATCH FOR THE THIRD TIME IN THREE MIN-
UTES AND THEN CRANE MY NECK TO SEE THE CLOCK
OVER THE LIBRARIAN'S DESK. It's definitely 6:17 p.m. and I
am definitely running out of time if I'm going to meet with Drew
before Jenna arrives.

I pull out my new burner phone and scroll through the text
messages I exchanged with Drew this afternoon to double-check
the time we set, but there's no mistake. Drew agreed to meet me
here at the public library at six o'clock, right after his basketball practice. That's not what I told Jenna, though. I told her we
couldn't meet until six thirty, so I'd have plenty of time to run my
proposal past Drew first.

If I'm lucky, Jenna will be running late as usual. I chew on my
lip and then tap out a text to her. *Got here a bit early. Are you on
your way?*

The three blue dots that indicate she's typing a message

appear right away. *I'm on the bus. Put your spreadsheets away & chill out.*

I smile despite myself and glance at my laptop, already open to the spreadsheets. Jenna knows me so well.

I started keeping the spreadsheets in ninth grade, when Mr. McAllister almost cheated me out of 3 percent in math class. I'd kept all my assignments and tests, so when I saw my final grade was a disappointing 89 percent, I pulled out the folder and went over and over the numbers. I got the same result each time: 92 percent. I created my first grades spreadsheet to present to him as evidence.

He was less than impressed.

But when the vice principal compared Mr. McAllister's records to my spreadsheet, we discovered that he hadn't bothered to enter a major test on linear relations. *An entire test.* How does a teacher forget a whole test?

So, I started tracking my grades in all my classes to make sure I got credit for every percentage point I earned. As my dad always says: *The world doesn't owe you any favors.* I wasn't about to leave my fate in someone else's hands, especially not with dreams as big as mine.

Over the years, the spreadsheets have become more than just an insurance policy against teacher incompetence, though. They've become a source of comfort whenever life gets too stressful—all those orderly rows of numbers adding up to grades that will take me one step closer to my goals. Whenever I'm feeling nervous and overwhelmed, I open my spreadsheets and remind myself that everything is going to work out.

The trouble is, the spreadsheets aren't as reassuring this semester as they have been in the past. I'm taking English, law, calculus, and chemistry this semester. Guess which two are giving me an ulcer?

Not chemistry and calculus, that's for sure.

I knew English would be stressful. It always is. There's no one right answer. Everything is up for interpretation, and *how* you say something is just as important as *what* you say. It's virtually impossible to get a 95 percent in English class, and nothing is ever *finished*. You can't just get the answer and move on—you have to keep writing and rewriting over and over again.

And law. I'd expected law to be easy. Something is either legal or illegal. Right or wrong. But it turns out law is more complicated than that. And more fascinating. The great irony of this year is that the more interested in the law I become, the worse I perform in class. I get so wrapped up in legal arguments and obsessed with considering all the various interpretations that I overcomplicate things instead of just giving the simple answers that Miss Bailey seems to be looking for. Meanwhile, I'm being outscored on every test by my mouth-breathing classmates, who are all cheating their way to easy As.

I look at my law spreadsheet and sigh. I need this group project to bring up my grade. I cannot have anything less than an A on my transcript. I just can't. Even in an elective course like law. My father's voice plays on a loop in my brain: *Just getting good grades doesn't make you special, son.*

If I'm going to get into MIT, I can't just be good. I have to be *exceptional.* I wipe my sweaty palms on my pants and breathe deeply, reminding myself of my goals: *grades and money.* Those are the two most important things in my life right now, and I have to stay focused on those priorities. Grades to get into MIT and the money to pay for it.

I close the spreadsheet and move it into the Trash folder on my desktop. There's no time for panic and second-guessing myself. Not when there's work to be done.

I check the clock again and breathe a sigh of relief as Drew strolls through the front door of the library. *Grades and money,* I remind myself, pulling out the notes I prepared earlier.

Because Drew is going to be the key to helping me make money.

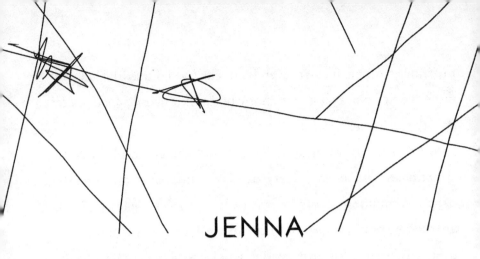

JENNA

I STEP OFF THE BUS AND SUCK IN MY BREATH AS THE
ICY WIND CUTS THROUGH MY BLACK LEATHER JACKET.
It's a completely impractical coat for early March in Canada, but
I love the way it makes me look—like I just swung off the back of
a motorcycle.

"Your vanity is going to give you pneumonia," my mom called
after me as I raced out of the house earlier. "Just wear your damned
parka, J.J."

"I left it in my locker," I lied, sprinting for the bus stop. "The
bus lets out right next to the library. I'll be fine!"

I put my head down and hunch my shoulders against the cold,
speeding as fast as my clunky Doc Martens will allow. It's only
one short block to the library doors, but it feels like the length of a
football field. My nose starts to run in the cold, and I raise frozen
fingers up to wipe it. I'd planned to make a big show of catching the bus later, like the independent badass I am, but it's too

damned cold to play the hero. I'll have to bum a ride with Mouse when we're done.

I relax my shoulders as the light spilling out of the library surrounds me. Even though I'm freezing my ass off, I stop to take in the sight of the rows of bookshelves visible through the floor-to-ceiling windows.

I've been coming to this library practically my whole life. My mom used to bring me here to story time when I was little, and I got my first library card the day I started kindergarten. I've come here with my mom, with my stepdad, and with little Jonah once he was born. This library has seen me as a knobby-kneed tomboy, a fashion-obsessed preteen with a mouth full of braces, a budding ballerina, and now an angry social outcast. I feel dizzy, suddenly. As though I'm standing alongside all those other versions of me.

I give my head a shake and pull out my phone to check the time. Mouse should be happy. I'm only five minutes late. That's practically early for me.

I hurry along the side of the building, peeking between bookshelves to catch a glimpse of Mouse at his favorite table. I'm expecting him to be bouncing his leg nervously and watching the door for our arrival, so when I see him sitting beside Drew with their heads bent together, I stop short. My first thought is: *How in the world did Drew beat me here?* And my second thought is: *What the hell are they talking about?*

I'm instantly transported back to last year, when I used to catch them whispering in the hallways between classes and passing thumb drives to each other like they were bags of weed.

I step off the sidewalk and slip through the bushes to get a closer look. Mouse is talking animatedly, pointing at something on a page between them. Drew starts out shaking his head but then leans in to Mouse and whispers intently. I rest my hand against the window, wishing I could hear what they're talking about.

"Oh my God, what are you doing, you psycho?"

I let my head fall forward to rest against the glass. I know that voice.

"I told you she was weird," Ella says to her friends. "I can't believe I ever hung out with her."

I squeeze my eyes shut at the laughter that follows, then whirl around to face them. The best defense is a good offense, after all.

Ella and her cronies are all wearing high heels and miniskirts with bare legs. I suddenly feel much less stupid for wearing my thin leather jacket.

"If heading to the library makes me weird," I say, stepping out of the bushes like it's totally normal, "then I guess I'm weird." I pause to eye Ella up and down. "I'm sorry. You probably don't know that word. *Library*. It's this place where they keep books that you can borrow to read. You know *books*, right?"

She gives me a withering look and then sidesteps me to peer

through the window. "Oh. My. God. Ew. You were totally *spying* on Drew!"

Her friends squeal and move to look through the window.

"Are you, like, stalking him or something? Because that's really messed up."

"Yes," I deadpan. "I'm stalking Drew, and I figured the most logical place to find him would be the *library*. Isn't that where all the jocks hang out?"

"Well, *I* knew he'd be here tonight." She flips her hair and exchanges a sly smile with Keisha. "He texted me earlier."

"Lucky you," I say, turning to head into the library.

Ella darts in front of me, surprisingly agile on her stilettos. "Where do you think you're going?"

"To. The. Library," I say slowly, like I'm speaking to a simpleton. Which, let's face it, I sort of am.

"Oh, no. No, no, no, no, no. *We're* meeting Drew. You stay away."

"You're not serious." I look away from her wild-eyed expression to the vacant stares of her friends. "You're not this stupid, Ella. You're in my fucking law class. You know I'm working with Drew and Mouse." I grab her by the shoulders and propel her back over to the window. "See—Drew and Mouse. And me. Law class. Project. Work."

I let go of her shoulders and shake my head in frustration as I walk away.

"He's not interested in you," she calls after me.

"I'll cry myself to sleep over that later tonight."

"I'm serious, Jenna. Guys talk, you know. He knows all about you."

I squeeze my hands into fists in my jacket pockets and keep walking. *She's not worth it.*

"Guys don't really go for the sluts. They might fool around with them, but they get tired fast and move on to nicer girls."

I'm almost at the door. I can just ignore her and keep walking. Get into the nice warm library and torment the hell out of her by laughing at everything Drew says and sitting way too close to him.

"What do you think he'll say when I tell him you were watching him through the window like some kind of creeper?"

Oh, hell. She's not going to stop until I smack her down. I turn and stalk over to her, enjoying the way she takes a nervous step back as I approach. "Go ahead, Ella. Tell him whatever you like. It's only fair, really. I mean, I did tell him all about your raging case of genital herpes." I give her a fake sympathetic look as she sucks in a shocked breath. "That wasn't a secret, was it?"

I smile sweetly at her friends as they laugh nervously. "Have a nice night," I tell them, turning to walk slowly into the library. Before the door swings shut behind me, I hear Keisha call out, "What did Troy ever see in you? You're so trashy."

I grit my teeth and shake the snow out of my hair as I peer into the library. Drew and Mouse are still deep in conversation, heads bent together. I slip past the librarian's desk and head for the bookshelves, looping around so I can sneak up behind them.

"I'm not saying your math is wrong," Drew tells a visibly frustrated Mouse. "I'm just saying that this is too much. It's just a hobby. I'm not trying to make a career out of this."

"Neither am I. But think of it this way . . ."

I slide over to peer through a gap in the books. Mouse flips over a sheet of paper and sketches out a graph. "This is your risk-to-reward ratio. Right now, you're taking all the risk with minimal reward. If you tap into the markets I can provide, the risk stays relatively stable, but the rewards multiply."

"So you say. But I don't know these people in your 'markets.' How do I know they're smart enough not to get caught with the goods, and that they won't rat me out if they do? Doesn't the risk go up when more people know what's going on?"

"Theoretically. But consider the markets. I'm talking about highly intelligent people who are motivated to avoid exposure. People like me. Their need for your product is high, but they have to consider their own risks. Possession of stolen goods does not help one's application to institutions of higher learning." Mouse holds up a hand as Drew starts to protest. "I don't care how you get the phones, and none of my acquaintances will, either. In fact, the more dangerous they perceive the endeavor, the better. The point is, they're motivated to keep it a secret—both from the school and from their parents. Their risk is essentially greater than yours."

"Hi, Drew!" Ella's voice comes out of nowhere, making me jump almost as high as Mouse and Drew. Mouse crumples the papers he's been writing on, and Drew leans away from him. "Hey, Ella," he drawls.

I see Ella's eyes hunting for me, so I slip down the row of books and head for the magazine section. I spot what I'm looking for, grab a few copies, and saunter back to where Drew and Mouse are sitting.

" . . . She's around here somewhere," Ella says in a dramatic stage whisper. "We found her out in the bushes watching you, and she came in, like, five minutes ago."

Drew sees me before Ella does, and cocks an eyebrow at me mockingly. I roll my eyes for his benefit and sneak up behind Ella. "Who are we looking for?" I ask, making her jump.

"Y-you're here."

"Of course I am." I drop the magazines on the table. "These are current issues. I thought we might find something useful in them."

I pull out a chair, accidentally-on-purpose banging it into Ella's leg. "Oops."

"*Wired, Computerworld, PC World* . . ." Mouse flips through the magazines admiringly. "Good thinking, Jen."

"I also brought this," I say, pulling my new laptop out of my bag and running my hands over it.

"No. Way!" Mouse exclaims, forgetting his sacred commitment to library etiquette. "Sorry!" he whisper-shouts to the librarian, who's in the process of standing up to chastise us. She shakes her head at him disapprovingly but can't keep the amused smile from turning up the corners of her lips. The librarians love Mouse. He spends almost every day in here after school and treats it like it's a cathedral.

"Way," I tell him quietly. "My stepdad helped me get a deal, but it made a huge dent in my savings. I'll be picking up extra shifts at work until the end of time, but it's totally worth it."

"That's a thing of beauty," Drew interrupts. "May I?"

I nod at him and he flips open my new MacBook. "Want to trade?"

"Not a chance," I tell him, sliding the computer back over to me. "I've waited *years* for a new laptop. Ask Mouse. I've been stuck with an ancient crappy laptop since ninth grade. This was way overdue."

Ella clears her throat behind me, and we all look up at her. "Are you still here?" I ask. "What do you want?"

She narrows her eyes at my tone but doesn't want to be a bitch in front of Drew. "I . . . I was just wondering what you're doing later."

She's obviously talking to Drew, but I can't help myself. "Gee . . . I'm pretty busy tonight," I tell her. "What about you, Mouse?"

"Homework," he says, smiling at me.

"I meant Drew," Ella snaps.

Drew looks back and forth between us, obviously amused. "Not sure yet," he says, giving me a wink and putting his hand on my knee. "What are our plans, Jen?"

Ella huffs and turns bright red. "I—I didn't know that . . ."

"It's just like you said," I say with a forced smile, "guys always end up with the nicer girls."

I wait until she storms away before smacking Drew's hand off my leg. "You're lucky my hatred for Ella is stronger than my revulsion for you."

He gives a low chuckle that takes me by surprise. "You're welcome."

I roll my eyes again and turn to face Mouse, who looks almost as shell-shocked as Ella did. "Relax," I tell him. "Drew's just messing around."

Drew cuffs him on the shoulder and nearly knocks him off his chair. "Mouse knows that, right, Mouse? We're buddies from way back."

"Speaking of which . . ." I narrow my eyes at Mouse, knowing he'll be the weak link. "What were you two conspiring about before I got here?"

"Our project," Mouse says, too smoothly.

"Mmhmm." I make a grab for the papers he scrunched up when Ella arrived on the scene, but he's too fast for me. "What are you hiding?"

"I'm not *hiding* anything," he says so confidently that I start to doubt myself, even though I overheard their conversation with my own ears.

"Really?" I ask, arching an eyebrow and holding out my hand. "Then pass me the papers."

"Just because I want to keep something private doesn't mean I'm hiding it. Hiding implies wrongdoing. I just don't want to talk about this."

I'm surprised by his backbone but annoyed by the games. I cock my head to the side and narrow my eyes. "I probably wouldn't want to talk about how I'm fencing stolen goods, either. Though I'm not sure how you've convinced yourself that there's nothing wrong with it."

Drew whoops out a laugh, earning another harsh stare from the librarian.

"You knew already?" Mouse asks, sinking down in his seat.

"You're not the evil genius you think you are," I tell him, folding my arms on the table and looking back and forth between them. "I don't care what shit you two get up to, but I do have one request. No, a demand. That you not hide things from me. I'm done with whispers and secrets, and nothing pisses me off more than finding out I'm the loser on the outside who has no idea what's going on."

Mouse opens his mouth to argue, but I hold up a hand to

stop him. "I don't want excuses or explanations. No more secret meetings before I get here. No more hiding things from me like last year. You don't have to include me in your plans, but don't treat me like an idiot and sneak around behind my back. Got it?"

Drew shrugs. "Fine with me. This was Mouse's idea anyways."

I turn to Mouse. "Of course," he says, not meeting my eyes. "No secrets and no hiding things."

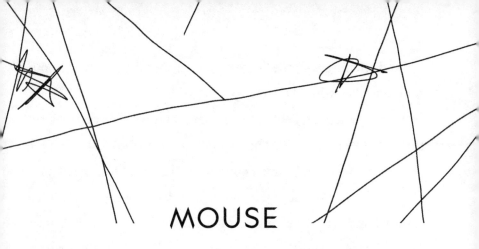

MOUSE

I'M NOT A JERK.

Drew is a jerk.

So why is Jenna getting into his car right now instead of mine?

I hold my frozen hands up to the heat vents in my mother's Corolla and count the cars in the library parking lot to calm my nerves.

Drew is still undecided on bringing me into his cell-phone business, Jenna thinks I'm a misogynistic creep, and they're both mad at me about the case study even though my topic makes the most sense academically.

I don't understand people. They're so illogical.

Once Ella left us alone and Jenna stopped lecturing us about keeping secrets, I tried to shift the focus back onto our project. We're only a week into it, and we're already behind everyone else.

"Did either of you get the chance to look up case studies?"

I asked them. I had the perfect one in mind, but I was hoping someone else would bring it up first.

Jenna pulled up a file on her new laptop. "I picked out two that I think could work. The first is the dude who's suing his cell-phone provider for giving a copy of his call logs to his wife. She found evidence in there that proved he was having an affair, the asshole, and now they're getting a divorce." Jenna looked up at us expectantly, and I gave her a weak smile. I prayed her second choice was the Heather Morningside case. "OK . . ." she went on. "I can see you're underwhelmed by that one. How about the woman who was fired from her job for posting complaints about her coworkers on Facebook."

"I vote for the second one," Drew said.

Jenna shrugged. "I'm good with that, but we should look at all the options first. What did you come up with?"

"Same two as you," Drew said, flashing her a blinding smile.

She heaved a sigh. "You didn't do the work, did you?"

"I have one," I interrupted, pulling out the article I'd printed off the Internet this morning. Drew caught a glimpse of it before Jenna did and grabbed it out of my hands.

"No, you don't," he warned, crumpling the paper. "Don't be an idiot."

"She can handle it," I told him. "Jenna's tougher than you think."

"It's not about toughness," Drew snarled. "It's about not being an asshole."

Jenna flicked her eyes over to Drew.

"Listen," I said, "I'm not trying to be a jerk here, but—"

"But you want to do the Heather Morningside case," Jenna said.

"Yes, but let me explain—"

"For the record, I'm against this," Drew said.

"I know," Jenna told him, before turning to me. "And I know why you want to do it. It's all over the news and you figure it'll get us a good grade."

Heather Morningside was a fifteen-year-old from Alberta whose boyfriend filmed her while they were having sex. He sent the video to his friends, who then each sent it to a few more friends, and eventually it made the rounds on social media. She killed herself three weeks later, and now the police have arrested everyone who forwarded or posted the video and charged them with both possession of child pornography and distribution of child pornography.

"It *will* get us a good grade," I said. "It's timely and it affects people our age. But it's not just that. Think how powerful this topic will be coming from you, Jenna. People will really pay attention to what you have to say about this."

My heart was pounding by that point. Jenna's fury isn't something I risk lightly, but I knew I was right.

"No," Drew said. "We do the Facebook one."

"Hang on," Jenna said, sitting back in her chair and watching me intently. "I might agree to the Heather Morningside topic, but only on one condition."

"Anything," I told her.

"I won't present. I'll do research and contribute to the written assignment, but I won't stand up in front of the class and talk about this."

"But—"

"No buts. I won't do it."

"This is a bad idea," Drew said. "Let's pick another case. Who gives a shit about the grade. It's a stupid fucking project for a stupid fucking class. There's no reason to get into topics that make Jenna upset."

"The topic doesn't make me upset," she said, never taking her eyes off me. "The expectation that I'm going to become some kind of spokesperson for this issue makes me upset."

"That's the beauty of this, though, Jen. You can take what happened to you and make it into a positive. I *know* you," I said, leaning forward and lowering my voice. "I know the worst part of this is that you feel powerless. This could be your chance to take charge. To change that."

She narrowed her eyes and I willed myself to hold her gaze, feeling sweat bead on my forehead. "What about you, Drew?" she asked, without looking away from me. "Do you think this would be good for me?"

Drew paused, sensing a trap. "He makes some interesting points," he said cautiously.

Her shoulders relaxed and she looked off into space, thinking.

I let out a relieved breath, but just as I thought she was about to agree, her eyes snapped back onto mine and she said, "Bullshit."

"Wh-what?"

"It's bullshit. And stupid. And insulting. Just because a bunch of guys can't resist plastering my picture all over the Internet, I'm supposed to realign my whole world to take on the cause? It's supposed to be *my* job to work for change? Screw that. I didn't ask for all this to happen to me. If it's anyone's job to change, it's you guys. *All of you.* Everyone who looked at, retweeted, or passed around my pictures. You're the ones who have something to learn here, not me."

I shook my head. "But I didn't—"

She stood up so fast her chair fell over. "We're doing this topic. Not because I have something to prove, but because you guys have a lot to learn."

I watched her storm off toward the bathrooms. *You guys have a lot to learn.* Did she mean me, too?

My thoughts were interrupted by Drew punching me in the shoulder. Hard. "What the fuck is the matter with you?" he hissed. "All we have to do is keep our shit together for a few weeks, and you go bringing up the one topic we need to avoid?"

"It's the best topic," I said weakly.

"I don't give a shit about this project or what grade we get. Do you have any idea what you've done? We're gonna have to spend the next few weeks talking about all the ways it's a crime to pass around naked photos of girls. We're gonna have to stand up in front of our class and discuss the legal consequences of even having a copy of those photos. You don't think that's gonna make people talk?" He poked his finger against my chest. "I'm gonna make this really clear, Mouse, because you're officially the stupidest genius on Earth. If this comes back on me in any way, I'm taking you down with me. The minute anyone asks me about girls sending me pictures, I'll sing like a canary about how you set up the database and kept track of every picture the team collected. Got it?"

I felt my blood run cold. "I didn't mean to—"

He looked over my shoulder and sat back in his chair. "Jenna's coming. Keep your mouth shut and stop being so goddamned eager. We're going to do the minimum to get by on this assignment and you're going to sit back and shut the fuck up."

I spent the rest of our work session resisting the urge to retrieve my grades from the Trash folder on my laptop. I *need* an A on this assignment. We can't do the minimum. We just can't.

The heater in my mom's Corolla finally kicks in, and I sit back in the seat and check the clock. 10:17. They've been sitting in Drew's car for more than nine minutes now, and he hasn't even brushed the snow off the windshield yet. It makes my stomach churn, wondering what they're talking about for so long over there. I squint my eyes and try to make out their silhouettes through the layer of snow separating us, but it's impossible.

I give my head a shake and pull up the Notes app on my new phone.

How I know that Jenna isn't interested in Drew, I type out. I tap my right forefinger against my chin three times to help me think, and then I type:

1. He's Troy's best friend and she hates Troy.

2. She doesn't trust athletes.

3. He's a player.

4. He's not a nice guy.

I check to see that Drew's car is still in the lot (it is) and then look back down at what I've written so far. Numbers three and four are complicated in ways I don't want to think about too much, but in the interest of thoroughness, I know I have to.

I'm sort of to blame for Jenna knowing that Drew is a player. But only sort of. I'm sure she could have pieced things together herself, but they were becoming friendly last year and there was the day she went shopping for Troy's birthday present alone with Drew and I just couldn't handle that . . .

So, I told her about the contest. Well . . . I told her *some* of the information about the contest. Everything I said was the truth. Just not the whole truth.

"What do you mean, they're collecting nude photos of girls? Like trading cards?" she asked, her eyes flashing in an alarming way.

"You make it sound gross," I moaned.

"That's because it *is* gross. Who all is involved?"

"Drew, Devaughn, Alex . . . basically the whole team."

"Troy?"

I wanted to say yes, but the truth was, he refused to ask girls for pictures. "He knows about it," I said.

"But is he in the contest?"

I shook my head, hating the way her shoulders relaxed in relief.

"I knew it," she said, smiling. "Troy would never do something like that. But Drew . . . I'm gonna give him a piece of my mind the next time I see him."

"No!" I said, my heart hammering in my chest. "I told you that in confidence, Jen. You can't say anything to anyone. They'd know it was me who told. No one on the team would ever turn on anyone else."

"What do you care if they know?" she asked, arching an eyebrow.

"Please," I said, putting my hand on her arm. "This is the first time in my whole life that Troy and I have gotten along. He *trusts* me, and it's changed my life. No one harasses me in the halls anymore and people actually listen to what I have to say. Please, Jenna."

She sighed. "Fine. But I hope you know what this is costing me, Mouse. You're asking me to pretend not to know something huge that shouldn't be a secret. Think of the girls at school—our *friends*. Don't you think they deserve to know what's going on?"

She looked at me expectantly, obviously hoping that her guilt trip would work. I was in too deep, though, and if she started talking about the competition, then I'd be caught in the cross fire.

I check the clock again. 10:26. What are they *doing* over there? Drew's BMW is worth more than my dad makes in a year. There's no way it's not warmed up yet.

I look back at my list and consider point number four: *He's not a nice guy.*

When I was nine years old, my parents took me on my first and last carnival ride. It was called the Gravitron, and it was a giant circular space that spun around so fast that you stuck to the wall even when the bottom dropped out. I cried all the way through the ride, my tears tracking sideways to pool in my hair. When it was done, I took three wobbly steps out of the ride and then threw up everywhere.

Trying to figure out what Jenna wants from a guy makes me feel just as dizzy and sick as the Gravitron did.

Consider the evidence:

1. Jenna's real dad took off as soon as her mom got pregnant. He was supposedly this super rich, popular guy whose parents picked up and moved to get him away from the situation. As far as I know, he's never contacted Jenna or even acknowledged that she exists.

2. Her stepfather is a total nerd, but she adores him. He's this tall, skinny guy with thinning hair and a fondness for knock-knock jokes. You just know he's the guy who got picked on in high school, but Jenna thinks he walks on water and she'd beat the crap out of anyone who said anything bad about him. (I know, because I once joked that he was a loser and limped for a week afterward.)

3. Things she's said to me over the years that give me hope: "You're such a nice guy, Mouse," "I wish all guys could be like you," and (my personal favorite), "You're going to make a great husband someday."

Sounds like I'm her exact type, right? Except . . .

4. She was head over heels for Troy, even though he's more like her real father than her stepfather.

5. She knows that Drew took part in the contest last year, and yet she's sitting in his car right now doing who knows what behind a thick layer of snow, even though she knows that I'd drive her home in a heartbeat and that I live closer to her than he does.

I look up as movement catches my eye, and I see Drew slide out of his car with a snow brush to clear off the windshield. He's laughing, and I feel like someone has reached through my chest and ripped out my heart. This isn't supposed to happen. Jenna's supposed to see me and Drew side by side and realize that even though I'm not six feet tall or an athlete, I'm the better person.

But then, she hasn't called me *nice* in a very long time, and she didn't even look surprised today when she heard that I wanted in on Drew's cell-phone business . . .

I'm beginning to think she doesn't really care if I'm the nice guy anymore. In fact, I'm beginning to think she doesn't see me as a guy at all.

TODAY . . .

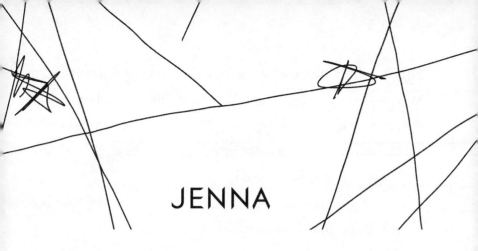

JENNA

@YRWRSTNITEMARE.

A blog with seven semipornographic pictures of Miss Bailey. The same seven pictures we agreed to delete just a few days ago.

I rub my hands over my face and try to focus on Mr. Williams and his lesson about derivatives, but I'm in no mood for calculus. Not after our little meeting in the parking lot this morning.

"We're golden. There's nothing tying us to those pictures. No one knows we had them, and we had Mouse's big brain covering our tracks the whole time. We officially know nothing about anything." Either Drew really believes we're in the clear, or he's a great liar.

I tap my pencil against my chin and go back over our early-morning conversation. There's something eating at me, and it takes me a minute to figure it out. Drew texted me this morning at six o'clock, calling an emergency parking-lot meeting at seven, but he obviously talked to Mouse in the middle of the night. Why didn't they message *me* when everything went down? Why wait to talk to me until morning? I rerun the conversation in my head.

They basically just told me about the tweet and dismissed my worries about getting caught. We didn't talk game plan at all. So, the purpose of the meeting was . . . to break the news to me? Or did they have their own meeting before I got there?

Those two and their secrets.

I check the time on the clock. 9:05. I can't get my hands on Drew's phone, but I know where his laptop is.

"Any questions?" Mr. Williams looks around the classroom and sighs at our glazed expressions. "Page eighty-seven, questions one through eight are homework. Get started now so I can help you when you get stuck."

I shift in my seat. Only twenty minutes till the end of class.

I wait till Williams sits down and then slide out of my chair and make my way up to his desk. His eyes crinkle up at the sight of me; he's sure I'm coming for extra help. He never gives up hope, ole Williams.

"Bathroom," I say, veering toward the door.

"Mmhmm," he says with a little shake of his head. "Try to make it back before the bell, Bradley. I don't want to have to babysit your stuff for you."

I slip into the hallway and scurry down the back stairwell, my heart fluttering in my chest. Drew has gym first period today, so his laptop should be in his locker.

I twirl the dial on the lock and dart glances up and down the hallway. When I'm sure the coast is clear, I open the door to find his laptop right where it belongs. *Thank God.* I grab it and head for the girls' washroom. I have about fifteen minutes before the bell goes and the hallways start swarming with students.

I duck into a stall and sit down, balancing the laptop on my lap. I wipe sweaty hands on my shirt and then open Drew's email.

I click through the screens as quickly as I can, looking for emails between him and Mouse. When I'm satisfied, I check the clock and shut the laptop. I have five minutes to spare, and everything is as it should be.

I stroll out of the washroom and head back to Drew's locker, feeling lighter. I put his laptop back where he left it and breathe a sigh of relief.

THREE WEEKS AGO . . .

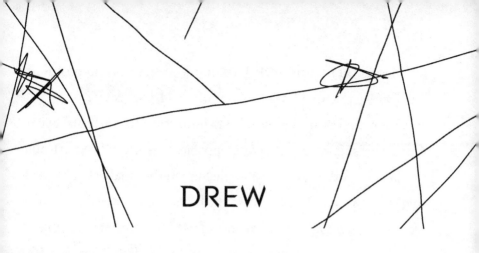

DREW

MY TIMING IS OFF AGAIN.

I plant my right foot and swivel, reaching back for the ball, but I'm too far out of position. Number 21 from the opposing team, a two-hundred-pound beast named Malcolm, knocks me over as he stretches an impossibly long arm out to grab hold of the ball.

I scramble to my feet, ignoring the groans from our bench. There's less than a minute left, and I may have just cost us the game.

"C'mon, D," Troy shouts, clapping his hands at me as he races past. "Snap out of it!" I wipe the sweat from my eyes and sprint after him, trying to shut out distractions and focus on the ball. I can already see the headline in tomorrow's paper, though: *Edgewood Eagles grounded by Wilson blunder.*

Ever since Troy stepped foot on the basketball court in ninth grade and took our school from last in the division to first, the entire town has rallied behind the Edgewood Eagles. Local businesses support us, little kids know our names and positions, and every game we play is in front of a sold-out crowd.

Troy's the reason I moved up from B team to starter last year. Our friendship made us an unstoppable pairing on the court, able to read each other's minds and pick up on the smallest cues. Troy might be the star, but I'm his right-hand man, always in the perfect position for a pass. Or, at least, I used to be. My timing's been steadily falling apart this season, and I don't know why. It's like the connection between us is all screwed up and I keep misreading his cues.

Malcolm's shot bounces off the rim, and Troy is there to catch the rebound. I head down the court, dodging and weaving to shake my coverage, getting into position for Troy. There are ten seconds left in the game and we're down by one point.

Troy dribbles the ball, his eyes darting between me and Kevin. Kev's a super-tall Asian guy, with a solid two inches on me and a hook shot that can bring tears to your eyes. He's got two guys all over him, though, and I'm wide open. I plant my feet and get ready for the pass that doesn't come.

Troy fires the ball into Kevin's hands and time stands still as we watch Kevin pivot and line up his shot. The ball leaves his hands just as the clock winds down to zero and the whole gym goes silent as the ball arcs up into the air.

My stomach clenches as the ball swishes into the net and the crowd goes wild.

That was my shot. I was wide open.

Troy roars his approval at Kevin, grabbing him in a bear hug and then pumping his fist in the air. I give my head a shake as I realize that the whole team is celebrating while I stand here stunned.

I paste a smile onto my face and jog up to Kevin. "Beautiful shot, man!" I say, clapping him on the back. My voice sounds hollow, but no one seems to notice. Devaughn and Jackson swing Kevin up onto their shoulders, and the crowd laughs at the sight of them trying to support his weight.

This is a good thing, I remind myself. We needed this win.

I can see the new headline, though. *Maguire and Lee clinch win in last-second stunner.*

In the locker room, Troy snaps his towel at me before pulling two beer cans out of his bag and tossing me one. "Don't be a jerk about this," he tells me. "We won. That's what matters."

"Don't be a jerk about what?" I ask, like I have no idea what he's talking about. I check to make sure Coach has left the room and then pop the top on the can.

The corner of Troy's mouth turns up. "You think I can't tell that's a fake-ass smile? You're pissed I didn't pass you the ball."

I shrug. "You made the right call. Kev nailed that shot."

"Damn right I made the right call. I'm gonna say this as your captain and as your friend: You're all over the place out there, and if you don't get your shit together, Coach is gonna put you back on the bench."

I take a long pull off my beer and then meet Troy's eyes. "I'd've made that shot."

He cocks his head to the side. "Maybe. Maybe not."

"*That's* the problem," I tell him. "You've lost faith in me."

"No. The *problem* is that you're overthinking everything and not trusting your gut. You've lost your edge, and I can't rely on you."

He's not saying anything I haven't already said to myself, but it still stings to hear the words.

I drop onto the bench and kick off my sneakers. "I don't know what's happening, man." I tell him. "I think the pressure's getting to me."

He nods and sits down beside me, clapping a hand on my shoulder. "The pressure's there for all of us. But you gotta learn to *use* it to drive you forward, not let it drag you down."

"It's not just that," I say. Troy can do no wrong on the court. He doesn't know what it's like to be constantly under the gun. "Do you have any idea how hard it is to be the only white guy on the team, constantly battling for respect?"

"I *know* you didn't just play the race card with me." Troy laughs.

"I'm being serious. Every time I walk out there, I have to prove myself all over again. If the team sees that you've lost faith in me, then I'm done."

"Please. No one gives a shit if you're white or black. Least of all me. Kev's the only Asian out there, but you don't see him whining about it."

"Kev's a giant."

"Stop making excuses. It's not about size or race or anything except how you perform on the court. You get your shit together, I'll pass to you every time. You play like my mom, and I'll find someone else to rely on."

I chug the rest of my beer and let his words sink in. No more getting distracted. I need to focus and then everything can go back to normal. "I don't know," I deadpan, tossing the can into the trash. "Your mom's pretty baller."

"My mom's the shit," Troy says, yanking a clean T-shirt over his head. "Now get dressed and find your balls, white boy. It's time to party."

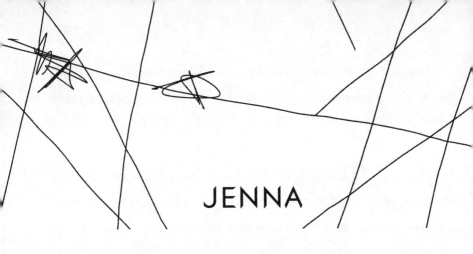

JENNA

I LEAN AGAINST THE COUNTER AT FRANNY'S FROYO AND WATCH FAT SNOWFLAKES FLOAT TO THE EARTH OUTSIDE THE FLOOR-TO-CEILING WINDOWS. There's nothing more excruciatingly boring than working at a frozen yogurt joint during the winter.

I probably should have quit Franny's ages ago, but my stepdad made me give up my late shifts at the diner after a girl got assaulted out back by the Dumpsters, and the movie theater down the street let a bunch of us go when business dropped off after the holidays.

"It's all Netflix's fault," my manager, Carl, said, handing me my last paycheck. "They're destroying the moviegoing experience."

Personally, I think the run-down building and dirty washrooms did more to wreck the moviegoing experience at Carl's theater, but I wasn't about to tell him that. Carl's dad runs the drive-in outside of town, the Dairy Queen, and the new A&W. I'm not about to burn that many potential employment bridges in one go.

I wipe the already spotless countertop and check the depth of snow in the parking lot for the millionth time. I left the house for my shift in a pair of Converse sneakers without considering the weather. A good two inches of snow has fallen since I've been here, and I'm going to have to trudge through it to get to my bus stop.

It looks like a scene from a Christmas card out there, which is so misleading. How is it that the pretty, gentle-looking snowfalls are the ones that accumulate into massive piles that have to be plowed and shoveled and trudged through, while the menacing-looking sleety snow just melts away and disappears?

The door chimes as a group of middle schoolers comes in, sans parents. Lovely. I paste on a smile and get ready for attitude.

I watch the girls fill their bowls with multiple flavors of frozen yogurt and pile on the toppings. I can tell by looking that their allowances aren't going to cover the cost of their creations.

"Hurry up, Sasha," a lanky blond snaps at a brunette who's clearly in the midst of an epic awkward stage. "My dad's picking us up in twenty minutes."

Poor Sasha, who's been deliberating over flavors, lurches toward the closest one and pulls the lever. I'm pretty sure she'll regret her choice. The coconut tastes like ass.

She fills up her bowl with toppings and rushes over to the scale, plunking the bowl beside the others and knocking their towers of toppings all over the place.

"Geez, Sasha!"

"You're such a spaz!"

"Who invited her anyway?"

It's too bad this place is self-serve, because I'd like to spit in all their froyos right about now. Well . . . everyone's but Sasha's.

"That'll be $39.50," I tell them, rocking back on my heels and waiting for the explosion.

"$39.50?" The blond wails. "That's ridiculous. It's yogurt and fruit."

"It's by weight," I explain patiently, looking longingly at the clock.

The girls grumble and empty their wallets out on a tabletop, counting their money.

"Sasha should have to pay extra for all that *candy* she heaped on," one of the girls announces. I watch Sasha shrink into herself, and I have to dig my fingernails into my palms to avoid exploding. *You need this job*, I remind myself. *Don't freak out.*

Sasha pulls a five out of her wallet and blinks back tears. "This is all I brought."

"You can't be serious. Five dollars?"

I take in Sasha's frayed jeans and scuffed boots and make a decision. "Sasha?"

She looks over at me, tears in her eyes. "Y-yes?"

"Were you the last one to put your froyo on the scale?"

"Um . . . yes?"

102

"Sorry, ladies, I gave you the wrong total." I take Sasha's order off and reweigh their bowls. "That'll be $31.20."

"Why?" a skinny brunette with way too much makeup asks.

"Because Sasha's our one-hundredth customer this week, so her order is on the house."

I pass Sasha her froyo and give her a little wink. "Put that five away," I tell her quietly. "Save it for people who deserve it."

She blushes and nods, going over to sit down at a table.

"Since we're a group order, shouldn't we *all* be free?" the brunette asks.

"Sorry," I say as cheerfully as I can. "That's not the way it works." *And I'll be paying for Sasha's order out of my own pocket. There's no way in hell I'm paying for yours.*

"Do you have a manager or something?" the blond girl asks, pulling out her cell phone and tapping away on the screen. "There must be somewhere to file complaints."

This is why I don't do nice things, I think to myself as I debate dumping all their orders in the trash and kicking them out. I'd like to keep this job, but I'm no saint . . .

Just before the little divas throw a shit fit that will inevitably trigger a meltdown of my own, the door chimes again and Drew walks in.

What the hell?

I blink at him, confused. "What are you doing here?"

He shrugs. "Getting frozen yogurt, of course." He smiles at the girls crowded around the cash register and I can see their little hearts start fluttering. "You ladies almost done?"

"Oh! Yes. For sure!" The blond girl snatches up the pile of bills they've been organizing and thrusts it at me.

I don't know whether to be thankful or insulted that Drew unwittingly saved my ass. Why is it that my best efforts to be polite and civil (not to mention stick up for the underdog) resulted in hostility, but one flash of Drew's dimples and the girls melted?

I give the blond her change and she actually drops it into the tip container. Seriously?

"Thanks for all your help," she chirps at me. "We'll just be over there." She smiles at Drew and flutters her eyelashes, and I nearly puke into the tip jar.

"Friendly girls," he mutters, too low for them to hear.

"Only because you walked in."

"I know. I was watching from my car. You looked like you needed some help. I figured it'd be better for both of us in the long run if I stepped in and broke things up instead of having to drive the getaway car after you beat them to death with the cash register."

"You're a real hero," I mutter, hating that he thinks he did me a massive favor.

"So, you really work at Franny's Froyo," he muses, stepping behind the counter and looking around. "What do you do here? I mean, besides taking money from middle schoolers."

"The usual stuff—cleaning up, prepping the yogurt and top-pings, end-of-day paperwork . . ." He looks far too interested in what I'm saying, and a sudden realization washes over me. "You've never had a job, have you?"

He shakes his head, looking sheepish. "Nah. My parents want me to focus on school and sports."

"Must be nice," I mutter.

"Not really," he says, clueless. "I'd love to have a job like this." He runs his hands over the counter and looks out at the store like a king surveying his domain. "Think about it—your boss trusts you to manage all of this . . . to be in here all by yourself and han-dle everything."

I snort as he walks toward the back room and stops in front of the schedule posted on the wall. I don't bother telling him that Franny triple-checks everything I do, convinced I'm trying to rob her blind.

He taps the schedule and shoots me a crooked smile. "Your name is up on the wall and everything," he says.

I'm about to make a joke about how easily impressed he is when I catch sight of a group of elderly ladies picking their way carefully along the snow-covered sidewalk outside. *Shit.* I recognize one of Franny's friends among them, so there's no doubt they're headed in here to check up on me. I push Drew into the back room. "Stay in here until I tell you it's safe to come out."

"Are you offering me a job?" he asks, reaching for an apron hanging on the wall.

"Not even close," I say, slapping his hand away from the apron. "Stay in here and keep your mouth shut, so you don't get me fired." I smooth down my uniform and scurry over behind the cash register before the door opens.

"Good afternoon," I say brightly, wincing at the idea of Drew listening to me suck up to customers. I wish he'd just stayed in the car and let me have it out with the middle schoolers.

"Good afternoon," the women chorus, looking around like they're casing the joint. I sneak a peek over at the toppings counter and breathe a sigh of relief that the girls didn't totally destroy it.

A piece of crumpled paper hits me in the side just as the women move over to the yogurt machines. I glare into the doorway of the back room, where Drew is pantomiming me picking up and opening the paper. I flap my hand at him, motioning him back just as one of the ladies looks over at me. I start waving my hand like I'm swatting away a fly instead.

"Are you OK, dear?" she asks, craning her neck to see around the machines and into the back room.

"Fine," I chirp. "Just thought I saw a fly." A fly. In the middle of winter. Nice.

Drew snorts in the back room and I cough to try to cover up the sound. Now all the women are staring at me and my face is flaming red.

"Could you recommend a flavor?" asks a tiny woman with gray hair and a purse that probably costs as much as a small car.

"Sure," I say, bending down quickly to snatch up the crumpled paper. "The mango is my favorite. Followed by the strawberry banana. The only flavor I wouldn't recommend is the coconut."

Out of the corner of my eye, I see Sasha's head snap up and the girls around her start laughing. *Shit. Sorry, Sasha.*

I'm sweating now, and I can feel the dampness in the underarms of my cheap polyester uniform. I wait for the ladies to go back to the froyo machines before shooting Drew a murderous look and unfolding his note.

Lookin' HOT, Bradley.

I swipe the note aside and reach under the counter for my phone, peering at my reflection on the blank screen. *Oh, good God.*

I whip off the bright-green visor Franny makes me wear and swipe underneath my eyes. I have huge mascara raccoon eyes and my apron is all lopsided. It's like I got dressed in the dark and then rolled through the snow to get here.

I pat my hair down as discreetly as I can before checking my reflection again. *Jesus.* The visor left a big red mark on my forehead that makes me look demented. I pull it back on and give up on looking like anything other than a complete disaster. What is he doing here, anyway? There's no way he jumped in his car in the middle of a blizzard and decided he had a hankering for frozen yogurt.

I knew driving home with him the other night was a mistake. But it was freezing outside and his car is so nice and Mouse was getting on my nerves and I hate taking the bus . . .

I force a smile onto my face as the old ladies bring their yogurt to the scale. I use my chirpiest voice and give them all extra napkins and even carry their tray over to a table for them, but not one of the old biddies leaves a tip. I make a mental note to put my application in at Starbucks first thing tomorrow morning. Especially if Drew the wonder boy is going to start popping up at my places of employment.

"Everyone all right here?" I ask, making a big show of wiping the toppings counter before slipping into the back room.

"How did you even know I work here?" I whisper, keeping half an eye on the storefront, so the old biddies won't tell Fran that I disappeared into the back.

Drew shrugs. "What makes you think I came here to see you? Maybe I just wanted frozen yogurt."

"Mmhmm. Likely story." I can't resist a smile, and it pisses me off.

"I called your house and your dad told me you were working here."

"You called my *house*? Who does that?" I can't believe the nerve of him. He might as well follow me home and peek in the windows.

He shrugs. "You didn't answer your cell."

"Because I'm *working*."

"I figured that out. After I called your house."

I sigh and lean back out the door again, checking on Franny's friends. Why do old people eat so freaking slowly?

"So, what's the emergency?" I ask. "Why the sudden need to track me down on a snowy Sunday afternoon?"

He twists one side of his mouth up into a flirtatious smile and steps closer to me. "I thought we could hang out. Just the two of us."

"You're joking," I say sarcastically, folding my arms over my chest. "One ride home and you think I'm into you?"

"One ride home and I think *I'm* into *you*."

I can't help myself. It's such a classic Drew move that I burst out laughing.

The smile slides off his face, and my stomach swoops in sudden panic. He can't be serious. This is *Drew* we're talking about. He shamelessly flirts with every girl who crosses his path. "I—I mean . . ."

I twist my hands together, trying to figure out how to deal with this. I can't have Drew interested in me. Not seriously, anyway.

His face breaks into a dazzling smile. "Gotcha," he says, with a low laugh that I can feel rumbling in my own chest.

I reach out and smack him on the shoulder. "You jerk. I thought I hurt your feelings or something."

"Haven't you heard?" he asks with a shrug. "I don't have any feelings."

His tone is light, but there's an edge beneath his words. I'm beginning to feel like it's going to be harder to manage Drew than I expected. I somehow have to find a balance between being friendly enough to make it through the next three weeks of working together and being distant enough not to encourage his affections.

"Excuse me," a tremulous voice calls out behind me, interrupting my thoughts.

I whirl around to find the old lady with the massive handbag staring at us with pursed lips. "Yes?" I ask innocently, stepping in front of Drew as though I might erase his presence from her memory.

I hear Drew fumbling on Franny's desk behind me and send him a silent plea to quiet down and stay out of sight.

"Do you work here?" the lady calls out, tapping on the counter. "I don't think you should be back there."

Just as I open my mouth to make excuses, Drew steps around me holding a clipboard.

"Sorry to interrupt, ladies," he says confidently, "but I've finished my inspection and I'm due at the next location in less than an hour."

I blink at him. "You've finished your . . . ?"

"Top marks for cleanliness for both the storefront and the back room. The stickers on the machines indicate that you're due for service within the next year, but you're still within guidelines." He taps a pen on top of the clipboard. "Please let the owner know that I'll be mailing out my report within the week."

Drew nods his head at Franny's friend. "Sorry for the

disruption, ma'am." He saunters over and lets himself out from behind the counter, then walks out of the shop without even looking back at me.

I'm still standing in the doorway of the back room, stunned, when the lady at the counter turns back to me. "Well," she says, "that was certainly the most charming health inspector I've ever seen. And the youngest, too."

Her eyes are sparkling, and a little laugh escapes me. I can't tell if she's onto me or if she really was charmed by Drew.

"He's young," I tell her. "I'll give him that. But charming? I'm not sure. I think he was a little too full of himself."

Her laugh rings out in the tiny shop, making her sound much younger than she appears. "The handsome ones always are, dear."

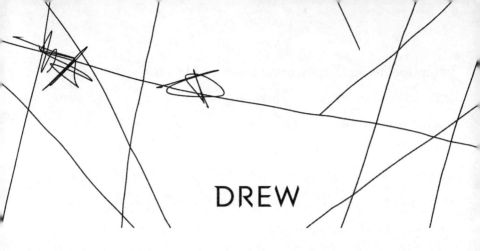

DREW

WHERE THE HELL IS MY BLUE TIE?

I kick at the stack of clothes piled on the floor of my closet but can't find it anywhere. This is why I never clean my room. I have a *system*: The clothes draped over my desk chair or piled on top of the hamper are still clean; the ones by the foot of my bed are questionable but could do in an emergency; and the ones thrown on the bathroom floor have passed the point of no return.

When Jenna texted earlier today and suggested we meet at someone's house instead of the library, I was all over it. I hate everything about the library—the uncomfortable chairs, the constant *shh* from the librarians, and the slow-ass Wi-Fi. So, when Mouse said his house was out of the question and Jenna failed to offer hers up, I invited them both here.

Which explains why I had to do a rushed cleaning job and why my laundry system got all fucked up when I dumped the entire contents of my room into my walk-in closet and pulled the door shut.

But that doesn't explain why I'm in desperate need of a solid-blue tie on a Wednesday night.

I have my brother, Harrison, to thank for that.

Harrison's not supposed to be here till the weekend. But, as my mother informed me when she came home early to prepare, he finished his last midterm today and couldn't wait to come home. So my mother decided that a formal family dinner was in order. Of course. How else would we welcome the Golden Boy home?

I rifle through my dresser drawers, trying to remember the last time I wore that blue tie. It must have been a Game Day, which means it's probably rotting in my gym bag. I peek my head out of my room to make sure my mother isn't outside. I should be dressed by now, and she'll lose her shit if I'm not ready when Harrison walks in.

The coast is clear, so I take the steps two at a time and then skid to a stop in front of the hall closet. I grab my gym bag from where I tossed it inside and race back upstairs when I hear the garage door opening.

He's back.

I yank the tie out of my bag and start to fasten it around my neck before the smell hits me. Jesus.

"Andrew!" my mother calls, rapping on my door. "Your brother's home."

"Just a sec," I say, darting into my en suite bathroom and

feeling my heart drop. The tie is a wrinkled, smelly mess. The only one I have clean has red and black stripes, and I'm wearing a blue checkered shirt. Even *I* know that shit won't fly.

I can hear my mother rushing down the stairs and calling her hellos as I whip the door of my closet open again. I need a solid shirt, but my hangers are all bare. When my brother went off to school, Mother decided we were all grown-up enough to start doing our own laundry. "I don't want you children being spoiled," she told us right before instructing our housekeeper to stop collecting our dirty laundry. Hence my flawed system and clothing crisis.

I weigh my options. I can risk a polo shirt or sweater, which my mother will inevitably see as an insult to my brother; I can wear my current shirt with either the clashing striped tie or the wrinkled dirty one; or I can wear a wrinkled white button-down with the striped tie. I yank a white shirt out of the pile and cringe. It looks like I slept in it.

Harrison hammers at my door on his way to his room. "Hurry up, loser. I'm starving and mom's waiting on your lazy ass."

Terrific. I tie the clashing tie around my neck and check my phone. It's six thirty already, and Jenna and Mouse are supposed to be here by seven thirty. With any luck, they'll be late. Very, very late.

▲ ▼ ▲

"There you are," my mother says, depositing a vase full of flowers on the front-hall table. "What took you so . . ." Her voice trails off as she catches sight of me.

"What in the world are you wearing?" She sighs, her heels tapping on the floor as she approaches. "I swear, Andrew. It's like you were raised by wolves."

She pulls me into the library and smooths down my hair. "Take off that hideous tie. Where's your blue one?"

"Laundry."

She frowns and takes the tie from me. "Having you do your own laundry was supposed to make you more self-reliant, not turn you into a street person."

I can't resist a smile. "I'm hardly a bum, Mother."

She adjusts my collar and brushes at my shirt. "Clearly you need ironing lessons."

It takes all my effort to keep from rolling my eyes. My mother doesn't even know where the laundry room is.

"What is your father going to say?" she muses as she leads me out of the library.

Nothing good, I'm sure. But then, my father would find fault with me even if I was dressed by Calvin Klein himself.

"What is your father going to say about what?" Dad asks as we step into the hallway. He drops his briefcase on the front table and looks up at us. "Ah. I see the Great Laundry Experiment is still on."

"Shush," my mother laughs, hitting him playfully on the arm. "Andrew is still learning."

"Jesus Christ," Dad mutters. "He's almost eighteen years old." He turns to me and I can feel the lecture coming. When my father was my age, apparently, he was already a god among men. "What are you, some kind of moron?" he asks. "You can't manage to get dressed without your mommy?"

I force out a strangled-sounding laugh and clench my jaw until my back teeth ache.

He opens his mouth to say something more but is interrupted by the sound of Harrison on the stairs.

"There's my boy!" Dad calls out as Harrison strides over to us, his hand held out to our father.

"What's this?" Dad teases, brushing aside the handshake and pulling Harrison into a hug. "You're too grown to hug your father?"

"I brought you a present," Harrison tells him, retrieving a small wooden box from the bottom step. "My chemistry professor says they're the best cigars around."

Dad's face breaks into a wide smile as he lifts the lid of the box. "Thank you, son, but you shouldn't have. If you're spending money, spend it on your mother."

"He did," Mother says, gesturing at the giant arrangement of flowers on the front table. "Aren't they lovely?"

"Good to have you home, Harrison," my father says proudly,

116

putting an arm around my brother's shoulder and leading him into the dining room. "I'm hoping you'll rub off on your siblings."

Mother looks at her watch and sighs. "Speaking of siblings, where is your sister?"

I shrug, hoping Ange is upstairs in her room. I've been so preoccupied thinking about all the ways tonight is going to be hell for me that I forgot to factor in the wild card that is my sister.

"Do me a favor," Mother says, straightening my collar again. "Go let Angela know that it's time for dinner. I'd hate to hold everyone up."

I take the stairs two at a time, muttering to myself as I go. I want this dinner over and done with as soon as possible, so I can sneak Jenna and Mouse upstairs without any drama.

"Angie," I call, pounding on her door. "Get downstairs! Mom's gonna shit herself if you hold up dinner."

No answer.

"I'm coming in," I warn, jiggling the doorknob.

When she doesn't screech at me to stay out, I push open the door to find her room empty. *You've got to be kidding me.* I stomp over to her bathroom and peek inside, but there's no one there. Where the hell is she?

By the time I make it downstairs, Harrison and my mother are already sitting at the table, with my father pouring the wine. Mother raises her eyebrows at me and I shake my head.

"Let's get started," she says brightly, picking up a platter and passing it to my father.

Dad looks over at Angela's empty chair and shakes his head, his lips turned down in a frown.

According to my father, the world is split into winners and losers, with the default setting being loser. To be a winner, you have to expend special effort. To be a winner, you have to actively *stop* being a loser.

Harrison is a winner.

Angela and I are borderline losers.

It doesn't matter that I play varsity basketball and soccer, or that I have a solid B average, or that I can get any girl I want. None of that matters because Harrison has already done all that and *more*.

"How was your day?" Mother asks, trying to distract Dad from Angie's empty chair.

"Fine. Fine," he says, waving off the question. "Same as always. Although . . ." His eyes light up. "I heard some rather interesting news today. You remember Ben MacDonald, don't you? From the pharmacy?"

"Oh, yes," Mother says. "Nice man. Bad teeth."

"Yes, well, I heard he just filed for bankruptcy."

"No! With the business they do in there?"

"Rumors of gambling," Dad says, shaking his head in fake sadness.

Harrison meets my eyes and smirks. This is our parents' favorite game: Name the Loser.

"His son goes to my school," I say, just to stir the pot. "Total druggie."

For the first time all night, Dad looks at me with something resembling interest. "Really? I wonder if there's a connection to the pharmacy."

"I don't think they sell E at the pharmacy," Angie laughs, breezing into the room dressed in denim overalls and a ratty T-shirt.

"Oh, *Angela*," Mother exclaims. "You can't sit down to dinner dressed like that! Go change right this instant."

"Mom, please. I'm starving!" Ange plops down next to me and spears a potato off my plate. "Thanks, bro," she says, through the wad of food.

"Angela!"

"I was painting, Mom. Chill. Harry doesn't care, do you, Harry?"

"Not in the slightest," Harrison says, winking at her.

Mother sighs and shakes her head at Ange. "Well, at least explain to me what E is, then."

"Oh, no," Ange laughs. "You'll have to ask Drew about that."

"Yeah, right! You're the one who hangs out with the *artsy* crowd. If anyone knows about the drug scene, it's your hippie friends."

"Andrew!" Mother exclaims, just as the doorbell rings.

"Jesus Christ," Dad says, tossing his napkin onto the table. "It's like a circus around here tonight."

"I'll get it, Dad," I say, leaping up out of my chair. I figure I'll stash Mouse and Jenna up in my room and then come back down to finish out dinner. No need to make introductions. I can just imagine the look on my father's face if he met Mouse and Jenna.

"Sit," Dad commands. "I'm perfectly capable of answering the door."

Shit.

Ange raises her eyebrows at me, but I ignore her and start shoveling food into my mouth. "This is great, Mom. Delicious." I stand up and toss my napkin onto the table. "I'm gonna go see—"

My mother stands, and I can tell from the look on her face that my cover is blown. I turn to see my dad ushering Mouse and Jenna into the dining room.

"Angela," Mother scolds, maneuvering around our chairs, "you should have told us you invited friends over. We'd have set a place for them at the table."

Ange rolls her eyes. "They're not here for me, Mother."

"No?" Mom asks, holding out a hand in greeting to Mouse.

"No. They're friends of *Drew's*," Dad says pointedly.

"Oh . . . Oh! Of course . . ." Mom falters.

"I'm Matthew," Mouse says, after an awkward pause. "And this is Jenna."

"Hey, Mouse," Harrison calls out. "Long time no see."

Mouse startles, obviously surprised that my brother knows his name.

"Mouse is Troy's cousin," my brother explains. "And Jenna is . . . ?"

I search his face for any sign of recognition. Harrison's met Jenna before through Troy, but I can tell by the look on his face that he doesn't recognize her, not that that's surprising. Jenna's no longer the carefree blond that she used to be.

"A classmate," I say, a little too firmly. Harrison arches his left eyebrow, and I curse myself for piquing his interest. "The three of us got *assigned* to the same group in Bailey's law class."

Jenna shoots me a withering look that I ignore.

"Well, Troy's family is our family," my Dad says, clapping Mouse so hard on the back that his knees buckle. "Pull up a chair and have a seat, both of you. There's plenty to go around."

My parents love Troy like he's their own son. Hell, they probably love him more than they love me . . . Maybe even more than they love Harrison.

"Absolutely," Harrison says, with a big shit-eating grin on his face. "If Drew's doing schoolwork on a Wednesday night, it's got to be one interesting project." He shifts his chair over and smiles at Jenna. "Maybe I can help. I aced Bailey's law class."

"Everyone aces Bailey's law class," Jenna says levelly. "I think we've got it covered."

I can't resist laughing at the expression on Harrison's face. "We really need to get to work," I tell my mother, who's studying Jenna. I turn to Mouse. "You guys ate already, didn't you?"

121

Mouse nods his head so fast that he must be doing damage to that big brain of his. "We're really behind," he says apologetically. "Thank you for the invitation, though, Mr. and Mrs. Wilson."

I give Mouse a little push toward the door and hurry out of the dining room before my father's face can turn any redder than it already is. I know he'll have a lot to say about Jenna's manners as soon as we leave, but I don't care. It was worth it to watch her shoot Harrison down.

"That was awesome," I tell her, slinging an arm around her shoulder at the base of the stairs.

She shrugs me off and stops, crossing her arms over her chest. "Which part was awesome? The way you made a point of how you got stuck with us as partners? Or when your parents slobbered all over Mouse while pretending that I didn't exist?"

"You're cute when you're mad," I tell her, pinching her cheek and then dodging her left hook. "Relax! My parents are superficial idiots and I saved you from the agony of having to sit through a meal with them."

"Well, at least now we know where you got it from," she mutters.

I meet her eyes and my heart stutters. She must feel it, too.

"Guys?" Mouse interrupts, startling Jenna. "Are we getting to work, or what?"

"After you," I say, gesturing up the stairs.

Mouse gives me a hard look before starting up the steps. Jenna moves to follow, and I reach out and touch her arm to stop her.

"You want to hate me, I know," I tell her. "But you can't help liking me. I'm just too damn charming."

"You're an idiot," she declares, her expression unreadable. "Mouse, tell Drew he's an idiot."

But Mouse just shakes his head and keeps walking.

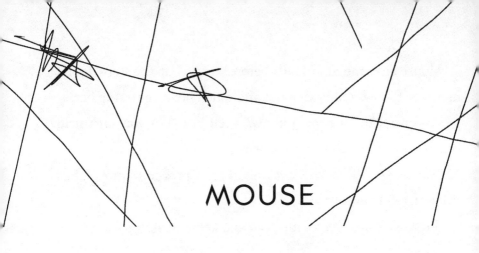

MOUSE

WE SHOULD HAVE GONE TO THE LIBRARY.

Drew's room is ridiculous. His parents must print money in the basement or something, because there's no way any seventeen-year-old should have a brand-new iMac, a laptop, every game system under the sun, *and* a flat-screen TV in their room.

"You've got to be kidding me," Jenna breathes, walking into his room behind me. "Who are you people? Is your father a mobster or something?"

Drew shrugs, but I can tell he loves the attention. Drew loves all attention.

"Can we get down to work?" I ask sharply as Jenna wanders through his room. She runs her hand along his dark wooden desk and then sits in his leather chair and jiggles the mouse of his iMac, bringing to life a computer screen larger than my family's television.

"How do you not have straight As with a setup like this?" she asks, twirling the chair around and putting her feet up on his desk. Drew presses his lips into a straight line, and I wonder how many times his parents have asked him that same question.

"Mediocrity is my superpower," he quips, grabbing his laptop and heading for a pair of leather couches on the far side of the room. "Come work over here. It's more comfortable."

I hitch my backpack up on my shoulder and follow Drew, shaking my head at the excess, until I see something that makes my knees go weak with want—floor-to-ceiling shelves filled with what can only be . . .

"You into comics?" Drew asks as I drop my bag on a couch and gape at a setup that's a comic-collector's dream. The shelves are clearly custom and are divided into a series of glass-fronted drawers that pull out to provide access to the carefully packaged comics inside. I think of my own comics at home, stored in cardboard boxes stacked in my closet, and feel a pang of jealousy. Is there anything Drew *doesn't* have?

"Check them out if you want," Drew says. "I have a pretty impressive *Batman* collection."

Of course he does.

I shake my head and tear my eyes away from the comics as Jenna flops down next to Drew and pulls out her laptop. "Where should we start?"

Right. Drew might have every luxury under the sun, but *I'm* the brains here. I open my mouth to take charge, but Drew steps in before I can get a word in.

"I started researching last night," he says, pulling out a notebook and flipping through the pages. "This case is way more complicated than I thought, and . . . What?"

Jenna and I are both staring at him with our mouths hanging open.

Jenna recovers first. "You started researching?"

He rolls his eyes. "Don't be so surprised. This case is crazy. Look at this . . ." He flips through his notes and then taps a page. "Heather Morningside's family claimed she didn't know that her boyfriend . . ." He flips another page and checks his notes. " . . . Aaron Ducet . . . was filming when they had sex, but when the police checked her phone records, they found that she'd been sending him raunchy photos of herself for weeks and that the two of them had discussed filming themselves having sex the day before he shot the video."

I lean forward, interested. "But her parents probably didn't know that when they made their statement, right? I mean, it's not like Heather would have shown those texts to Mom and Dad."

"That's where things get interesting." Drew flips the page and reads from his notes. "According to Detective Kaden Miller, the texts and images were recovered by investigators from the computer forensics team." He looks up. "Did you know that was even a thing?"

"Of course," I tell him. "They analyze tech associated with criminal activity."

Drew nods. "Well, they can do shit I didn't even know was possible. Not only did they find every message, photo, and video ever deleted from her phone, but they also determined the date and time each one was erased."

"And . . . ?" Jenna asks, drawing out the word. "Who cares that she deleted her messages or when she did it? As a matter of fact, who even cares that they were there? This case is about the fact that her boyfriend posted the video, not whether she knew she was being filmed."

"All that's true," Drew tells her, "except for one thing. Heather didn't delete the messages. According to the investigators, all of Heather's messages were deleted on October 17."

I open a browser tab on my laptop and do a quick search to be sure. "Two days after she died."

Drew sits back on the couch, nodding his head. "Two days *after* she died. Which means Ma and Pa Morningside, who sang the praises of their virginal daughter, found the messages, deleted them, and then pretended they never existed."

Jenna raises her eyebrows. "That's a big leap, isn't it? I mean, what if the boyfriend got ahold of the phone and deleted the messages to save his own ass? Or a friend or sibling or someone who wanted to protect her image?"

"All questions the police asked, because Heather's parents denied having any knowledge of the missing messages. But they caught her father in a lie about where the phone had been and who had access to it, and eventually, her parents confessed to deleting everything related to Aaron Ducet."

Jenna shrugs. "So what? So her parents are idiots. What does that have to do with the case? You can't figure out what happened to Heather before she died by the actions of her parents *after* she died."

"That's faulty logic," I tell her. "How people behave before, during, and after a crime are all part of criminal behavior analysis. There are whole branches of police forces dedicated to the study."

"You've been watching too much *CSI*."

I ignore her. "Besides, if they were willing to lie about the messages, what else are they lying about? This throws all their testimony into question."

"And too much *Law & Order*," Jenna mutters. "I think you guys are reading way too much into this. Heather Morningside was fifteen years old. In the course of a few weeks, her parents found out that she was having sex with a predatory asshole, that she unwittingly starred in an amateur porn video that was sent to all her friends, that she was so bullied afterward that she took her own life, and that she'd been sending compromising pictures of herself from a phone they probably bought for her. Why are you even surprised they'd want to erase all traces of her mistakes? Is that what you'd want people to remember about someone you love?"

"It's not so much that they erased the photos," Drew says,

tapping his pencil on his notebook. "It's that they went out of their way to deny her involvement. They lied."

"And not just lied," I jump in. "They presented a false image of her to the press and to the police. That's got to qualify as interfering with a criminal investigation."

Jenna rubs her hands over her eyes. "I get what you're saying, but I think you're both missing the point. Her parents aren't the ones on trial here. The scuzzy boyfriend is. *He's* the one who posted the video online. He's being charged with possession of child pornography and distribution of child pornography. What her parents knew or didn't know is beside the point."

"Huh." Drew draws the corners of his mouth down and nods appreciatively at Jenna. "Good point."

"Don't look so surprised," she quips. "I'm not just a pretty face."

There's something pulling at the back of my mind, though, and I'm not about to give up the argument as quickly as Drew. "But maybe her parents *did* commit a crime. Maybe they *should* be held accountable."

Jenna levels her gaze at me. "For trying to protect their daughter?"

"No. For trying to shift all blame onto Aaron Ducet. Just hear me out, because I think we could have a really unique way of looking at this case."

Jenna crosses her arms over her chest and glares at me, and I feel my confidence falter for a moment. I know she doesn't like where I'm going with this, but she's a smart girl. Smarter than other people give her credit for. She's going to see the brilliance of my idea. I just need her to be able to look at things objectively and recognize that what happened to Heather Morningside is nothing like what happened to her.

"Think about it this way," I say. "She was only fifteen years old, and she had unsupervised use of a cell phone and enough freedom that she could maintain a secret relationship with an eighteen-year-old. Does that seem right to you?"

Drew's eyebrows knit together. "So, you're saying this happened because her parents let it?"

I do a quick Google search and find what I'm looking for. "Parental negligence. I'm sending you both a link."

Their laptops ding as my email finds its way to them.

Jenna gets to the message first and reads aloud. "Parental Duty to Supervise." She skims through the article and then pushes her laptop aside. "This only pertains to young children," she says. "It's about parents having to control and supervise kids who are too young to understand the consequences of their actions or control their behaviors. Heather Morningside was fifteen."

"Yes," I say, "But . . ." I send them another link, this time to a newspaper article. "Check this out."

Drew's face pales as he reads it, and he shoots me a quizzical look.

"The laws are changing," I explain. "When the majority of the

Criminal Code was written, there was no Internet. No online world to contend with. This shows that lawmakers recognize we need to reexamine the law to take into account the unexpected consequences of Internet use."

The new law will make it a crime to post or distribute intimate photos of anyone, regardless of their age. Which means that people will no longer have to rely on child pornography laws as their only recourse if someone passes around compromising pictures of them.

Jenna's eyes are bright when she looks up from her laptop screen. "This is good," she says. "I just wish it'd happened earlier."

Drew gives me a warning look that I ignore. "But you didn't need it last year. You were still under eighteen and the child pornography laws would have applied," I tell her.

"*Would have*," she says. "Except that nobody took what happened seriously enough to call it child pornography. It took Heather Morningside's *death* for this kind of change to be possible."

"But I don't get why this is necessary," Drew interrupts. "Heather Morningside was fifteen. The old laws protected her and that's what they're charging the boys with. Why create this new law?"

"You're joking, right?" Jenna snaps. "You don't think this is long overdue?"

"I think it sounds like a classic case of overcorrection. All of a sudden people's activity on the Internet is going to come under scrutiny because of a couple of bullying idiots. Why should my rights be limited because of the actions of others?"

"How are your rights limited? This only applies to nude or sexually explicit photos. If you're not betraying anyone's trust and being a total dickhead, this will never apply to you."

"But what about shares on Facebook or reposts on Instagram," Drew says, leaning forward. "What if I repost a photo of a swimsuit model. Am I going to get charged with a crime?"

Jenna rolls her eyes. "Did you even read the article? Or did you just freak out immediately and let your brain shut down? Because it says right here," she says, tapping her screen, "that it only applies to photos where there is a reasonable expectation of privacy. Meaning, if I sent you a nude shot that was just for your eyes and you decided to pass it around to your teammates. A swimsuit model who poses for a photoshoot obviously does not have an expectation that the photos are private."

"OK," Drew says, deflating. "That makes sense. But I still think it seems overdone to extend the law beyond eighteen. A woman over eighteen is an adult and knows the risks when she sends those kinds of pictures. She's old enough to understand the consequences of her actions."

"And so is anyone who decides to post her pictures without her consent. Which is why they should be within reach of the law."

"We're getting off track," I interrupt them. "The reason I

showed you this article was to support my argument for parental negligence in Heather's case."

"I don't see what one thing has to do with the other," Jenna says, her eyebrows furrowed. "Are you trying to say that because her parents are the adults in the scenario they should have to pay the price?"

"No. Not entirely." I stand up and pace in front of them. There's an idea forming in my brain, but I haven't quite grasped it fully. "Give me a minute," I say, grabbing my laptop and heading over to Drew's desk. I'm so close to something, and I need to read without distraction. I type "Parental Duty to Supervise cases" into Google and skim through the search results. I'm dimly aware of Jenna and Drew arguing behind me, but I push their voices out of my head and lean in to the screen.

It's the seventh link that pulls everything together, and I leap out of Drew's chair. "In Parental Duty to Supervise cases, the key factor in whether parents are liable is how well they prepared their children to face dangerous situations. Kids who run in front of cars or cause an accident while on their bikes, for instance. If the parents can prove that they educated their children on traffic or bike safety, they're not found liable. If they didn't provide adequate supervision or instruction, they *are* liable."

"But again, these are *children*. Like, kids under five," Jenna points out.

"Yes, which is why it's important that the laws around Internet use are in flux. The law as it stands assumes that as children get older, they need less supervision. My argument is that in the case of Internet safety, kids between ten and fifteen or sixteen need *more* supervision. Did Heather Morningside's parents monitor her Internet use and teach her about online safety? Or did they just hand her a cell phone and hope for the best? Because those are skills that *have* to be taught later, I think we can argue that the parental duty to supervise should be extended."

I'm breathing hard by the time I'm done with my pitch, and my heart is pounding. I know my idea is good, but I need both of them on board.

Drew gets up and paces between the couches. "I like it," he says finally. "I didn't really want to go crazy with this project, because it's just Bailey's class, but I think this could be really interesting."

Jenna snorts.

"What?" he asks her. "You have to admit he's onto something here."

"No. What I have to admit is that I've been paired with a couple of morons. I really thought you two would be smarter than to be distracted by all the noise around this case."

I knew she'd be difficult about this. "What's that supposed to mean?"

"It means that every time a guy hurts a girl, the world goes crazy trying to figure out all the ways she's to blame for what happened to her. And you're both falling into that trap."

"But I'm saying she *wasn't* responsible. You should be happy about that. I'm not blaming Heather Morningside."

"Yes, you are. You're still saying it's her fault, but with the insulting disclaimer that she's too young and stupid to be held responsible. Instead of putting the blame on Aaron Ducet, which is where it belongs, you're saying she never should have sent the photos in the first place because her parents should have taught her not to. Whether you hang her out to dry or blame her parents, it still comes down to blaming the victim."

"Jenna," I say in my calmest voice. "This is what Miss Bailey wants. She wants us to use case law and apply it to an ongoing case. This is *gold*. We'll get an A for sure, *and* we'll provide new insight on laws related to Internet use."

I see it coming an instant before it hits. I've pushed her too far, and her eyes flash as she rounds on me. "I don't give a fuck what Bailey wants. Bailey is a complete idiot and a raving bitch who loves putting kids down. Why are you trying so hard to impress someone you despise?" She clenches her fists and closes her eyes, trying to get her temper under control. "When are you going to learn, Mouse, that an A is not worth compromising your values. I'd rather fail this project than put my name on something that blames Heather Morningside or her family for what her boyfriend did to her. End of discussion."

Drew blinks at us, taken aback. "OK. Let's calm down for a minute." He runs his hands through his hair. "Maybe it's not such a bad thing that we see things differently here. The law isn't black and white, right? Isn't that what Bailey's always saying?" He holds up a hand as Jenna starts to object. "Just hang on a second. What if we produce two different views of the case, with research to back up each one. Mouse and I can work the parental negligence angle, and you can argue against it."

"I like it," I say, getting excited. "That ties in to the main theme of the course—that the law can be interpreted multiple ways and that it's all about how you make your argument."

They both turn to stare at me. "There's a theme to the course?" Drew asks.

"Absolutely. And we just figured out a way to tie our project in to it."

Drew and I both look at Jenna, who's still quietly seething.

"You won't have to endorse my interpretation of the law. You'll just have to recognize it as an alternative to yours," I tell her. This is the answer to all my worries about this project.

Jenna bites her thumbnail and considers my proposal. "I can do whatever I want with my section of the project?"

"Anything you want," I assure her.

"All right, then," she says, sweeping her hair into a stubby ponytail and grabbing her laptop. "You're on."

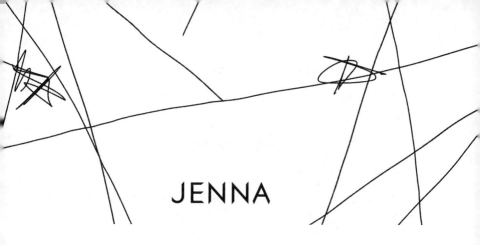

JENNA

HOW COME YOU HATE BAILEY SO MUCH?

I squint at the screen of my phone and then check my bedside clock.

It's one in the morning, I type back.

That's not an answer, Drew responds, making me smile despite myself.

I'm trying to think of a witty comeback when he messages, *Did I wake you up?*

Nope. Was reading.

Lies. No one reads at 1 a.m. What are you "reading"?

Schoolwork, I lie.

I stick a bookmark between the pages of my novel and toss it onto my bedside table. There's no way I'd admit to Drew or anyone else how addicted I am to the Stormgirl series. If there's one thing I hate, it's a cliché, and me reading stories about a girl who devotes her life to training as a fighter so she can seek vengeance on her enemies by kicking ass all over her kingdom is more than a little cliché.

I burrow under the covers with my phone. *Who says I hate Bailey?*

Well . . . you called her a bitch and an idiot today.

Just stating facts. You've said similar.

Maybe. Seemed more personal than that, tho.

Why does he care? *You're reading too much into this. I hate everyone, remember?*

Even me?

Fishing for compliments? Didn't peg you as needy.

It takes a moment before his reply appears. *Ouch.*

I'm heartless, remember?

I don't believe that.

I flex my fingers over the phone, trying to resist the urge to type what I already know I'm going to write: *I thought everyone on the team knew I was a heartless bitch after I tried to take down your beloved captain.* I hesitate for a second before sending the message and then hold my breath for his response.

We've never talked about that before.

That's cause I don't talk about it, I reply.

You're the one who brought it up.

Temporary lapse in judgment.

Can I ask you a question without you getting mad?

My heart takes a little leap. *Doubtful. But you can try.*

How come you never got revenge?

I did. I lit his fucking truck on fire.

138

No. I mean real revenge.

I narrow my eyes at the screen. Where is he going with this? *Like what?*

I dunno. He must have sent you pics too. Why didn't you post his photos?

Oh, please. That's not revenge.

No?

No. You guys pass around pictures of your wangs like it's nothing. I'd just save you all time by posting your dick pictures.

Did you just say "wangs"?

I laugh out loud before clapping a hand over my mouth. Drew's going to make me wake up the whole house. *Yes, smart-ass, I did.*

Just checking. So . . . you want a picture of my wang?

And just like that, all the fun is sucked out of the conversation. Why can't guys go two minutes without making things sexual? *No, I do not want a picture of your wang. Go to bed, Drew.*

Can't blame me for trying. Good night.

I set my phone on my nightstand and debate picking up my book again, but everything I didn't tell Drew about what happened with Bailey is bouncing around in my brain. Instead, I turn off my lamp and burrow under the covers, waiting for the memories to run their course so I'll be able to fall asleep.

Less than a week after my photos went viral, I was walking down the hallway with my head held high, daring anyone to mess with me. Inside, though, I was shaking. Inside I felt like all my nerve endings were firing at once. Like I was made of flame.

People averted their eyes or whispered, and I pretended I didn't care. Ella and my former friends looked through me like I didn't exist, and I pretended I didn't care. My heart was broken and I missed Troy so badly it hurt, and I pretended I didn't care.

Before I met Troy, I hated my body. The way my belly curved out instead of being flat, no matter how many hours I spent in the ballet studio, and the way one of my boobs was noticeably bigger than the other. I hated the faint spider veins on my legs and the way my arms were just a little too thick. When I looked in the mirror, I saw all my imperfections.

So when Troy and I first started dating, I was petrified to let him see me naked. I kept putting him off, convinced that if he saw my body, he'd be disgusted. It didn't help that he was absolute perfection—all sculpted muscles and smooth, perfect skin.

After months of insisting on completely darkened rooms whenever we fooled around, I finally relented and allowed him to leave the lights on. And I'll never forget the look on his face when he saw me. He was captivated by the sight of me. He loved everything that I hated about my appearance. He nicknamed my boobs Big and Little and loved to rest his head on the gentle curve of my belly. He made me feel beautiful. I started to see myself through his eyes—the eyes of someone who loved me—and it made me think about my body in a whole new way.

Until my pictures went up on the Internet.

Seeing my naked body displayed on Twitter stripped away all that magic and laid my flaws out in the cold light of day. I went back to seeing myself through the eyes of people who *didn't* love me, and it was devastating. The comments and laughter and replies to the tweet all reaffirmed every terrible thing I'd ever thought about myself and my body.

So when Miss Bailey, a teacher I'd never even had before, stepped up that day and asked to speak with me, it was a welcome distraction from the train wreck in my brain. I followed her into her classroom and sat down across from her desk.

"I heard what happened to you, Jenna, and I can't imagine what you're going through."

I felt something in me reach out to her. Miss Bailey had a reputation as a mean teacher, but she was offering me kindness when I most needed it. I opened my eyes wide and let the tears fall. Tears I'd been holding back with every last bit of my willpower. I hadn't realized how exhausting the effort was until I let go.

Bailey shifted uncomfortably as I cried. There was a box of tissues on the far corner of her desk, but she didn't offer me any, so I wiped my face on the sleeve of my hoodie.

"I can see this is very upsetting for you. I'd really like to offer you the opportunity to share your story. I think it might help you feel better."

"Thanks," I mumbled, not sure if I was ready to talk quite yet. "I haven't had many people to talk to, so I appreciate you listening."

Her eyebrows drew together. "Well yes . . . I suppose I'll be there, too. It is my class, after all."

"I . . . I don't understand."

"I'd like you to talk to my senior law class. To share your story so that others can have the benefit of learning from your mistakes."

All my whirling emotions crystallized into a sharp point as her words sunk in. "My mistakes?"

"I think you could really help people with your story, Jenna. The girls in this school need to learn about the dangers associated with sharing certain types of . . . *information* online. I've talked about this in class, but I don't think I'm getting through. It would be so much more powerful for them to hear from you about how it feels to be exposed like that." She gave a little shudder. "And I think that they would really benefit from hearing you talk about the ways that this will impact your future."

I blinked at her. "My future?"

"Of course! You won't be in high school forever, but those pictures will always exist online. How do you think this will affect you when you're trying to get a respectable job?"

Looking back, I don't know why I was so shocked. Everything I'd heard about Bailey should have prepared me for the things she was saying. But I felt fooled all over again—just like I had when I first saw my naked body posted from Troy's account. I felt ashamed and stupid and worthless, like it was all my fault and I should have seen it coming. So I raced out of her classroom and didn't speak to her again until the first day of this semester, when I sat defiantly in senior law.

Because here's the thing: I don't lose. I don't give up and I don't run away.

It's no accident that this year's project topic is Privacy and the Internet. I know she's still trying to get her way and have me talk about all my mistakes and how I ruined my life. But this time I'm ready. I'm not easy prey anymore. This time no one will take me by surprise. And this time, I'll say all the things I should have said last year.

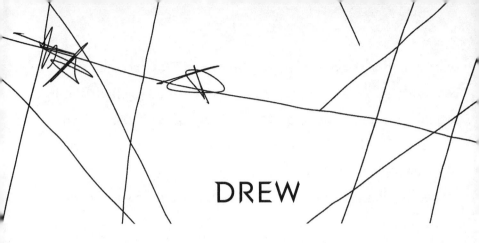

DREW

I'M ABOUT TO KNOCK ON JENNA'S FRONT DOOR
WHEN IT SWINGS OPEN AND A MAN CARRYING A
BAG OF GARBAGE NEARLY TRIPS OVER ME.

"Whoa!" he says with a laugh. "That was almost a messy disaster." He strides over to the edge of the porch and lowers the bag into a garbage bin below before turning around to face me.

"What can I do for you?" he asks, wiping his hands on his pants.

I open my mouth to respond but no words come out. This guy doesn't look like he's related to Jenna at all. He's tall and skinny in the most awkward way, with a nose that looks out of place on his face. I'm suddenly convinced I have the wrong house.

"Wait a minute . . ." the man says, stepping forward and studying me closely. "You're number 16. Andrew Wilson. Edgewood Eagles!" His eyes light up and he breaks into the Eagles fight song right there on his front porch.

"What in the world is going on out here?"

I turn around, and now I'm sure I have the wrong house. The

woman at the front door can't possibly be Jenna's mother. She's barely five feet tall, with short black hair and bright blue eyes. She's strikingly beautiful, but in an entirely different way than Jenna.

"We have a bona fide Eagle on our porch, here, Marie," the man says, pumping his fist in the air.

"Oh, really," she says, putting her hands on her hips. "Is Jenna expecting you?"

"You . . . you must be Jenna's mother," I say, stepping forward to shake her hand.

"Indeed, I am," she replies, keeping her hands on her hips. "And you are?"

"Drew, ma'am. Drew Wilson. I'm a classmate of Jenna's. We're working on a group project together."

"I'm Jenna's stepdad," the man says, stepping in to shake my hand and rescue me from the awkwardness. "You can call me Gary."

"Jenna has plans tonight," her mother says, side-eyeing Gary.

"Yes, I know. We're working on our project at my house. I just happened to be in the neighborhood and I thought I'd see if she needed a ride."

Gary plants a kiss on top of Jenna's mother's head. "Isn't that nice?" he asks pointedly. "Let's invite the young man in."

She sighs and pushes him through the door, before turning back and giving me a once-over. "The boys on your team treated Jenna horribly last year."

"Yes, ma'am."

"I'm not saying you were involved, but you'll understand why I'm not thrilled to have you show up on my doorstep. You mess with my daughter and you'll have me to deal with."

"Yes, ma'am."

She leads me into a tiny family room with a television tuned to the Discovery Channel. "Have a seat. I'll see if Jenna's ready to go."

I sit down on a faded blue couch and look around the room. It's the complete opposite of my house but in a cozy, lived-in way. I try to imagine my mother sitting on the mismatched furniture or decorating the room with family photos instead of art prints, but I can't.

I hear a knock from down the hall and I get up and move to the doorway, curious about how Jenna will take my surprise visit.

"Hey there, Butterfly. You didn't tell me that you're working with someone from the team," Jenna's mom says. "Or that he looks like an underwear model."

I look down at myself and smirk. Mrs. Bradley has better taste than I thought, given Gary's physique.

"An underwear model?" a boy's voice asks. "Like, from the Walmart flyer?"

Jenna's laugh rings out down the hallway, and I can imagine the way her eyes must be crinkled up at the corners right now.

"Not exactly," Jenna's mom replies.

There's a pause and then the boy says, "He *is* fully clothed, isn't he?"

I hear footsteps in the hallway and race back over to the couch.

"Oh, good," a boy of about seven or eight says. "I was worried you weren't wearing a shirt." He's thin almost to the point of looking unhealthy, with massive brown eyes that dominate his face.

I give a little chuckle and look down at my clothes. "Nope. I remembered to put everything on this morning."

He nods his head, a serious look on his face. "I sometimes forget to put things on, too. One time, I went to school with no shoes."

I cock my head to the side, trying to figure out if he's messing with me. "Seriously?"

"Joe's always serious," Jenna says, sweeping into the room and enveloping him in a bear hug that he quickly wriggles out of.

"It's Jonah," he says, shooting her an exasperated look. "And I already know who the underwear model is."

"Jonah!" Jenna says. "Some conversations are private."

"He's from the basketball team. Andrew Wilson. Number 16. Seventeen years old, 6'1", 180 pounds . . ."

"Thank you, Jonah," she says, resting her hands on his shoulders and maneuvering him toward the door. "I think sharing time is over."

"But I have questions."

"Another time, Jonah," Jenna's mother says, appearing in the doorway. "Your sister and her friend need to be on their way."

"Just one thing," he says, catching my eye. "I read in the paper that you're close friends with Troy. He said he'd teach me to play basketball. Would you like to join us?"

I sneak a look at Jenna, who looks panicked. She meets my eyes and gives her head a little shake. She obviously hasn't told Jonah about their breakup, and I'm not about to blow her cover.

"Of course, big man. It would be my pleasure."

"Big man," he says, nodding his head seriously.

"All right, big man," Mrs. Bradley says, ushering him out of the room. "It's time to get your homework done."

He looks over his shoulder at me as they leave, and I can't help but smile. One look at Jenna, though, and the smile drops from my face.

"Why so cranky, Butterfly?" I tease. "I'm here to give you a ride."

"Don't even," she warns, picking up her bag. "There is one person on Earth who's allowed to call me that, and you just met her."

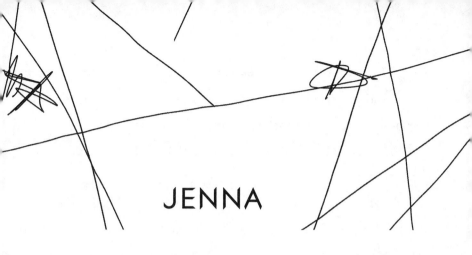

JENNA

I PICK AT A HOLE IN MY BLACK TIGHTS, MAKING IT SAT-
ISFYINGLY BIGGER. I've been trying to focus on my research,
but all I can think about is Drew standing in my living room
talking to my family like he belonged there. First my workplace
and now my house. What is *wrong* with him? He's like some big
dumb puppy who just goes wherever he pleases without consider-
ation for anyone else.

I look over and catch him staring at my ripped tights as though
my outfit offends his preppy sensibilities. "What?" I ask him, propping my legs up on the arm of his couch and crossing my ankles
to show off the secondhand pair of black boots that I touched up
with a Sharpie.

He shakes his head at me, amused. "Nothing. I just . . . I miss
your old look."

"Of course you do," I say drily. My old look was cheerleader
meets preppy schoolgirl. Completely vanilla. Completely like
every other girl in school.

"Don't take it the wrong way," he says, flopping back on his bed and picking up his book. "I get why you're doing the whole rebellious thing right now and all. But I'm looking forward to the day when you're done being mad and can go back to being hot."

I narrow my eyes at him and twirl a strand of black hair around my finger. He doesn't fool me. If he preferred fluffy blonds, he'd be late-night texting Ella, not me. "I didn't think it was possible for me to have any less respect for you than I did five minutes ago. But there you go, taking misogyny to whole new levels."

He snorts behind his book. "It's not misogyny. It's just fact. All guys have a look they go wild for. Right, Mouse? I happen to be hot for your old look, that's all."

Mouse startles and looks at me like a deer caught in head-lights. I know I shouldn't pick on him—it's Drew who's pissing me off, not him—but I can't resist deflecting the attention away from myself for a minute. "And what look are you hot for, Mouse?"

"I . . . I don't know. I . . . I like the way you look. And your old look. I like . . . I'm not sure."

Drew gives a cruel laugh and sets his book aside. "I think he's trying to say he has the hots for you."

"Or perhaps he's more evolved than you and sees the person beneath the clothes."

"I'm sure he wants more than anything to see beneath your clothes."

Mouse jumps up off his chair, letting his laptop clatter to the ground. "Oh, no," he says, picking it up and tapping gently on the keys. "Please please please please."

I sigh. I'm still irritated, but I can't help feeling sorry for Mouse. "Is it OK?" I ask him.

He finishes tapping away at the keyboard and then looks up at me with relief in his eyes. "It's OK." He slumps back in his chair, hugging the laptop to his chest. Despite what Drew says, I know that Mouse could never love anyone as much as he loves his laptop.

"Besides," I say, turning back to Drew, "I'm not going through a *rebellious phase*, as you so condescendingly put it. I'm dressing this way because I like it. I got tired of dressing the way everyone else wanted me to, and I decided to dress for myself."

"And it was your lifelong dream to look like you just walked off the set of *The Walking Dead*?"

"That's a bit dramatic, don't you think? Dressing in black hardly makes me one of the undead."

"I just think you could make your life easier, that's all."

"And being your definition of pretty would make my life easier? Not even close. You have no idea how much easier life has been since I changed my look."

"Whatever," Drew says, opening his laptop and dismissing me. "I'm just trying to help you."

You don't need to explain yourself to him, I remind myself. But I want to, and it frustrates me.

I bite my lip and turn to Mouse. "Do you remember that project we did on animal adaptations in seventh grade science class?" We were partners for that project and worked on it together every day after school for two weeks.

"Of course," he says. "You were obsessed with that spiky lizard that shot blood out of its eyes."

"Whoa," Drew interrupts. "Hold up. There's a lizard that shoots blood out of its eyes?"

"The Texas horned lizard," I say, unable to hold back my smile. "An adaptive marvel. If a predator manages to get past the spikes on its body, it can actually increase its own blood pressure to burst vessels in its eyes and squirt blood out of them to scare the predator away."

Drew looks at me like I've lost my mind. "That's disgusting."

"That's survival. And that's what this is," I say, gesturing at my outfit. "These are my spikes and horns and blood coming out of my eyes. This is me surviving."

"This is you scaring people away, agreed," Drew says. "But I wouldn't call it surviving. I'd call it prolonging the agony."

"What's that supposed to mean?"

"Has it occurred to you," he asks, crossing his arms over his chest, "that by dressing like that, you're actually reminding people of what happened every single day? Your whole naked photo thing would have completely blown over by now if you'd just moved on."

I gape at him, unable to believe the words that just came out of his mouth.

"He's right, Jen," Mouse says. "If you'd just go back to the way things used to be, everyone would forget about what happened."

I'm so shocked that I can't even find the words to respond for a moment. Mouse is supposed to be smarter than this. He's supposed to understand me. I give my head a little shake and force my face to go blank. I don't even know why I bothered opening up to them about this stuff. "Forget it. You guys don't get it."

Drew shrugs his shoulders and looks back down at his laptop, but Mouse moves over to sit beside me. "Just think about it," he says softly. "Don't you want to go back to the way things used to be?"

I'm up off the couch and pacing in front of him in an instant. I'm not supposed to care this much about what they think, but I'm so disappointed in them both that it's like fire in my veins. "There is no going back, Mouse. Do you really think the way I dress or do my makeup will let anyone forget what happened? Everyone's already decided who I am, and it has nothing to do with me. Dressing like I used to didn't protect me from being labeled a slut, so what makes you think it will rescue me from the gossip mill?"

He opens his mouth to respond, but I'm not done yet. "What you're asking me to do is act like you. To use *your* adaptive behaviors instead of my own." I stop in front of him and lean down so we're eye-to-eye. "You're an opossum, Mouse. You remember those from our project, right? They lie down and play dead to escape predators. Just like you."

His eyes widen in shock and go shiny with unshed tears. He blinks hard and then looks away from me, unable to meet my eyes anymore.

"You two are so fucking dramatic," Drew interrupts with a dismissive laugh. "You talk about *survival* like we're in the wild. We live in the suburbs, for Christ's sake. Don't glamorize your screwed-up coping mechanisms by calling them *adaptations*."

"Spoken like a true predator," I say, earning a reluctant chuckle from a wounded Mouse.

"Now I'm a predator?" Drew says, shaking his head at us. "You're being ridiculous. What have I ever done to you?"

I put my hands on my hips and stare hard at him, letting him connect the dots himself. Letting him think about all the ways he and his friends have done me wrong. I don't break my stare until he looks away. Until I know he's gotten the message.

He's not a clueless puppy dog, I realize. He's a lion. And the reason he thinks he belongs everywhere is that the savanna seems pretty tame to a lion. If he tried walking around in the gazelle's shoes for a while, he'd have a whole new appreciation for the dangers of the environment.

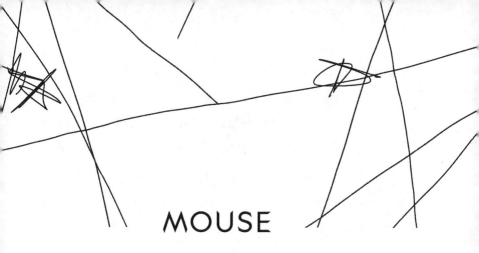

MOUSE

AN OPOSSUM.

An ugly, hissing creature that deals with stress by going into extreme shock and entering an involuntary comatose-like state that makes it look dead.

I throw off my covers and reach for my glasses so I can see my bedside clock. Three thirty in the morning.

Goddamn it! I hate that Jenna can do this to me. I have a calculus test second period and a chemistry lab after lunch. I need to focus. I need sleep.

I whip off my glasses and push the heels of my hands into my eyes until lights flash behind my eyelids. I wish I could pull her out of my brain. I can picture her in there like a virus, invading my neurons until she's branched into every area of my mind. I imagine reaching into the base of my skull and pulling, the threads of her emerging like an intricate spiderweb. It would feel so good to tug them free. It would be a relief.

After her photos went viral last year, I'd thought I was finally free of her. She shut out the whole world, and we went for more than six months without talking. And while at first it hurt so badly that it was hard to breathe, over time her hold on me slowly started to recede. After a while, I could think again. I could stop seeing myself through her eyes and worrying over her every word and action. I threw myself back into my studies and focused with a new intensity.

And then she started calling me again at the end of last semester. She begged me to take Miss Bailey's law class with her and invited me over for dinner and to study. She found her way back into my mind, and it was like the previous six months had never happened. She was different, but she was still Jenna. And I still loved her as fiercely as I had in seventh grade when she punched Devaughn Miller in the nose for giving me a wedgie during gym class.

I realize most people would laugh at me for this, but the truth is that Jenna and I are soul mates. We're similar in all the ways that really matter, though we look like complete opposites on the outside.

Take Jenna and her makeover this year. She can call it survival all she wants, but I understand her motivations better than she thinks, because I'd love to shed my misleading appearance, too. Before last year, Jenna was all silky blond hair, doe eyes, and the face of an angel. But underneath her cotton-candy exterior was a girl who never backed down from a dare, who had a dark sense of humor, and who was far more intelligent than she let anyone see.

I resent how easy it was for her to shed her old image and reinvent herself. I'm trapped in my body, and I can't change it no matter how hard I try.

I get up to look in the mirror over my bureau, even though I know it will only make me feel worse.

I don't look the way I imagine myself. When I'm walking around during the day, I feel bigger than I really am. More impressive. Not a giant like Troy; I'm not delusional. But formidable. Confident. Smart and capable and at least moderately attractive.

But then I'll catch a glimpse of myself in a classroom window or in a mirror in the washroom, and I'll come crashing back to Earth.

I study my reflection, turning my head from side to side and then backing up to try to see my whole body in the mirror. I'm too skinny, and my dad's right when he calls me girly, because there's something feminine and dainty about me. No matter how many of Troy's protein shakes I drink or weights I try to lift, I stay so agonizingly thin that my head looks too big for my body. I step closer to the mirror again and check out my face. I have clear skin, which is good, but it gets shiny when I'm nervous, which is most of the time. My eyes are huge and make me look permanently surprised, a look that isn't helped by my thick glasses.

I turn away from the mirror and slump on my bed. Somehow, I got the short end of the stick in the genetics department. I'm not like Troy, or my dad, or even my grandfather. They're all strong, athletic black men who command attention when they walk into a room. They have *presence*. And me? I am absence. I am forever defined by what I am not.

But if there was one person who I thought saw past my appearance to the real me, it was Jenna. Jenna, who is so much more than the way she looks.

But she called me an opossum.

She doesn't remember the Indonesian mimic octopus at all. Or else she just doesn't see that I am one.

She fell in love with the blood-shooting lizard during our project, but it was the Indonesian mimic octopus I chose to focus on. It avoids predators by arranging its body into different shapes that resemble other types of marine life. It can make itself look like a sea snake, a jellyfish, a stingray, you name it.

It had the ability I wanted more than anything else: the ability to transform its appearance. I studied everything about it and realized that even though I couldn't alter my looks, I could still change myself in other ways. I became an expert at transforming myself into whatever people needed me to be. So when the basketball team needed a computer genius to design a database for their contest, I was their man. When Jenna needed a faithful friend who never judged or criticized her, that was me. When I realized my mother needed a son who'd be the gentleman my father failed to be, I was there for her. And when my father needed a scapegoat for all his disappointments—a punching bag ⋎ never fought back—I became that, too.

Because if there's one thing I've learned, it's that people don't like it when you surprise them. They don't like things that defy their expectations or challenge their view of the world. My survival strategy is sensing what people expect from me and fulfilling that expectation. And it works. As soon as I became useful to Troy and his friends, I stopped getting stuffed into lockers and beat up after class. And as soon as I accepted my father's temper without offering a shred of resistance, I gained the ability to defuse his anger and minimize the fallout.

Of course, I've also had to stop being me, but that's just temporary. As soon as I get accepted to MIT and move far away from here, I can shed these survival strategies like a snake's skin and be free to be myself.

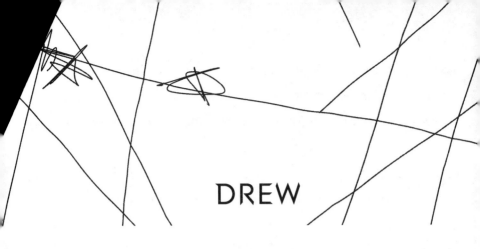

DREW

"YOU KNOW, WE DON'T NEED TO WAIT FOR HER TO GET STARTED," MOUSE SAYS, INTERRUPTING MY CONCENTRATION FOR THE THIRD TIME IN FIVE MINUTES. Jenna's late, as usual, and he's freaking out about the loss of productivity.

"Would you quit pacing around," I tell him, leaning forward to try to block him out of my peripheral vision. I'm ten seconds away from completing this mission, and . . . "Shit!" My car careens off the track and I throw my Xbox controller down in disgust.

"Sorry," Mouse mumbles, pushing his glasses up higher on his nose.

I exit the video game and load up a new one. "Come here."

Mouse perches beside me on the couch and clears his throat. "I'm not trying to annoy you, but—"

"This is Assassins VI," I interrupt, thrusting a controller into his hands. "And we're going to play right now, because I have the sudden urge to shoot you in the face."

"But—"

"But nothing. You're the dude on the right side of the screen, and I'm on the left. Use your radar to track me. Your goal is to try to find and kill me before I kill you. First to five kills wins."

Mouse squints at the screen as I start the game. I give him a few minutes to get used to the controls and then start pursuing him as he maneuvers his character down a hallway. I've played this map about a thousand times, so it takes all of three seconds for me to sneak up behind him and blow his head off. "That's one for me!"

"That's not fair," Mouse says, a muscle jumping in his jaw. "You've played this before."

"All right, then," I say, exiting to the main menu. "We'll start over and use a map I don't know. May the best man win."

I expect him to argue or give up, but Mouse slides off the couch and onto the floor to get closer to the screen.

I score two more quick kills and start to feel bad for him. "Do you want me to set a handicap? I can up my difficulty and lower yours, so it's more fun."

"Shut up," he says, right before his character rounds the corner in front of me and he gets his first kill.

"Nice. Now you're getting it."

I re-spawn and pick up some ammo packs and then track him down to where he's hiding in a far corner of the map. He's a sitting duck in the middle of the room but somehow manages to dodge a hail of my bullets and dive through a doorway. I follow, but when

I get into the room, he's gone. I pan the camera, looking for whatever exit he escaped through, and he jumps out from behind a stack of crates in the corner and punches me in the face before unloading his submachine gun on me.

"Oh yeah," he shouts, pumping his fist in the air. "You're dead now!"

"Lucky shot," I say, flexing my fingers around the controller.

We spend almost five minutes stalking and avoiding each other before I narrowly get the next kill.

"Fuck!" Mouse shouts, shocking me. I don't think I've ever heard him swear before.

"Just a game, dude," I tease, enjoying his intensity.

But then he kills me twice in a row and I'm not fooling around anymore.

We're tied four kills to four kills when Jenna bursts into my room. "Holy shit, you guys!" she yells. "You have *got* to see this."

"Not now," Mouse snarls, throwing a grenade into the room I'm hiding in. I leap out at the last second but take enough damage to bring my life down to 50 percent. I loop through the main building and grab a health pack just before Mouse manages to get there, and I fire a few rounds at him before he retreats.

"I'm serious, you two," Jenna says. "Turn off that stupid game and come see this."

I squint at the screen and try to block out her voice. There's no way I'm losing this game to Mouse. I'm *king* of Assassins VI.

I see from the radar that he's right above me on the second floor of the map, so I loop around and take the stairs to sneak up behind him.

He darts in front of me right as I reach the top of the stairs, and we both shout in surprise. It's going to be whoever is quicker on the trigger, and—

The screen goes black.

"What the—"

I blink in shock as Jenna waves the power cable for the Xbox in front of us.

"What the hell are you doing?" Mouse shouts.

Jenna jumps and drops the cord.

"I-I'm sorry," he sputters. "It's just . . . that was a really key moment."

"No. Way," I command. "Do not apologize to her." I pick up the power cable and wave it at Jenna. "That was shitty, Jen. You don't get to walk in here late and then interrupt us when we're having fun."

"Whatever," she says, waving her hand at me dismissively. "When you see what I've found, you're going to thank me."

Mouse sits down with a resigned sigh, the little puppet, but I'm not going to be so easily won over. "There's absolutely nothing you could have that would—"

"Stop talking and just listen," she says, reaching into Mouse's bag and pulling out his laptop. "On my way here, I had to run back to the school because I left my phone in my locker. On my way out of the building, I passed by Bailey's classroom and the lights were on and the door was open. I couldn't resist peeking in, because, really, who'd have thought Bailey would be the kind of teacher to stay late, right?"

"Get to the point, Jenna," I say.

"I'm getting there! Bailey was at her computer all alone in the classroom, and I remembered that Mouse had been nagging at me for losing the presentation outline handout, so I figured I might as well ask her for one since she was there."

Mouse perks up. "You actually went and talked to Bailey? Like, without someone forcing you to?"

"OK. It's weird, I know. But she was in there and I figured, *what the hell*? Plus, I figured it was safer to admit I'd lost our sheet when she didn't have an entire classroom to humiliate me in front of. But anyways . . . that's not the crazy part . . ."

"Wait," I exclaim, in mock surprise. "You mean there's *more* to this gripping tale?"

"Oh, shut up," she tells me. "You're going to feel like an idiot when you see what I've got."

I roll my eyes but lean in closer as she taps away on the keyboard.

"So, I walked into the room, but I guess she didn't hear me. When I walked up behind her, she was on a *dating* site. I saw her profile."

Jenna turns the computer around and there is Bailey in all her glory. But not the Bailey we see in class every day.

"I think I'm going to be sick," Mouse squeaks, his eyes wide.

I grab the laptop and take a closer look. It's Miss Bailey, all right. Sprawled across a bed, wearing a tiny red dress.

It's disgustingly perfect. Or perfectly disgusting.

"What did she say when she saw you?" I ask, hardly believing that Jenna got out alive with this information.

"Are you kidding me? As soon as I realized what I was seeing, I snuck back out and then knocked on the door before walking in. She practically shat herself and freaked out about me interrupting her *work* before turning off her monitor." Jenna starts laughing.

"Did you get the handout?" Mouse asks, like a complete idiot.

She ignores the question and sits down beside me. "So, am I forgiven?"

"Oh, you're forgiven," I tell her, scrolling through Bailey's profile. "Listen to this: Single female, thirty-two years old, open-minded and adventurous—"

Jenna snorts. "Yeah, right."

" . . . Looking for hot thirtysomething male to fulfill fantasies."

"That's disgusting," Mouse says, coming over to sit on the other side of me. "Ew. Close that window. I can't look at that anymore," he says, but he doesn't stop staring at her picture.

"Do you think she's had any responses?" Jenna asks.

I check the date on her profile and shrug. "She's been a member for more than two years now. If she's had zero interest, I feel sorry for her."

"Well, she obviously hasn't found Mr. Right, because she's still actively checking her profile," Mouse points out, still unable to tear his eyes away from Bailey's picture.

"What kind of guy do you think she goes for?" Jenna asks with a laugh.

I open a new tab in the browser window and do a Google image search for *Guys teachers find sexy*, then scroll through the photos of shirtless men that appear.

"No way," Jenna laughs, grabbing the laptop from me. "Bailey hardly qualifies as a teacher, and I'll bet her tastes run far raunchier than this." She types *Hot tattooed men* into the search bar and finds what she's looking for. "This one," she says matter-of-factly. "She'd go wild for this one."

"You think?" I ask, feeling suddenly inferior. Is this what Jenna finds hot?

"Definitely. In fact . . ." her eyes take on a gleam that takes my breath away. "Mouse . . ."

"Whatever you're thinking, the answer is no," he says, shaking his head. "I know that look. That look means things are about to go very wrong."

"Now, Mousie," she says playfully, batting her eyelashes and reaching across me to rest her hand on his leg. "You love to help me out, don't you?"

He doesn't stand a chance.

Mouse groans and rubs his temples. "What do you want?"

"If we wanted to test my theory and message Bailey through this site without it ever being traceable to us, how would we do it?"

"You're kidding, right?"

She nudges me in the arm and jerks her head toward Mouse. "Tell him this idea is brilliant."

She's an evil genius. "This idea is brilliant," I tell him. "If it'll work."

Mouse takes the laptop from Jenna and clicks through the site. "Nope. We're out of luck. You need a credit card to register and pay the yearly fee, and those are traceable."

I shrug, disappointed, but Jenna isn't deterred.

"What about one of these," she says, pulling a card out of her wallet.

"Tell me you didn't steal someone's credit card," Mouse says.

"Of course not! It's a prepaid Visa. A gift card. Supposedly you can use it anywhere that accepts Visa cards."

Mouse narrows his eyes. "Where did you get that?"

"It was a birthday gift, Mr. Suspicious."

"And you've been holding off on spending it for three months?"

"I forgot I even had it. Chill out. Now, will it work?"

"I'm not sure. Do you have to register it or something?"

"I don't know. Just try it and see what happens."

Mouse looks to me for guidance, but I'm the last person to be the voice of reason. This seems like way too much fun to me, and if there's no way I'll catch any blowback, then I'm all for it.

"We have to sign up for the site," Mouse says, clicking the Register button. "What should our name be?"

Jenna taps her index finger on her nose, thinking. "He looks like a Tom to me. Tom Anderson."

"That's the most vanilla, boring name I've ever heard," I tell her.

"We want vanilla," she says. "Bailey will Google the name and we want one that'll have a gazillion hits, not one so unique that only a few possibilities show up."

"Huh. That's smart," I say grudgingly. "You're scary good at this."

She shrugs. "Tom Anderson," she repeats, watching while Mouse types it in.

"Oh God. We need to give an address."

"Just make up a fake one," I tell him.

Mouse types in *123 Street Road, Toronto, Ontario* and then looks up a postal code that looks semi-legit.

"Nice job," Jenna says, handing him the Visa card.

"What should our password be?" he asks, after typing in the number.

Jenna and I look at each other, excited. If this works . . .

"How about *Bailey*," Jenna suggests.

Mouse types it in and presses the Submit button, and we all hold our breath waiting for the transaction to process. It seems to take ages, and I'm just about to lose hope when our Registration Confirmation comes up, prompting us to log in again.

"Yes!" Mouse whoops, surprising me. I thought he was against this, but he seems even more excited than I am.

His fingers fly across the keyboard as he logs in and finds his way to the New Profile page. "Let's grab that photo you chose, Jen," he says, saving the picture and then uploading it to Tom Anderson's profile.

Jenna meets my eyes and smiles so wide that it cracks something inside me. "Let's get to work making Miss Bailey's dream guy, gentlemen!"

The stats are easy to come up with, but Jenna busts our balls over the harder questions. "You can't write *porn* for turn-ons," she tells us.

"Why not? It's the truth. Ask any guy," I say.

"These profiles aren't about truth. They're about attracting the opposite sex. No woman drools over a guy who brags about his dedication to porn."

"So, what do we say, then? *Long walks on the beach*?"

"Jesus, no! Nothing cheesy like that. How about: skinny dipping, dirty talk, and smart women."

"Smart women?" I scoff.

"We want Bailey to think she's found her soul mate, right? Well, I'm pretty sure she thinks she's smart."

We finish up the profile and then look at each other, suddenly nervous. "Should we message her now or wait and think on this?" Mouse asks.

"Now!" Jenna says. "I just spent my birthday money on this adventure. There's no chickening out at this point."

Mouse hands her the laptop. "You do it."

She smiles at me before navigating to Miss Bailey's profile and clicking on Send Message. "How do I start?"

My fingers are itching. This is the part I'm good at. "Let me."

She passes me the laptop and I crack my knuckles before starting:

Hello Beautiful,

At the risk of sounding creepy, I've been staring at your profile, trying to work up the nerve to message you.

If you're still available and looking for a match, I'd love to hear from you.

Tom

"That's it?" Jenna asks as I hover the mouse pointer over the Send button. "Shouldn't we add some more detail?"

"Not yet," I tell her. "We want her to be intrigued and eager to find out more."

"You two kind of freak me out," Mouse says, shaking his head.

"I'll take that as a compliment. Should I send it?"

Jenna raises an eyebrow at Mouse. "What do you say? We good?"

He shrugs and looks at me. "What do you think?"

I don't bother to answer. I just click Send and watch Mouse's eyes go wide. "It's done now," I tell them. "There's no turning back."

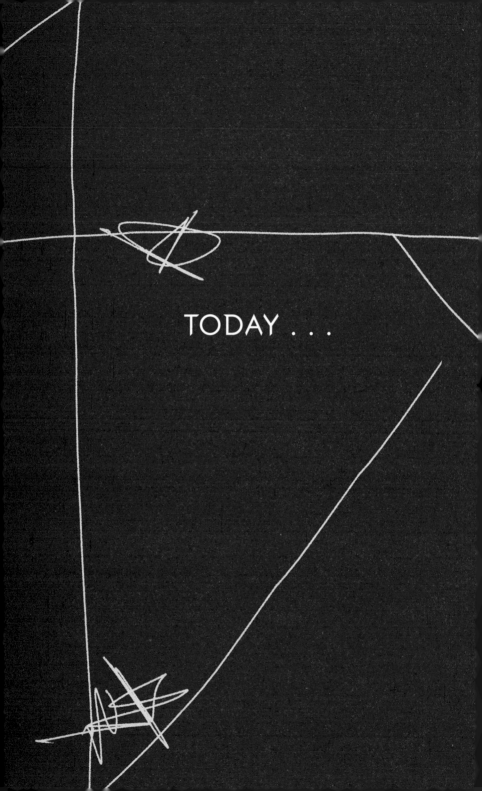

TODAY . . .

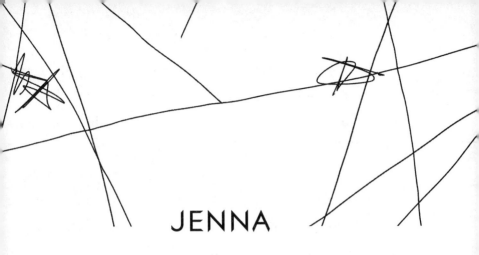

JENNA

I MAKE IT BACK TO CALCULUS CLASS WITH TWO
MINUTES TO SPARE AND FIND MR. WILLIAMS ON THE
CLASSROOM PHONE.

He looks relieved as I stroll through the door. "Of course she's
here, Mrs. Isaacs. I'll send her right down."

Williams hangs up the phone and turns to me, trying his best
to look stern. "I seem to remember telling you to make it quick.
Did you get lost on your way to the bathroom?"

"You said to be back before the bell rang," I remind him. "So,
I'm actually early."

He cracks a smile and shakes his head at me. "Grab your stuff
and get down there. *Directly* down there. Mrs. Isaacs doesn't sound
like she's in a playful mood today."

In my experience, Mrs. Isaacs is never in a *playful mood*, so
I don't start to worry until I walk through the office doors and

catch sight of Miss Singh. She looks up from her desk and greets me with a tight smile and a warning shake of her head.

"Mrs. Isaacs would like you to fill out a form today," she says pointedly.

I stop short and take a good look around the office. It's way too quiet in here. The VPs are usually buzzing around, sipping coffee and plotting how to make our lives miserable. Today, everyone's holed up in their offices behind closed doors. Even the other secretaries have their heads down. I bite my lip. This doesn't feel like a routine check-in. So much for all Drew and Mouse's assurances that everything will be fine.

"Cell phone?" Miss Singh asks, tapping a laminated copy of the Edgewood High School Responsible Use of Technology policy, which has mysteriously appeared at the corner of her desk. She has got to be kidding me. No one pays attention to Edgewood's rules about technology. Especially me. I shoot her a look that tells her just how weird I think she's being and am rewarded with the tiniest of smiles and a quiet chuckle. Thank God. I was beginning to feel like I'd slipped into an alternate universe.

I retreat to a far corner of the waiting area, tossing the Office Referral form in the recycling bin as I go.

Miss Singh watches as I pull out my cell phone and fire a quick text to Mouse and Drew.

Just got called to the office.

I run my fingers over the phone and will one of them to reply. It's not even nine thirty yet, and I'm the only one of us down here, so it's still possible that this meeting isn't about Miss Bailey at all. My thoughts are interrupted by Miss Singh clearing her throat loudly, and I slide my phone into the waistband of my jeans just before Isaacs appears in front of me.

"Good morning, Jenna. Come on back."

I follow her to her office, thinking about how long it's been since I've been in here. Isaacs took me seriously when I cut off our check-ins four weeks ago. I look around her office and bite back a smile. Everything is exactly the same as I remember it—even her Internet Safety bulletin board. There's something weirdly soothing about that.

"You've certainly made a lot of changes since we last met," she says, perching on the edge of her chair. "Your attendance has improved, your grades have risen, and you haven't been kicked out of law class once. To what do we owe this remarkable transformation?"

There's an edge beneath her words, and I lean forward, interested. "I thought you'd be happy I'm finally moving forward. Isn't that what you said you wanted?"

The corners of her mouth turn down. "Of course I'm happy. I'm thrilled with your progress. Which is why I'm sorry we have to have the conversation I called you down here for. You've made a great deal of progress, and I'm hesitant to bring up subjects that might get in the way of that . . . but I'm afraid this is unavoidable."

Here we go.

She leans forward and folds her hands on her desk. "Something terrible has happened to a teacher at this school. Something I know you can relate to."

I take a deep breath and concentrate on keeping my face neutral.

"It appears that a student or group of students has somehow gotten access to her personal information online and posted it publicly, causing her considerable embarrassment and distress."

I bite the inside of my cheek and fight the urge to quote Isaacs's lectures from last year. *There is no such thing as personal information on the Internet, Jenna,* was a common refrain. As was *You should never put anything online that you wouldn't want your mother to see.* I'm guessing Miss Bailey missed out on those little pearls of wisdom.

"What kind of personal information?"

"That's not important right now. What *is* important is finding whoever is responsible, as I'm sure you, of all people, will agree. I'm hoping you can help us with that."

Isaacs is watching me intently, so I force a smile onto my face and try to swallow down the bitterness. "I'd love to help, but I don't know anything more than what you just told me."

"But you could find out."

"*How?*" I narrow my eyes at her. "You told me yourself last year how difficult it is to make a case in situations like this."

She gets up and closes her office door to give us more privacy. "Let me be honest with you, Jenna. I know kids are talking about this situation. And I know that none of them will be willing to discuss it with me. As soon as we start investigating, everyone will conveniently develop selective amnesia." She smiles wryly. "But I'm hoping that with your . . . experience . . . in this area, that you might be willing to break that cycle of silence and help us investigate. You can help us make a difference, Jenna. We can catch whoever is responsible and send a clear message that online harassment won't be tolerated here at Edgewood."

"You have *got* to be kidding me," I say, seething. "Where was all this urgency when *I* was the one with my boobs plastered all over the Internet? How come I was a stupid kid who got lectures and judgment and Miss Bailey gets to be a victim? How come the people who posted pictures of *me* got off with a warning, while you *won't tolerate* what's happening to her."

Isaacs nods once and gives me a tight smile. "I see."

"You *see?*" I'm breathing hard and primed for a fight. She should know me better than this by now. She should know my temper.

"Yes. I see quite clearly where we're at. For someone who knows nothing more than what I've told her, you certainly know a lot about this situation."

I freeze and try to remember what I've said.

"I never named Miss Bailey as the teacher involved, and I never mentioned anything about topless photos."

Isaacs sits back in her chair with a self-satisfied smirk that makes me downright hostile. She thinks she's so *smart*.

"*Everyone* knows about Miss Bailey," I snap. "The whole school has seen the photos. Doesn't mean I know anything about who posted them."

"So why lie to me about it, then?"

"Because telling you the truth has never done me any good."

She looks hard at me for a moment, then shakes her head. "I'd hoped we could do this the easy way, Jenna. Especially after all we've been through together. But since that seems to mean nothing to you, we may as well lay things out on the table. I know much more than you think I do. I *know* you have information that could help us. I'd hoped that I could appeal to your sense of empathy for Miss Bailey's situation, but since that's not an option, you are now officially part of the investigation. Please take a seat outside. I'll call you back in when I have more questions."

TWO WEEKS AGO . . .

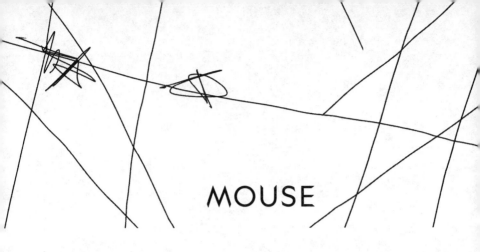

MOUSE

I NEED TO GET READY FOR SCHOOL, BUT I CAN'T SEEM TO GET UP OFF MY BED. I check my laptop screen again and try to wrap my mind around what I'm seeing.

On behalf of the Admissions Committee, it is my pleasure to offer you admission . . .

I got in. To MIT. *I got in.*

For the past year, I've spent countless hours fantasizing about this exact moment and how I would feel when I got my acceptance, but now that it's here, I'm completely numb. I have the dizzying sensation that I might be dreaming . . . that none of this is real.

I scan the letter again and try to process the details and instructions. There are forms and deadlines and decisions to be made. And I'll have to tell my parents. God, I'll have to admit to my father that I applied without his permission . . .

Am I really going to do this? *Can* I really do this?

I feel panic welling up in me. I've been focused on getting accepted for so long that I never stopped to think about what I'd do if it actually happened. It was such a long shot. A dream. A fantasy I used to escape from reality. And now it could become my reality.

My phone chimes on the nightstand, startling me. For a panicked second, I have the irrational fear that it's my father and that he somehow knows what's happened. I take a deep breath and smile at my own paranoia. My dad doesn't even know about the phone, let alone my acceptance.

I find a text from Drew, sent to both Jenna and me: *Drop what you're doing and log on to the dating site. Tom Anderson just got a reply . . .*

I didn't think it was possible for this day to get any more surreal.

Jenna replies almost immediately: *OMG! Did you read it already?*

Of course, he writes. *Want me to tell you about it?*

NO! Have you seen it, Mouse?

I smile and type, *Not yet . . .*

WAIT FOR ME! I'm on the bus. Be there soon.

My heart swells in my chest. *I can be there in 15 minutes*, I type. *Meet by your locker?*

Too crowded. Arts hallway in 15.

I take a last look at my acceptance letter before closing my laptop and shoving it into my bag. If I'm going to make it to school in fifteen minutes, I have to hurry.

▲ ▼ ▲

By the time I reach the arts hallway at school, Jenna is already sitting on the floor by the music room, with Drew standing beside her. My heart throbs in my chest, and I'm suddenly convinced that they've already checked Bailey's reply together, without me. I slow to a stop, unable to tear my eyes away from the sight of Jenna smiling up at Drew.

I'm standing there, frozen, when she looks over and catches sight of me. Her face is flushed and her eyes are dancing, and I suddenly feel my knees go weak.

"We waited for you," she calls out, patting the floor beside her. "Hurry up—before the bell rings."

I rush over and sit beside her, relief flooding through me.

"Someone's eager," she teases, before opening her laptop and logging in to the dating site. "Four messages?" she asks, when Tom Anderson's profile comes up.

"Holy shit!" Drew says, sitting down on the other side of Jenna. "There was only one when I checked this morning."

Jenna opens the first message and I lean closer so I can read it over her shoulder.

Thanks so much for your message, Tom. I'd love to chat more.
—Allison

"Not bad," Jenna says. "She doesn't sound half as desperate as I thought she would."

"That's what I thought, too," Drew says. "But I suspect the next three messages might push her into desperate territory."

"Good point," Jen says, closing the first message and opening the next one.

Hi again. I'm heading to school in a minute, so I won't see your messages until later in the day. If you message, that is. I hope you message. And I'll reply as soon as I'm home.

"Oh boy," I mutter. "Even *I* can tell that's not cool."

Jenna's laugh echoes down the hallway. She opens the next message:

Just to clarify—I'm a teacher, not a student. Because I said I was going to school...

The next message is time stamped just one minute later.

Sorry for all the messages. Just excited to hear from you. Talk soon! —Allison

"If Tom Anderson were real, he'd be running for the hills right now," Drew says darkly.

"I don't know," Jenna muses. "Maybe he'd be charmed by how enthusiastic she is."

I snort loudly and Jenna turns to me, a surprised grin on her face. "What's so funny?"

"I think guys and girls might have different definitions of *enthusiasm*," I tell her, earning a fist bump from Drew. "Miss Bailey's coming across as the kind of person Tom might find hiding in the bushes outside his house."

Jenna cocks her head to the side. "Harsh, but accurate." She hits the Reply button under Miss Bailey's last message and hovers her fingers over the keyboard. "What should Tom say?"

"Nothing yet," Drew tells her. "Let her sweat it out for the day. We can meet at my place tonight and respond when we have more time."

My head snaps up in surprise. "Tonight? It's Friday night. You have nothing better to do on a Friday night than hang out with us?" I ask, echoing his words from a couple of weeks ago, when he mocked me for suggesting we work on a Friday.

Drew appraises me. "Nice burn. Respect."

"We can't just leave her hanging all day," Jenna cuts in. "She'll be able to see from Tom's profile that he's been online."

"So what? That'll just pique her interest. She'll be wondering about him all day and then be hyped when he finally responds to her tonight. Trust me."

"Sure. But in the meantime, she'll be a total bitch in class today," Jenna points out.

"Damn," Drew concedes. "You raise a good point."

"Let's say something like: *Good to hear from you, too. Can we chat tonight?*" I suggest.

Jenna types out my words and then looks to Drew for approval.

"Drop the *Good to hear from you, too* from the beginning and just send *Can we chat tonight?*" Drew says. "Or better yet, just *Chat tonight?*"

"Ooh, I like it," Jenna says, making the changes. "Gives her a bit of hope but still leaves her hanging." She presses Send and then looks up from her computer. "I can't wait to see Bailey in class today. When do you think she'll check her messages?"

"Probably in the next five minutes or so," Drew quips. "She did send four messages before eight o'clock this morning, after all."

I feel a smile stretch across my face and I suddenly see the three of us the way we must look to people passing by in the halls. We look like three friends having a good time before school. I feel like I'm a part of something, and I'm nearly bowled over by the irony of it all. The MIT acceptance on my laptop is my long-awaited ticket out of this place, and it arrived just as I'm starting to feel like I finally belong.

"How pathetic is it that I'm actually sorry that it's a Day 2 and we don't have law until after lunch?" I ask.

Jenna bumps her shoulder against mine. "Not pathetic at all, 'cause I was thinking the same thing." She slides her laptop into her bag and stands, holding out a hand to help me up. "Thanks for waiting for me, Mouse."

Her hand is soft in mine, and I can't find the words to respond. I want to pull her into a hug. I want to tell her I got into MIT. I want to stay here in the hallway and feel her shoulder against mine for the rest of the day.

I *don't want* this feeling to end.

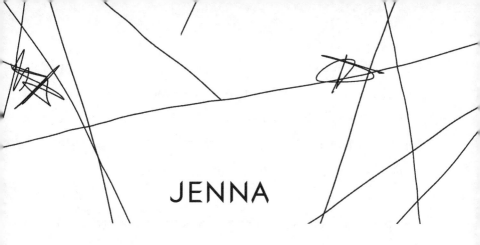

JENNA

"CAN'T THIS OLD THING GO ANY FASTER?" I ask Mouse on the ride over to Drew's house. Bailey was hilarious in class today, and I can't wait to see her response to Tom.

Mouse accelerates infinitesimally. "I have some news," he says.

I rummage in my bag for my phone. I'm sure Drew's already on the site, and I don't want him messaging Bailey before we get there. "What news? . . . Damn it, Drew!"

"What's wrong?"

"He says if we're not there in five minutes, he's starting without us." I tap out a reply on my phone. *The hell you are! You send so much as one message and you'll have me to deal with.*

Drew sends back a devil emoji and I laugh out loud. "He's an idiot," I tell Mouse. "And he wouldn't dare . . . but hurry up just in case."

Mouse shakes his head and turns down Drew's street. "How many messages do you think she sent today?" he asks.

"My money's on at least three," I say. "Did you notice how she kept finding excuses to look for something in her desk drawer? I'm sure she was checking the site on her phone in there."

Mouse pulls into the driveway and I send Drew a text. *We're here. Come let us in.*

Door's open and parents are out, he responds.

Up in Drew's room, he's got his laptop open and a selection of drinks laid out on the coffee table in front of his couch.

Mouse and I dump our bags by the door and make our way over to him. "You throwing a party or something?" I ask. He's got a six-pack of beer, along with bottles of rum, whiskey, and vodka on the table.

"I didn't know what you guys liked to drink," he says, looking up from his computer. "And I figured tonight warranted a celebration."

Mouse groans and reaches for a bottle of Coke. "I take it you don't plan on getting any work done tonight."

Drew gestures at the soda in Mouse's hand. "That's for mixer. Loosen up and add a little something to it. And no, we're not getting any work done tonight. It's Friday, and we have more important business to attend to."

Mouse hesitates. "I can't drink. I drove us here."

I look back and forth between them, making a decision. "One drink won't kill you," I tell him, dropping onto the couch and grabbing a beer. "Drew's right. Let's have fun tonight."

Mouse looks surprised but nods and grabs a red plastic cup, filling it with Coke before splashing in a tiny amount of rum.

"You're a wild man," Drew teases him, grabbing a beer and tapping it against mine. "Ready?"

We gather around the laptop and open Bailey's last message.

I'd love to chat. How about 8:00?

"That's it?" Mouse asks. "Jenna and I were sure there'd be a ton of messages after this morning."

I check the clock. "She'll be online in half an hour. What should we write?"

"Nothing yet," Drew says. "Let's have a drink and wait for her." He pops open his can of beer.

Mouse takes a timid sip of his drink and grimaces, making me laugh.

"There isn't enough alcohol in there for you to even taste it!" I say, grabbing the rum and adding a generous amount to his cup.

He laughs nervously but settles back on the couch and takes a sip.

"We should turn this into a drinking game," Drew says. "Every time Bailey adds an emoji to one of her messages, we need to take a drink."

"Yeah, right," I scoff. "We'll all be hospitalized for alcohol poisoning by the end of the night. I'm betting she's a huge over-user of the smiley face."

Drew laughs loud and deep, and I find myself noticing that his smile is more real than I've seen it in a long time.

"My hands are sweating all of a sudden," Mouse says, wiping them on his pants. "Why am I so nervous?"

Drew looks at him like he's crazy, but I get it. I'm a little nervous, too. I take a long drink of my beer and imagine Bailey sitting in front of her computer watching the time tick down till eight o'clock.

"What's there to be nervous about?" Drew asks. "It's not like she'll know that it's us."

Mouse sputters and chokes on his drink, prompting Drew to add another pour of rum to his cup. "You need to relax, my man. Tonight is going to make every shitty law class we've ever had to sit through completely worthwhile."

I look down at the laptop screen and see that a green dot has appeared beside Bailey's name. "She's online."

Drew chugs some more of his beer and then sets it down and pulls his laptop onto his lap. "Show time."

I smile into my drink as I take a sip.

Hi beautiful, Drew types into the chat bar.

Three dots appear right away, indicating that Bailey is typing. The dots disappear, then reappear for a long time. Then disappear again. When she finally responds, it's just an emoji with a blushing smiley face.

"Drink," Drew commands.

We all take a sip and then watch as Drew starts typing again.

So, you're a teacher. What do you teach?

Social sciences. Mostly law this semester. What do you do?

Drew looks up at us.

"Firefighter," Mouse says excitedly.

"Firefighter?" I ask, laughing. "Where did that come from?"

He looks embarrassed. "I don't know. He looks like a firefighter. Or a cop."

Drew looks to me for approval. "It's hot," I concede. "Can't you just see Bailey bragging to her friends about dating a firefighter?"

"Firefighter, it is," Drew says, typing in the reply.

That's exciting. You must be very strong. Bailey adds another blushing smiley face to the end of the message.

"Drink," I say. "And I'm glad we're drinking, because I want to gag right now."

"She's totally into him," Drew says, after taking his drink. "Do we go there, or make her work for it?"

"Go where?" Mouse asks.

"Definitely make her work for it," I tell him. "Let's see Bailey get her flirt on."

Drew rests his fingers on the keyboard and hesitates. "Ideas?"

"Let me," Mouse says, reaching for the laptop.

Drew smiles at me. "I think the rum is loosening Mouse up." He hands over the laptop and sits back, his shoulder touching mine.

Mouse types: *Tell me more about you.*

There's a long pause, and then Bailey writes: *Oh gosh. It's hard talking about myself. What do you want to know? I'm a teacher, but you already know that. I've never been married, but was engaged once. I have 2 brothers, I love cooking . . .*

You were engaged once? Mouse types. *That sounds like an interesting story.*

Drew pretends to fall asleep and snore loudly.

"Shut up," Mouse says. "Tom's showing an interest in her."

"Tom's boring as shit right now," Drew says, taking the laptop back. "Pour yourself another drink, and when you've finished that, you can have another go at Bailey."

Drew hands me the laptop and gets up to put some music on. I check Bailey's response: *No way! That's an embarrassing story that I'll share when we know each other better.*

I finish my beer and type: *I'll show you mine if you show me yours . . . I have an embarrassing story, too.*

"Drink, everyone!" I announce, when Bailey responds with the blushing smiley face again.

"We need a new game," Mouse says. "I'm not going to be able to drive home if we keep this up."

"You can crash here on the couch," Drew says, leaning over my shoulder to read the messages.

Mouse looks shocked. "I . . . um . . . I was Jenna's ride, so I can't really do that."

"Relax, dude. My buddies crash here all the time. I'm not hitting on you or anything."

"And I can get my own ride home," I assure him. "I'll just text my stepdad later."

Mouse looks down at the drink in his hand and then at the computer where Bailey is typing another reply. "OK," he says tentatively. "I just have to call my dad first. I have my mother's car."

Mouse gets up and grabs his cell phone, then hesitates. "My dad doesn't know I have this phone."

"You can't be that drunk already," I laugh. "He won't know it's yours . . . just tell him you're calling from Drew's cell."

"Right," Mouse says. "Hang on."

Drew and I check out Bailey's reply. *Oh God. OK. I was 25 and my fiancé broke off our engagement one week before the wedding. I don't think you can get more embarrassing than that . . .*

"Whoa. No wonder she's so bitter all the time," I say.

"That guy dodged a bullet, though, right?" Drew laughs.

We hear Mouse behind us, arguing with his dad. "It's no big deal. We're working on a project and want to stay late. I'll be home first thing tomorrow morning . . . No, sir . . . I'm not with . . . her." He darts his eyes over to us nervously.

Drew gets up and motions for Mouse to hand him the phone, but Mouse turns away. "No, sir . . . yes . . ."

Before Mouse can stop him, Drew reaches out and plucks the phone out of his hand. "Good evening, Mr. Maguire," he says smoothly. "My name is Andrew Wilson, and I'm a teammate of your nephew, Troy."

Mouse's shoulders slump.

"Yes, sir," Drew says. "I agree, sir . . . he's here with us . . . tutoring the team." Drew makes an apologetic face at Mouse. "Yes, sir. We're very lucky to have him tonight. He's going to save us all from getting benched over our marks." Drew laughs. "We'll have him out very late, and we'd hate to disturb your family. If it's OK with you, we thought he'd stay over . . . of course. Thank you so much, sir . . . I'll let him know . . . OK. Good night."

Drew ends the call and hands the phone back to Mouse. "Holy shit, man. Your dad is a ballbuster."

"You're telling me," Mouse mutters. "But I'll bet his mood changed completely when he heard the name *Troy*."

Drew smiles ruefully. "Let me guess—your dad compares you to him all the time."

"You have no idea."

"Oh, I can guess. *My* dad compares me to him, and we're not even related."

They both look over at me and startle, guilt transforming their features. "Sorry, Jen," Mouse mutters.

I grit my teeth, irritated that they think I'm so fragile that I can't handle hearing Troy's name. "Forget about it," I say. "Bailey's waiting."

I hold up the laptop so they can see Bailey's last message: *Are you still there?*

"We need to come up with an embarrassing story for Tom," I tell them.

"An embarrassing moment for a good-looking, athletic firefighter? Does such a thing even exist?" Mouse asks.

"What's *your* most embarrassing moment?" Drew asks him.

"When I got pantsed in the hallway in ninth grade," Mouse says, without hesitation. "Your buddy Devaughn did it. He got my underwear and everything. I was completely naked from the waist down in the middle of the hallway one week into my high school career." Mouse laughs, and I'm amazed at how casually he discusses it. Up until this year, he couldn't even think about it without crying.

"What about you?" Mouse asks Drew.

Drew looks at me and then back at Mouse. "I can't believe I'm actually going to say this out loud, but in eighth grade I went on my first date—Elsie Campbell. She was gorgeous. Anyways . . . I let her choose the movie, and it turned out to be this horrible story about a kid whose mother dies of cancer. I couldn't help it—I started crying at the end of the movie. Like, actually sobbing. When the lights came on, I was a complete mess, and she hadn't even cried one tear. She told all her friends about it, and kids called me Crybaby for the rest of the year."

"You win," I tell him. I start typing, and Tom's embarrassing moment becomes the time he took a girl on a date and cried.

"You don't get off that easy," Drew protests, grabbing another beer. "What's your most embarrassing moment, Jen?"

I cross my arms over my chest and stare him down.

"Oh shit," he says. "Right. Boobs on the Internet."

Mouse buries his face in his hands, and I actually have to laugh. I must be more drunk than I thought. I look back at the computer screen where Bailey has responded: *That's adorable. Next question: What are three things you look for in a woman?*

"Ugh," Drew groans. "Girls love that question, and it's such a trap."

"What do you mean, a trap?"

"Please. No one asks that question and wants to know the truth. Bailey doesn't care what Tom really looks for—she just wants to hear him say things that describe her. Say something like: intelligent, caring, and good with kids. She'll eat that up."

I type out his suggestion and hit Send. "What about you, then," I ask. "What are the three things you look for? For real."

"For real?" he asks, taking a drink.

"Of course. I'm not looking to be your girlfriend, so you can be honest with me."

His mouth turns down in a frown. "OK. The truth. I like a girl with a good body, who has a sense of humor, and who's adventurous."

I roll my eyes. "Like you couldn't tell any girl that . . . What about you, Mouse? What's your perfect girl like?"

He thinks for a long moment, before draining his glass and answering: "Kind, ambitious, and intelligent."

"Lies," Drew mocks. "You forgot to mention *hot*."

"That's thing number four I look for."

"Fair enough," Drew laughs. "What about you, Jen?"

"I won't lie—attractive is one. The others are honest and loyal." I look back at the screen. "Bailey's are: *athletic, ambitious, and independent*. What's our next question?"

Mouse takes the computer from me and types: *Person in your life that you admire the most?*

"My mom," I say, without even thinking. Mouse and Drew both nod, but I wave them off. "I know, I know . . . everybody loves my mom. But it's more than that." I find myself telling them the story she told me about my father and grandmother, and how she built her new life out of the ruins of the old one. "She has this thing she taught me—the 24-Hour Rule." I don't know why I'm sharing all this with them, but I can't seem to stop talking. "She taught me that no matter what happens, you take twenty-four hours to be upset and freak out, and then you pick yourself up and take control of your life."

"And that's what you did," Drew murmurs.

"And that's what I did."

By the time we finish talking about our own answers, we realize that we've left Bailey hanging again. Drew yawns and looks at the screen where she's asked *Are you still there?* five times.

"Time for Tom to call it a night?" he asks us.

I stretch my arms over my head and check the clock. It's almost midnight. "Absolutely."

Mouse types: *So sorry—something came up here. Can we chat another night?*

Sure! Bailey responds, with one last blushing emoji.

"There's no way I can drink anything else," Mouse says, closing the laptop. "That woman uses way too many smiley faces."

"I should text for my ride," I say, as Mouse curls up on the couch.

"We should have asked about her proudest moment," Mouse mumbles, closing his eyes. "I had a good one for that. I got into MIT."

I almost drop my phone. "What? Mouse! Why didn't you say something sooner?"

He shrugs and fights to open his eyes. "Haven't even told my parents. They'll never let me go. My dad doesn't even know I applied."

"You're going to turn down MIT for your dad?" I ask, incredulous.

"Course not," he says, his eyes fluttering closed again. "That's why I need money. That's why I need in on Drew's cell phone business and why I did all that stuff for the team last year."

"All what stuff?"

He mumbles something that I can't make out. "What did you say?" I ask, leaning forward to hear him better. "Mouse?"

His brows knit together, and he mumbles, "I'm not an opossum, you know." Then his face goes slack and he passes out.

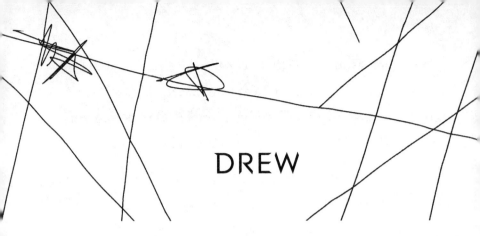

DREW

DRUNK MOUSE IS A STUPID MOUSE. *It's why I did all that stuff for the team last year.* Thank God he passed out before he could say anything else.

"Your ride coming?" I ask Jenna, hoping to distract her. I grab a blanket off my bed and cover Mouse up with it, then motion for Jenna to join me on the other side of the room.

She takes off his glasses and puts them on the coffee table, then looks down at his sleeping face. "MIT," she says, sounding impressed.

"I'm proud of the dorky little dude," I tell her, surprising myself with how much I really mean it. Mouse is annoying and neurotic and socially inept . . . but he's also brilliant and resourceful. I can't believe he's pulled this off all on his own, without his parents even knowing.

Jenna comes and sits beside me on my bed. "Do you think he'll actually go? To MIT?"

"Why wouldn't he?"

"His dad's a total asshole. He treats Mouse like shit."

That gets my attention. I know a thing or two about asshole dads. "What do you mean, treats him like shit? Does he hit him or something?"

"Only once, that I know about. But that's not even it. It's the way he talks to him. The way he puts him down all the time. His dad wants him to be just like Troy and makes him feel like a failure because he's not athletic and social and popular."

I shake my head and think about how fucked up life is. "My father would kill to have a son like Mouse. He'd trade me in a second. And it sounds like I'm his dad's ideal kid." I lie back on my bed and look up at her. "Do you think sometimes nature gets it wrong? Drops a kid into the wrong family?"

She blinks at me, a surprised look on her face. "Trust me— you wouldn't want Mouse's dad as your father."

I shrug. "My dad's hardly a gem. You never know. Maybe my life would be different if I had a dad like Mouse does."

"And you'd trade living in this palace for living at Mouse's little house?"

"Money isn't everything, Jen."

She laughs. "People with money just *love* saying that."

I open my mouth to protest, but she waves me off. "Enough about Mouse. What about you? What do you see yourself doing after high school? I mean . . . other than getting drafted by the NBA and serial-dating supermodels . . ."

I shake my head. "See, you don't really know me at all. I'll let you in on a little secret about me—I don't really like basketball."

"Lies."

"No, seriously. It's not basketball I care about—it's being part of the team. I love having fans cheer us on during a game and being recognized around town. And I love the feeling I get when I wear my team jacket—like I'm a *part* of something, you know?"

She looks away, and for the first time I realize how much she must miss being connected. How much it must hurt to be on the outside this year. I want to say something about it, but I can't find the words.

"So, what'll you do next year? When you graduate and aren't on the team anymore?" she asks me.

I shrug. "My grades aren't like Mouse's or yours, but they're strong enough, and I have tons of extracurriculars. I'll get into college somewhere and study business."

"And then . . . ?"

"And then I'll find a job where I can make enough money to buy a nice house, get married, and have a couple of kids."

Jenna gapes at me. "*That's* what you want? Some generic job and a family?"

"You say that like it's a bad thing."

"It's just—most people have all these grand plans for how rich and famous they're going to be, or how they're going to change the world."

I shrug. "I'm not like most people, I guess. I don't need to go to MIT to feel successful. I figure ten years from now, no one will care where we went to school or what our graduating average was. I don't see the point of running around stressing about things that don't even matter in the long run. Things always work out, you know? Better to enjoy life along the way. That's my philosophy."

"Huh. You make it all sound so easy."

"Isn't it, though?"

"Not everyone has the luxury of *enjoying life along the way.*"

"Everyone has challenges," I concede. "But I think the trick is to focus on the positives."

She shakes her head and smiles grimly. "I wish I had your confidence that things will all work out in the end. That hasn't been my experience so far."

"Well, maybe that's because you haven't reached the end yet," I tell her. "There's still lots of time for everything to work out."

She cocks her head to the side. "I hope you're right," she says thoughtfully. "I hope this *does* all work out in the end."

She stares into my eyes intently, and she's both intimidating and vulnerable all at once. I want to hold her and protect her and apologize for everything she's been through. But she's also a lizard that shoots blood out of its eyes, and I'm afraid that if I reach out for her, she'll go on the attack.

Her phone chimes while I'm debating what to do, and she

checks her messages. "My ride's here," she says, climbing off the bed and picking up her bag.

I don't want her to go. There's so much I want to say.

"Jen—" I call out, right before she walks out the door. She turns and looks at me, and all sense flies out of my head. "Those pictures of you last year . . . that didn't, like . . . ruin your life or anything, did it?"

There's a flicker of surprise in her eyes before she looks away. "You heard what I said about my mom's advice. You get over it. You pick up the pieces and take control of your life." She looks back at me. "Why do you ask?"

"I just . . . care, I guess."

The corner of her mouth turns up in a sad little smile. "My ride's waiting," she says, gesturing at the door. "I gotta go."

I watch her walk out the door, a giant hole opening in my chest. I flop back on my bed, feeling like I've lost something. Like I've wasted an opportunity that I might never get again.

There's a quiet knock at my door, and I spring up, thinking for a wild moment that Jenna's come back. But it's my sister I see in the doorway.

"Did I just see Troy's ex-girlfriend sneaking out of your bedroom after midnight?" she asks. Her tone is joking, but I can see the worry on her face.

"Relax, Ange," I tell her. "We were doing schoolwork." I gesture over at the couch. "Mouse is asleep right over there."

She steps into my room and looks at Mouse, then comes to sit beside me on the bed. "Everything OK?"

I shoot her an irritated look. "Of course. Why? Are you going to make a joke about me doing schoolwork on a Friday night?"

"No . . ." she says slowly. "Though that is massively suspect. I mean because you look . . . sad."

I force a smile onto my face. "Not sad. Just tired." I take a closer look at her. "Are you just getting in now?"

Her eyes sparkle the way they always do when she's up to no good. "Don't tell Mom and Dad."

"I can't believe they didn't wait up for you."

"Oh, they're still out. They think I got home hours ago. A notion that you will confirm tomorrow morning, being the loving brother that you are."

"Ange," I say warningly.

"Don't start," she says. "You sound like Mom. I was just out with Emma and Natalie, and we weren't doing anything wrong." She crosses her arms over her chest and glares at me. "It's so unfair. You and Harry have run wild your whole lives, but apparently I'm made of glass and must be protected at all times."

I sling an arm around her shoulder. "That's because you're a girl," I say lightly. "And you're only in ninth grade."

She ducks out from under my arm and sits cross-legged, facing me. "But it's not fair that they don't trust me. I've never done anything wrong! You've been in all kinds of trouble, so why aren't they monitoring your cell phone and giving you a curfew?"

"Partly because I'm almost eighteen," I tell her. "But mostly because they've given up on me."

"Don't be stupid."

I give her a look and then shrug my shoulders. "Whatever. Mom and Dad are just trying to protect you from guys. Guys are jerks, Ange."

"I have two brothers. You think I don't know that already?"

"I'm being serious. You're in high school now and you have to be careful."

She rolls her eyes and moves to get up.

"Hang on," I say, reaching for her arm. "Don't storm off. I'm just looking out for you. It's my job as your big brother."

She shakes off my hand. "Doesn't it strike you as weird that everyone *protects* girls by telling them what they can and can't do? Just because some guys out there are assholes, girls everywhere have to hide away and watch what they do, so they don't get victimized. Wouldn't it make more sense to punish the assholes instead of the victims?"

"Whoa," I say, putting my hands up in surrender. I peer past her to make sure she hasn't woken Mouse with her outburst. "I'm not saying that girls are to blame. And I know it's unfair that you have to be more careful than guys. But the solution to that is not to break curfew in protest and put yourself in danger."

"OK, then. What is the solution?"

"It sucks that some guys are assholes. I agree with you. And if I could change that, I would. But I can't. So, the best I can do is help you figure out who the trustworthy ones are."

"And you?" she asks quietly. "Are you one of the trustworthy ones?"

I'm so shocked that I can't even breathe for a second. My lungs feel like she grabbed them between her hands and squeezed. "Wh-what?"

"Are you one of the trustworthy ones?" Her voice is stronger this time, and she squares her shoulders defiantly.

"Of course I am!" I sputter. "Why would you even ask that?"

"The girls at school talk, Drew. Especially the older ones. They warn us about you and your teammates. About the way you ask girls for . . . pictures. And they say that Troy didn't post his ex-girlfriend's photos on Twitter—they think it was someone else on the team."

"And you want to know if it was me," I say dully.

A tear tracks down her face. "I'm sure it wasn't you. But they sounded so worried, and they said you'd asked them for pictures, too."

I take a deep breath and swallow down my anger. "Guys aren't the only ones who can be jerks," I tell her, when I regain some control. "I'm sure this isn't the first time you've run into bitchy girls. But think about it—if I'd posted pictures of Jenna, would Troy and

I still be friends? And would she be coming over here and staying late working on a project with me?"

Ange shakes her head and sits back down beside me. The trust is coming back into her eyes, and it makes my heart hurt that it ever left. Even for a minute.

"And as for the pictures . . ." I start. "This is embarrassing, but sometimes girls send guys those photos because they think it'll make them interested. It's the kind of thing I want to make sure you don't start doing. Because—and I mean this, Ange—no guy respects a girl who sends him X-rated photos. It's cheap and gross and I won't lie to you and tell you it's never happened to me, but I will say that I didn't ask for those photos."

She lets out a relieved breath. "So, you don't have some pervy collection of naked pictures on your phone?"

I get up and grab my phone out of my backpack. "The code's 7482. Check it out if you want."

She squeezes her eyes shut and shakes her head. "No. Thank you. I knew it couldn't be true. I mean, I know you're no angel," she says, laughing. "But I knew you wouldn't do something like that."

"Gee, thanks," I say wryly.

I watch her go and then toss the cell phone I'd offered her onto my nightstand before retrieving my real phone from my desk. I climb into bed and swipe my thumb across the screen, ignoring the long list of notifications that comes up. On the third screen, buried in a folder labeled Reference, is the photo album that I password-protected with one of Mouse's apps last year. I tap on it, and up it pops. My entire collection. There are photos of more than thirty Edgewood girls on here—a good fifteen more than anyone else on the team managed to collect before we had to prematurely call off the competition.

I scroll to the end. To the only photos that weren't sent to me directly. The three photos that I pulled off of Troy's Twitter account before they were taken down. Jenna.

It feels wrong to have these now, and my fingers shake as I select all three and then press the Delete button. I exhale in relief as the images of Jenna disappear from the album.

As far as I know, this album is all that's left of our competition last year. After Jenna's photos hit Twitter, Troy freaked out and went on a rampage, deleting the database and making sure every bit of evidence was destroyed. The other guys quickly followed suit, panicking they'd get caught—especially after the school warned us that we could be charged with child pornography.

I scroll through the photos, remembering how I got each one. There was an art to it . . . flirting with the girl just the right amount, asking without really asking, making it all seem like her idea. Some of these pictures took me weeks to get, and it was like a drug rush each time a new photo finally popped up on my screen, won through hours of late-night chats, countless hallway flirtations, and daily stairwell meetings between classes.

I was a legend on the team. Not even Troy could believe it. "How does a skinny white boy like you manage it?" he marveled, scrolling through my album. For six months, I wasn't Troy's sidekick—I was the badass player who had new photos to pass around every practice. They all wanted to know my secrets. They all wanted to *be* me.

I exit the album and stare at its icon on the screen. I hear Ange's voice in my head: *Are you one of the trustworthy ones?*

I select the album and hesitate, my finger hovering over the Delete option. I know I should nuke the album. I think about how I'd feel if Ange ever found out about it, or if Jenna knew. But I can't seem to make myself delete it. It's not even that I ever look at the photos these days—I haven't opened this album in ages. But it's like a part of me. Something I was good at. A time in my life when I was on top.

I turn off my phone and put it on my nightstand. I deleted Jenna's photos, and that feels like a big enough step for tonight. I'll sleep on it and decide what to do about the album tomorrow.

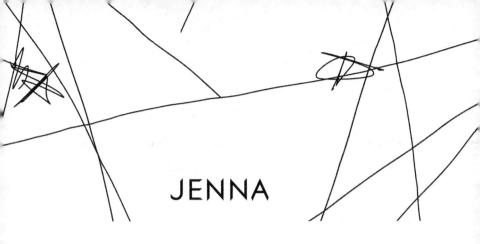

JENNA

"STILL NOTHING," DREW SAYS THE MINUTE MOUSE AND I WALK INTO HIS ROOM. He's sitting in front of his desktop computer, with the dating site open on the screen. It's been three days since Bailey last messaged Tom Anderson.

"Good," Mouse says, striding over to the desk and setting up his laptop beside Drew. "We have work to do, and this has been way too distracting."

Drew meets my eyes and gives me a look that says just how lame he thinks Mouse is. I can't help but smile in response.

"We'll hear from her in the next two days," I tell them. "Guaranteed."

"No way. The party's over and she's moved on," Mouse says.

"Yeah, right," Drew laughs. "He's a good-looking firefighter and she's . . . Bailey. She'll be back eventually—she's just punishing Tom for leaving her hanging on Friday night."

"OK, let me rephrase that: The party's over and we need to move on." Mouse pulls up a document on his laptop. "I had some new ideas for our argument, Drew. Did you finish the timeline of events?"

Drew leaves the dating site open on his desktop computer and gets up to retrieve his laptop. I slide into his desk chair and refresh Tom's messages on the site. I'm surprised Bailey hasn't contacted him at all, and I wonder if she's suspicious in some way. "Should we send her a message apologizing for Friday?" I ask them. "Just to smooth things over?"

Mouse looks up at me in surprise. "You've got to be kidding me."

I shrug. "We don't have to . . ."

Drew joins me at the computer, and Mouse drops his head into his hands.

"Go for it," Drew says, watching me type.

Allison,

I'm sorry about Friday night. I had a lot going on and was distracted. Can we try again soon?

—Tom

I give Drew a questioning look and he nods his approval.

"Can we please get back to work?" Mouse grumbles. "Who cares about Bailey's feelings right now?"

I lean back in the chair and put my feet up on the desk. "Where'd fun Mouse from Friday night go?" I ask acidly. "I think I like you better when you're drunk."

He shoots me a wounded look.

"Oh, come on," I tell him. "You already got into MIT. Why can't you relax for five minutes and just have fun?"

"I missed the memo that defined fun as sitting around a computer trying to hit on our law teacher," he says with surprising sarcasm.

Drew laughs and slaps Mouse's hand in a high five. God, they're irritating.

I get up and peer over Mouse's shoulder at the document he has open, and he slaps his hands over the screen to hide it from my view.

"What the hell?" I say, looking between him and Drew.

Mouse closes his laptop and turns to face me. "We're kind of in competition," he explains apologetically. "You're presenting a legal argument that challenges ours. Obviously, we don't want you to see our strongest points."

"Competition," I repeat, crossing my arms over my chest. "I thought we were working together on this, but just presenting two different ways of looking at the case."

"Well . . . yeah. But we both want to have the better argument, right?" He looks to Drew for backup, but Drew waves him off.

"You guys are taking this way more seriously than I am," Drew says. "I don't give a crap about *winning* or *losing*. I just want to get a decent enough grade to pull up my average."

I blow out an exasperated breath and move over to the couch to set up my own workstation on the coffee table. "Forget it."

Mouse turns and opens his laptop, then rubs his forehead and sighs. "Fine. You can read our work if you want."

"Don't need to," I say, loading up my own document. "I already know your argument is crap."

"Nice."

"I mean it," I say, not even bothering to look up at him. "If I waste time reading your lame-ass defense of Aaron Ducet right now, it'll just make me angry. And I'm not in the mood to be angry."

"Could've fooled me," he mutters.

I press my lips into a line and take a deep breath, determined not to let him get under my skin. "Honestly, I think you should feel guilty for even trying to take the blame off Aaron Ducet. But that's just me."

"We've already been over this," Mouse says slowly, like he's explaining something to a small child. "We're just presenting a legal argument. It's an intellectual exercise—a way of looking at the case in a new way, using legal precedent."

"An intellectual exercise?" I look down at my notes—a catalog of one girl's suffering—and I'm so disgusted I can barely speak. "That's something I'll never understand about guys. The way you can distance yourselves from situations so they're never personal."

"It's not distancing yourself if you're not involved. I don't even know these people. How could it be personal?"

Ugh. "It must be awfully nice to be a guy," I tell them. "Because when something happens to a girl . . . one way or another, we're all touched by it. When Heather Morningside commits suicide because she was bullied over a pornographic video, girls everywhere get the lectures and warnings about the choices we make and the consequences of our behavior. We all feel it and think about it and live it. So why isn't it the same for guys? Why don't you get lectures about your actions? And why don't you feel the weight of Aaron Ducet's choices?"

"I think some of your confusion comes from thinking emotionally instead of logically," Mouse tells me, in an infuriatingly condescending voice. "I don't feel responsible for Aaron Ducet's choices, because I'm not Aaron Ducet. Not all guys are the same, you know."

"And all girls are?"

"That's not what I said."

"It is, though. I asked why guys don't identify with Aaron Ducet the same way girls identify with Heather Morningside. Your response is that there are different types of guys, and so long as you're not an *Aaron Ducet* type of guy, then it has nothing to do with you."

"Well . . . yeah. Maybe guys are just better at looking at things objectively."

"Or you're just better at lying to yourselves."

"Lying about what?"

"There's no *Aaron Ducet* type of guy," I tell him. "You're not different. You just like to think you are."

He looks shocked. "I'd never do what he did, Jenna. I'd never post a video of a girl I had sex with. And I can't even believe you'd suggest that."

"Mainly because no girl would ever have sex with you," Drew pipes up from across the room.

I know Drew's just trying to lighten the mood, but I'm not about to get distracted from the point I'm trying to make.

"Do you guys mean to tell me that if Bailey sent us naked photos today, you wouldn't show them to anyone? Because I call bullshit on that right now."

Mouse turns back to his computer, dismissing my question, but Drew looks thoughtful.

"I'm not gonna lie," Drew says. "I'd show my buddies for sure. But I wouldn't post them online. That's just asking for trouble, especially after what happened with Tr . . ."

"After what happened with Troy?" I ask bluntly. "Don't censor yourself. If we're going to talk about this, let's be open and honest."

"OK, yeah. After what happened with Troy."

"But what if you couldn't get caught? What if no one could trace it to you? Would you post them then?"

"This is ridiculous," Mouse interrupts. "Why are we wasting time debating about something that hasn't happened and will never happen? There's no way Miss Bailey would send naked photos of herself to someone she's talked to for, like, five minutes online."

"It's an *intellectual exercise*, Mouse," I say pointedly. "And you're avoiding the question."

"I'm not avoiding anything. Of course I wouldn't post the photos. And I wouldn't share them with anyone, either. Because *I'm not that kind of guy.*"

"Stop kidding yourself, Mouse. You're just like any other guy."

"But I'm no—"

"You can't honestly expect me to believe that if you had nude photos of Bailey, you wouldn't share them around," I interrupt. "You'd do it, Mouse. Don't lie to yourself. I know for a fact you'd do it."

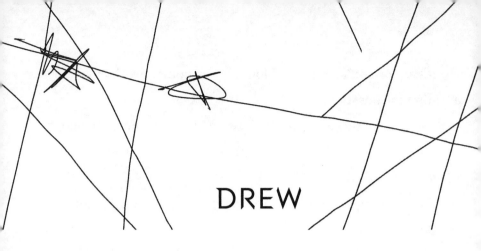

DREW

"WE NEED TO TALK."

I jump back, freaked out to find Mouse sitting on my mother's porch swing in the dark. He and Jenna left more than twenty minutes ago.

"Jesus Christ, Mouse," I say, pulling my car keys out of my jacket pocket. "What are you doing out here?"

"Thinking."

"You can't think at home?"

"We need to talk."

"Yeah," I say, striding past him and down the front steps. "You mentioned that."

I'm not in the mood for Mouse's neuroses.

"I'm serious, Drew. I think you should really listen to what I have to say."

"Look," I tell him, unlocking the car and opening my door. "I gotta go. Kevin's waiting for me and I don't have all night. Say what you want to say and let's be done with it."

"Jenna knows."

His words are a kick in the balls. I look up and down the street to make sure no one's listening. Goddamn, he's stupid. I told him never to bring this up.

"Jenna knows nothing, because there's nothing to know," I say slowly and forcefully to make sure he gets the message. "You need to get your shit together, Mouse."

"Just listen. I know what I'm talking about."

I let my head fall back in frustration. If I don't hear him out, he'll be obsessing about this forever. And an obsessive Mouse is a fuckup Mouse. Jenna's known him forever, and she'll see his paranoia written all over his face. Which means he'll get us busted out of fear of us getting busted.

"Get in the car."

"Where are we going?"

"Nowhere." I climb in and grip the steering wheel so hard that my knuckles turn white while he scurries around the front of my car and hops in next to me.

"Never," I say with ice in my voice, "never bring this up again."

He squares his shoulders and I can practically see him gathering his courage. "I think Jenna and Troy are back together, and I think she knows what we did."

I feel all the air leave my lungs at his words. Not at the *she knows* bullshit but at the thought of Jenna back with Troy. I feel . . . kind of sick and hot and sweaty and everything goes white for a second.

"You see it, too," he says with relief.

I swallow hard and will my heart to stop pounding. *Focus, Drew.*

When I can trust my voice again, I turn to face him. "I don't see it. At all. There's no way she's with Troy."

It occurs to me that he might be testing me. Mouse is a genius, after all, and he must wonder if there's anything going on between me and Jenna. Maybe he's just trying to get me all worked up so that he can tell if he's right.

"You don't know her like I do," Mouse says. "I can tell she's not mad at Troy anymore. And the only reason she'd get over her anger is if she knew it wasn't him. And if she knows it's not him, then she must suspect someone else . . . or several other people . . ."

I start laughing. I can't help myself. *This* is what he's freaking out about? He thinks Jenna knows what we did just because he suspects she's not mad at Troy anymore? "You're insane. Now get out of my car and take your crazy somewhere else."

I turn the key in the ignition, ignoring the look on his face.

"I'm not wrong."

"I thought you were supposed to be Mr. Logic, Boy Genius. Just because Jenna's happier these days doesn't mean she's not mad at Troy. It's been over a year now. She doesn't have to be angry every single day, you know."

"She said his name, Drew."

"You're not getting out of my car, are you?"

"She said his name."

I turn off the ignition and swivel to face him. "You've got two minutes. Spit it out."

"I've known Jenna for a long time. She doesn't forgive. Ever. If you cross Jenna, you're out."

"And?"

"The day after her photos went live on Troy's Twitter account, Jenna asked for my help. She wanted to cut him off completely and make sure there was no way for him to contact her. We blocked his number from her phone, erased all his messages, and unfollowed him on every social media platform she uses. He was done. Out. From then on, she refused to acknowledge his existence, and she went ballistic if anyone so much as uttered his name in her presence. I've spent time with her almost every day since the beginning of this school year, and I've never once heard her talk about him. Until today. Today she said his name. Like he was just some guy and not the person who ruined her life. Didn't you hear it?"

I had, but I'd taken it as a good sign. "She wasn't exactly talking about him," I point out. "She was completing the sentence I started and was filling in the blanks that I wouldn't post photos of anyone because of what happened with Troy."

"But she said his name. She said *Troy* without flinching. That means something."

I take a deep breath. "There are a million things that could mean. Maybe this project is mellowing her out. Making her see that what happened to her wasn't the end of the world. After reading about Heather Morningside, don't you think she'd get some perspective?"

"You don't know her like I do."

I grit my teeth. "You keep saying that, but I think you're beginning to realize that you don't know her nearly as well as you thought you did. And I think that scares the shit out of you."

"You're wrong."

"People aren't machines, Mouse. They're not math problems that you can figure out. They grow and change and mature. You want Jenna to be the person you think she is, but you might need to admit that she's her own person and you can't control her or predict her reactions."

"And if I'm right?"

"That she's back with Troy?"

"Yes. If she's back with Troy, then she knows the truth. That Troy didn't post her pictures. In which case, we're screwed."

"First of all, if she was back with Troy, I'd know. Troy worships Jenna. He'd tell me the *instant* they got back together. And second, your logic doesn't add up. Troy doesn't know it was us. If he did, we'd be grease spots on the floor right now. So even if Jenna *suspected* it was someone else, she'd have no way of knowing it was us."

"So you think I'm panicking over nothing."

"I think you're panicking over nothing."

He takes a shuddering breath, staring out the windshield.

"What about what she said to me . . . about how I'd post pictures if I had them."

I groan. "She was making a point, dumbass. She was saying that *all guys* would do it. It wasn't about you specifically. Not everything is about you."

"Then why did she say, and I quote: 'You'd do it, Mouse. Don't lie to yourself. I know for a fact you'd do it.'"

"You're worse than a chick. Do you make lists of things girls say to obsess over later? I'm only going to say this once, and then this conversation is over: Put yourself in her shoes. The guy she trusted completely . . . the guy she was *in love with*, posted naked photos of her online. Don't you think that would shake her confidence in guys in general? Don't you think she'd assume that we're all assholes now? She was telling you that you're just another guy, Mouse. Deal with it." I turn the key in the ignition again and put the car into reverse. "Unless you plan on coming with me to Kevin Lee's house to get drunk, I'd suggest you get out of the car now."

He pushes open the door and climbs out of my car, shaking his head. "I hope you're right, Drew. I really do. Because I'm hardly ever wrong."

I watch him walk down the sidewalk to where his car is parked. *Because I'm hardly ever wrong.* No wonder he has no friends. That guy is going to die a virgin.

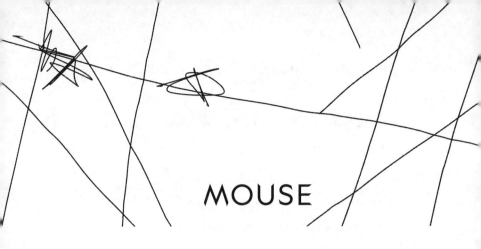

MOUSE

I THINK YOU'RE PANICKING OVER NOTHING.

She was telling you that you're just another guy, Mouse. Deal with it.

Drew's voice plays over and over in my head on my drive home, but his reassurances don't soothe me. Nothing would make me feel better except to hear Jenna tell me everything is OK, and that's impossible. What would I say? *So, Jenna, remember those pictures that Troy posted? Just checking to make sure that you don't think I did it.*

Because I did. Post the pictures, I mean. Not just me. Drew was there, too. Yet somehow he floats through life without giving it a second thought, whereas I live in constant fear.

It was an accident, he told me the day after it all exploded. *We were high, we made a mistake, and that's the end of it.*

I was ready to confess . . .

No, that's a lie. I felt like we *should* confess, but I didn't want to. Not one bit. People who cross Jenna don't get second chances.

So I let Drew talk me into keeping my mouth shut. He figured that if Troy and Jenna's relationship was strong enough, it would survive a mistake. *If they were meant to be together,* he'd reasoned, *this won't tear them apart.*

That sounded good to me, because I knew in my heart that they weren't meant to be together. I decided that the pictures would show her how wrong she was about Troy.

I pull into my driveway and turn off the car. My dad's truck is here, and I don't want to go inside yet. I'm barely keeping the panic at bay as it is, and a confrontation with my father will push me over the edge. I reach into the glove compartment for my notebook and pen. Time to think logically.

Signs that Jenna knows

She accused me of being like Aaron Ducet

She said Troy's name without getting angry

She's been more distant with me since last year

Signs I'm being paranoid

She hasn't perpetrated any violence against me

There's no evidence I was involved

She's closed off with everyone, not just me

This is getting me nowhere. I flip to a fresh page and tap my pen against my nose three times. To know what Jenna knows, I've got to think like her.

Which means I'm going to have to think about September 23. I've spent more than a year trying to forget that night, but Jenna wouldn't do that. Jenna would go over and over her memories searching for clues.

September 23. It was the first time I ever got high and the last time I'll ever touch drugs. Jenna had dragged me to a party at someone's brother's best friend's cousin's house. She insisted I go with her and said I needed to get out and be social. "You need more friends than just me, Mouse," she told me. "And besides, Troy will be there. You guys are family. You have to stop avoiding him."

She had no way of knowing, of course, that Troy and I were spending time together under the radar or that I was already friendly with the whole basketball team because they needed me to maintain their database. We'd kept our dealings quiet, since a group of jocks hanging out with a social leper like me would have raised all sorts of questions.

I got ready for that party like it was my wedding day. Jenna wanted me with her at the party, she wanted me to be happy, and I wanted to spend the night drinking and laughing with her. I day-dreamed about her realizing how perfect we were together, and I imagined kissing her at the end of the night.

When we walked into the party together, I felt like anything was possible . . . for about three seconds. That's how long it took Troy's *Jenna radar* to kick into gear. He was suddenly on top of us with his tongue stuck down her throat. It would be the understatement of the century to say that I instantly wished I'd never come to the party. And things only went downhill from there.

The next part of the night could be a Don't Do Drugs PSA. Or perhaps just a Don't Pretend to Be Cool When You're Not PSA.

In an attempt to escape the sight of Jenna glued to my cousin's lips, I wandered into a back room thick with smoke.

"Hey!" someone called out. "It's the little Mouse."

I gave a weak smile and started to back out of the room as the unmistakable smell of marijuana hit me. "Sorry, guys. I . . . uh . . . sorry."

"Come join us, Mouse," a familiar voice said. I squinted through the haze to see Drew patting the couch cushion beside him. I looked around nervously, wondering why he was being nice to me in public.

"I don't know if I . . ."

"You ever smoked, Mouse?"

"Like, cigarettes? Or those?" I gestured at the joint in his hand.

"These."

I shook my head, not trusting my voice.

"Well, then," he said, beckoning me over and offering me the joint. "Here's to trying new things."

I'd be lying if I said that I hadn't wanted to impress him in that moment. So even though I'd had a deep-seated fear of drugs ever since our Phys Ed teacher showed us a series of *This is your brain on drugs* ads in ninth grade, I sucked back that joint with the enthusiasm I normally reserve for video games and extra-credit assignments.

And then I had a beer. Or three.

And then, while Drew and I were sitting side by side on a ratty green couch with mysterious stains that I was trying hard not to think about, Drew said to me, "You're a pretty cool guy underneath it all, Mouse."

"Um . . . thanks." I felt awkward next to him . . . like my limbs were too long and attached to my body at odd angles. Everything about Drew was *right*. He could slide into any social situation and fit.

"Can you keep a secret?" I asked, suddenly confident that Drew would know what to do. My instincts were notoriously terrible, but Drew . . . Drew always said and did the right thing. He'd know how to help me.

Drew patted me on the shoulder. "Absolutely."

"I'm in love," I told him. "With a girl."

He laughed and sat back on the couch. "Excellent! Anyone I know?"

"Not really," I lied. "But she's out of my league . . . and she has a boyfriend. A big, scary boyfriend."

Drew shrugged and raised his beer to me in a toast. "I say you tell her. You've got the team to back you up, bro. Anyone messes with you, you tell us and we'll deal with it."

He meant it, I could tell. But then, he didn't know the guy I was talking about was his best friend.

"What if she doesn't like me back?"

"Then at least you'll know." He turned hooded eyes on me. "You wanna know what I really think?"

I nodded.

"I think it's about time you stopped being a little mouse. Aren't you tired of it? Get out there and take some risks. Be . . . what's your real name?"

"Matthew."

"Be Matthew. Mattie. Big Matt. Stop being Mouse."

Yes! I thought, standing up and squaring my shoulders. *I can DO this.* "Thanks, Drew," I told him, weaving toward the door. "I'm going for it."

I shake my head, frustrated. These are all *my* memories, but Jenna wouldn't know any of that. She did know I got high but only after we fought.

I rub my hands over my face and focus, trying to see the night through Jenna's eyes.

The next time she saw me, she was standing with a group of girls. I came hurtling toward them, amped up by Drew's pep talk and encouraged by the fact that Troy was nowhere to be seen.

"I need to talk to you," I said, ignoring her friends.

"Do you guys know Mouse?" she asked, not even batting an eye at my newfound confidence.

"I need to talk to you."

"OK. What's up?" This was the old Jenna. The blond, angelic-looking Jenna who was approachable and kind . . .

She looked into my eyes and smiled, and I lost all reason. "I love you," I announced in front of her friends.

"Aww, I love you, too, Mouse," she said, bumping her shoulder against mine and laughing.

"No. I mean, I'm *in love* with you."

"I see you took my advice about having a good time," she said. "How much have you had to drink?"

"Not just drink," one of the girls said. "Look at his eyes. He's completely baked."

"I'm not baked!" I said, grabbing Jenna by the arm. "Well . . . I am, but that's not why I'm saying this."

She looked down at where my hand was gripping her arm, and I pulled away quickly. "Sorry."

She rolled her eyes at her friends. "I think it's time to cut this one off," she joked.

"You're not listening to me!" I cringed at how whiny my voice sounded.

"C'mon, Romeo. Let's find you a way home." Her tone was light, but her eyes were steely.

She steered me up a set of stairs and down a hallway where things were quieter. "What's gotten into you?" she demanded, looking around nervously.

I stepped closer to her, emboldened by drugs and alcohol. "I just need to know," I murmured. "Do you feel the same way about me? *Could* you feel the same way?"

"Mouse," she said softly. "I do love you, but not like that. I love you like a friend."

"But that's how all the best relationships start."

The corner of her mouth turned up in a sad smile. "I don't see you that way. You're like a brother to me, Mouse. In fact, you remind me a lot of my brother."

I felt like throwing up. Her brother's a *little kid*. My shoulders tensed in frustration. She wasn't even *trying*. If she just gave me half a chance she'd see how perfect things could be.

I looked into her eyes and heard Drew's voice in my head: *Aren't you tired of being a little mouse?* And in that moment I was so sick of being me that I could barely stand it. So, I did the least Mouse-like thing I could think of. I went for it. I decided to show her that I wasn't the little kid she thought I was. I decided to show her I was boyfriend material.

I put my hands on either side of her face and kissed her. Hard.

It was electric. It was like in the movies when people kiss and discover the connection that was there all along. At least, that's how it was for me.

I'd like to think that if I'd been given a few minutes more, she might have relaxed and returned the kiss. I'd like to think that we were on the verge of a genuine romantic connection. But I'll never know. Because before any of that could happen, I felt myself pulled backward away from Jenna and thrown against the wall.

The hallway swam around me and I struggled to focus my eyes. I blinked heavily and Troy's face was in mine. "What the fuck do you think you're doing?"

I opened my mouth, but no sound came out. I looked to Jenna for help, but her eyes were flashing and her jaw was clenched. I could see the fury radiating off of her, and my stomach fell to the floor.

"Are you OK, Jen?" he asked, his eyes still on me. "He didn't hurt you, did he?"

"Of course not!" I shouted without meaning to. "I'd never hurt her."

Troy lifted me off the floor by my shirtfront. "I don't recall asking for your input here, you little shit. What did you think you were—"

Drew suddenly materialized beside us. "Yo, man. Ease up. This is on me."

Troy abruptly let me go and watched as I stumbled to the ground. "How is this on you?" he asked Drew.

"We were partying in the back room and Mouse came in. I let him smoke a joint with us and now he's all messed up."

"Shit." Troy flexed his hands and rolled his shoulders. "Are you kidding me? You should have known better, D. Lightweight can't handle the high."

He looked down at me and his mouth curled up in a mocking

smile. "You must be pretty far gone if you thought you had a chance with Jenna, coz." He shook his head, as if the thought of it was too outrageous to even contemplate.

I scrambled to my feet as he put his arm around Jenna and led her down the hallway toward the stairs. I was shaking with frustration and determined not to be left there on the floor in a disgraced heap. "What's wrong, Troy?" I called out, my voice cracking. "Are you afraid to leave me alone with your girl?"

Drew's face turned a shade of purple not normally seen in nature, and he grabbed me by the arm. "Are you fucking suicidal?" he hissed.

But Troy just laughed. "You really are fucked up." He pointed at Drew. "You did this. *You* clean up the mess. I don't want to see his face again until he sobers up."

I felt rage like I'd never felt before. Rage against Troy and my dad and everyone else who kicks me around and doesn't take me seriously. I was so *tired* of always being the punch line.

So later, when the party was dying down and I wandered into the living room to find Drew, Troy, and Jenna all cozied up on the couch, I marched right over to them. I still had things I wanted to say, and I was furious that no one wanted to listen.

As soon as I walked in, though, Troy took Jenna by the hand and left. I started to follow, but Drew pulled me back onto the couch by the arm. "Stop chasing trouble," he said. "He'll forget all about it by tomorrow."

"But I won't," I muttered.

"What exactly are you so pissed about?"

I shrugged. "Don't you ever get sick of it?"

"Sick of what?"

"Of always being in his shadow. Of letting him call all the shots."

Drew narrowed his eyes at me. "I think you're confusing me with you."

There was something behind his eyes, though. I knew I'd struck a nerve.

I shifted to face him, sure that I could win him over. "What the . . . ?" I felt something under the cushion. I reached down to investigate and pulled out a cell phone.

Troy's cell phone.

I stared down at it. Troy never let his phone out of his sight. It must have slipped out of his pocket when he was sitting there . . .

I swiped my finger across the screen. How many times had I watched Troy punch in his code? Unless he'd changed it recently . . .

I typed in 53662. Jenna's name. And the phone unlocked.

"Put that shit down," Drew said, his eyes flicking over to the doorway.

"Aren't you even curious?" I asked him, opening up Troy's photos. "Troy's the only one who's never uploaded anything to the database. Do you think he's that squeaky clean? Or is he just worried about getting caught if the rest of you go down?"

Drew took a long look at the door and then slid over next to me. "Be quick about it."

I scrolled through his albums and found one named Jenna.

"I don't think you're gonna find—Jesus!"

The album was full of shots of Jenna. Without her clothes on.

I started to sweat. They'd both kill me if they caught me. I moved to close the album, but Drew punched me in the shoulder. "Don't pussy out now," he said. "We'll never get this chance again." He tapped on a photo and it filled the screen.

"Oh my God," I breathed. She had no shirt on and was staring into the camera in this intense way that I'd sell my soul to have her look at me.

"Send it to me," Drew said, grabbing for the phone.

I swiveled so the phone was out of his reach. "No way! I'm sending it to myself!"

I dodged him while opening a new text, but then thought better of it. Through the fog in my head, I envisioned my dad checking my messages later and seeing her photo. I closed the text before sending it, my mind tripping over itself trying to come up with another way to get a copy of the picture.

"C'mon! C'mon! C'mon!" Drew urged, standing up in front of me to shield me from view in case Troy walked in. "Copy me on it."

Twitter, I decided. *I'll DM the photo to myself.* My dad knew all about checking my messages, my photos, and Facebook, but he still hadn't figured out how to work Twitter.

I opened Troy's Twitter and fumbled with the phone, struggling to attach the photo while Drew pulled at my arm and badgered me to hurry. I was about to send the message when I realized what an opportunity I was wasting. I'd never get this chance again, so it was foolish to attach only one picture. I pushed Drew off of me and closed the message, then opened Troy's photo album again.

Drew leaned over my shoulder and then smacked me on the back of the head. "Stop fucking around. Send the picture, dumbass!"

I reopened Twitter and started another tweet, attaching three photos at random before . . .

"He's coming," Drew snapped, grabbing the phone and clicking Send before I could stop him. He pushed the phone back into my hands and turned around just before Troy reached us.

"Hey," Drew said, completely casually. "I was just about to come find you."

I gaped at him, marveling over how smoothly he recovered. I let the phone drop onto the couch beside me and then knocked it back between the cushions as I stood up. "Troy, hey. I just . . . I want to apologize."

"Comin' down, are ya?" Troy said, searching the floor around the couch. "You guys seen my phone?"

"Nah," Drew said. "Where'd you have it last?"

"Right here." Troy felt around the couch cushions and came up with the phone in his hand. "Yes!"

My heart was hammering in my chest, and I must have looked

scared to death, because Troy clapped a hand on my shoulder. "Relax, Mouse. You're a dick when you're high, but something tells me you won't be taking up the party lifestyle full-time."

"So . . . we're good?" I squeaked out, wondering how I was going to get ahold of his phone again to delete the DM from his Twitter messages.

"We're golden," he said, before turning to Drew. "You coming with?"

"Be there in a sec," Drew told him.

"You good to get home on your own, coz?"

"Um . . . yeah," I said. "Sure."

"Good. Let's go, Drew, we're ready to roll."

Drew turned to me the second Troy left. "Hurry up, text me the photo."

"Where are you guys going?"

"After-party. Come on!"

"And I'm not invited?"

"Don't push your luck. Now quit fucking around and send me the photo."

I didn't want him to have a copy but knew he wouldn't leave me alone until he did. I pulled my phone out of my back pocket and looked for the notification that I had a new Twitter DM. There was none.

My stomach soured as I fought down panic. Maybe the notification just hadn't popped up yet . . .

I opened Twitter with shaking fingers and checked my DMs. Nothing from Troy. I looked up at Drew, panicking. "Did I send it to you by mistake?"

"What?" His eyes were wide. "What did you do?"

"Check your phone!" I hissed. "It's got to be there." If I didn't send it to myself, who did I send it to? I racked my brain to remember, but I couldn't recall choosing a recipient for the DM.

Drew tapped away on his phone and then sucked in his breath. "Jesus Christ, Mouse," he said. "What the fuck did you do?"

He turned his phone to face me, and there it was—a tweet from Troy's account. No text. Just photos. Up on Twitter for everyone to see.

TODAY . . .

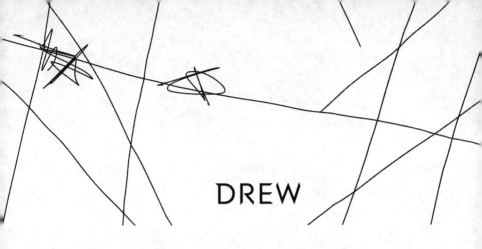

DREW

"WILSON!" MY GYM TEACHER BARKS AT ME AS I COME OUT OF THE LOCKER ROOM. "Office called. Barnes wants to see you."

"Thanks, Coach," I say absently, reaching into my backpack and pulling out my cell phone. One text from Jenna: *Just got called to the office.* I check the time. That was less than five minutes ago. Coincidence? I stash the phone and head to the office. There's only one way to find out.

"Hey there, Miss Singh," I say, as I walk through the office doors, "you're looking *fine* today."

There's no sign of Jenna, which means she's either in with her VP or they let her go already.

Miss Singh shakes her head at me, trying hard to look stern. "You're a scammer, Andrew. Don't think I don't know it." She taps a laminated sheet of paper on her desk. "You need to turn over your cell phone, please."

"Of course! I *always* play by the rules, you know that." I reach into my backpack and pull out my dummy phone. "Now be honest," I tease, dropping the phone into the basket on her desk, "you just want this phone so you can get ahold of my number, right?"

She frowns and then looks around before motioning me closer. "It's serious today," she whispers. "Don't mess around in there. I don't know what you've gotten yourself into, but they're debating calling the police."

I smile reassuringly at her. Miss Singh is adorable, the way she worries about me. "Not to worry," I tell her. "They've got the wrong guy."

Mr. Barnes steps out of his office and points at me. "You. In. Now."

I wink at Miss Singh before heading back to Barnes's office.

"Mr. Barnes. Good to see you again, sir. Have you been working out?"

"Don't be a smart mouth, Wilson."

I sling my backpack into the corner of his office and take a seat. "What's up?"

"What's up? What's up! You want to explain to me why your law teacher was in the office crying at seven o'clock this morning?"

I shrug. "Miss Bailey? No idea."

"No? You haven't seen or heard anything that might be considered upsetting?"

241

"I don't exactly hang with the teachers, sir, though I've heard rumors that she's banging someone up in math. Maybe check with him."

"Does a blog called *Miss Bailey Exposed* mean anything to you?"

"Not yet, but you can bet I'll be searching it out la—"

Mr. Barnes's fist hits the table with a bang that shuts me up. "Cut the crap, Wilson. I know you've seen the site."

"No," I say levelly, staring Mr. Barnes in the eye. "I have not."

"Is that so? Then explain this." He throws a stapled packet of printouts at me, hitting me in the chest.

I feel my temper rising as the papers fall to the floor. Goddamn, Barnes is an asshole. I'm not going to let him get to me, though. It's what he wants.

I clear my throat and then take my time picking up the pages, just to make him wait. Two can play this game.

Unsurprisingly, the pages are printouts from Twitter. The @yrwrstnitemare tweet is at the top, followed by pages and pages of comments.

"I didn't tweet this."

"Didn't say you did."

"I don't even know who . . ." I squint at the page, as though reading it for the first time, "@yrwrstnitemare is."

"Of course you don't."

"Then why exactly am I here?"

"Turn to page four and read the highlighted message."

I sigh loudly, pissed at being bossed around. When I get to page four, though, my breath catches. The message Barnes highlighted is mine. I mean, it's not *mine*, obviously, because I'd never have been stupid enough to reply to or retweet the Bailey message. But mine in that it was posted from my account. *Check out the tits on Bailey.*

"I didn't post this," I say dully, my mind reeling. "Someone must have—"

"Let me guess, Wilson," Barnes says cheerfully, swinging his feet up onto his desk and reclining in his chair. "Someone else must have stolen your password and posted from your account, right? Do you have any idea how many times a day I get that bogus excuse? Rates right up there with *The dog ate my homework*. I expected something a little more imaginative from you."

ONE WEEK AGO . . .

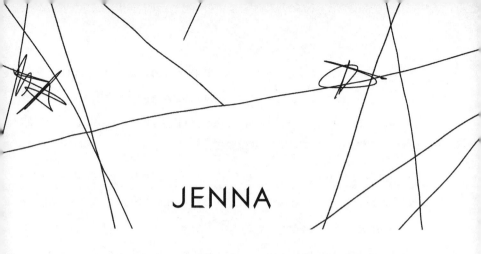

JENNA

WORKING ON PROJECT AT DREW'S FOR THE NEXT
HOUR, I TYPE, AS ANOTHER TEXT COMES IN. I press Send
and check the notification at the top of the screen. Drew.

Let's ditch the geek and fool around, he's typed.

I look up to find him waggling his eyebrows at me. *Focus,* I
respond, before pointedly turning off my ringer and stashing my
phone in my bag.

Drew groans and falls back on his bed, causing Mouse to look
up nervously. "What's wrong?"

"I'm dying of boredom," Drew says, propping himself up on
his elbow. "We've been working on this project for the last three
weeks and we're pretty much done with our section. Why don't
we just finish everything individually and then meet the night
before to put it all together?"

Mouse opens his mouth to respond but is interrupted by the
loud chime of a message coming in on Drew's desktop.

Bailey.

We abandon all coolness and race for the computer. She hasn't messaged in ages. Mouse was sure that she'd met someone else, but I was pretty confident that she was playing hard to get.

I get to the computer first and open the message. *Did you miss me?* Bailey wrote. *I've been away with friends for a few days, but I've been thinking about you a lot, and I think it's time we meet. Text or call me at the number in my profile and we can set something up.*

"Huh," Drew says, reaching into his pocket and pulling out a twenty-dollar bill. "Jenna wins. She was definitely playing hard to get."

Mouse groans and passes me a twenty. "But I don't get it. She's been in class every day this week. When did she go away with friends?"

"She didn't," I say, collecting my earnings. "She made that up to make herself sound like she has a life. She wants him to think she's not waiting around for him to message her and like it's no big deal if he's not into her."

Drew whistles. "Bailey's got *game*."

"How do you even know that?" Mouse asks.

"Simple human psychology, my friend."

Mouse reads the message again and sighs. "So, do we break it off, or just never message back?"

"What are you talking about?" Drew asks, striding over to his closet and pulling a box down off the top shelf. He roots around inside and then pulls out a cell phone. "Things are just getting interesting."

"We can't meet her!" Mouse's eyes bug out so far they threaten to make contact with his glasses.

"Of course not. But we can text her."

"To say what? That we don't want to meet?"

Drew tosses the phone to me and I raise an eyebrow at him.

"Bailey's not the only one who can play hard to get," Drew points out. "Maybe Tom wants to get to know her better before rushing into a meeting."

"Hold on," Mouse says, grabbing the phone out of my hands. "We can't text Bailey. She'll have this number. She could call it anytime. And what if she traces it back to us somehow?"

Drew plucks the phone from Mouse's hand and gives it back to me. "Impossible. And just because she calls the phone doesn't mean we have to answer."

"How do we explain never answering her calls?" I ask him. "That's a bit suspicious, isn't it?"

Drew shrugs. "Tom's a firefighter. He works shift work and isn't allowed to take personal calls."

I turn on the phone and open the messaging app. "This would free us up from the dating site," I point out to Mouse.

He looks pained, but I can see from the look in his eyes that he's tempted.

"C'mon, Mouse," Drew says, slinging an arm around his

shoulder. "I know there's a wild man in there somewhere. Let him out! Our project's almost done, and you've already been accepted to your first choice of colleges. Now's the time to *live*."

"Drew's right," I tell him. "I refuse to let you leave high school without ever doing a single reckless or irresponsible thing."

The corner of Mouse's mouth turns up ever so slightly into a smile, and Drew and I start to chant his name. "Mouse! Mouse! Mouse!"

"OK, OK," he says, laughing as we cheer. "You guys are crazy."

I swipe my thumb across the phone and the messaging app pops back up on the screen. "How about we write: *Meeting in person is a big step. Can we text for a while first?*"

Drew groans. "Guys don't talk like that, Jen."

"I disagree," Mouse says. "I'd write something like that."

"Exactly my point. Guys don't talk like that. Just write: *Got your message. Good call on the texting. Much better than using the site.*"

"And just ignore her suggestion that they meet?" I ask.

He gives me a thumbs-up. "Now you're thinking like a guy."

I tap out the message and press Send. "The deed is done."

"And it only took us twenty minutes of debating to decide to go for this little adventure. It's a wonder chicks ever get anything done, the way you agonize over every little thing," Drew says. "And I include you in the chick category, Mouse."

"Of course you do," he says, moving to pick up a textbook.

The phone chimes in my hand and we all freeze.

"So much for your theory about chicks agonizing over things," I tell him.

I flash the phone at them. Bailey has written *Hi handsome* and attached a blushing smiley face.

I type *Hi beautiful* and then look at Drew. He nods his head encouragingly, so I press Send.

Can I call you tonight?

"She doesn't waste any time, does she?" Mouse quips.

I hand Drew the phone, too nervous to type a response. He writes, *Sorry. Work phone. Can text, but can't take personal calls.*

That's too bad. I was looking forward to hearing your voice.

Mouse reaches his hand out tentatively for the phone, and Drew hands it to him with a flourish.

I'll bet you have a gorgeous voice, Mouse types.

Drew whoops and I mime throwing up. Bailey sends back her signature blushing smiley face.

"What do you think Bailey does at . . ." Drew checks the time on the phone " . . . eight p.m. on a school night?"

"She's probably watching reality TV and drinking a glass of wine all by herself," I muse.

What are you up to tonight? Mouse types.

It was a toss-up between messaging you and grading student papers. You won.

I'll take that as a compliment, Mouse writes before Drew takes back the phone.

Are the papers that bad? Drew types, the corner of his mouth turned up in a sarcastic smile.

The worst, she responds. *For some reason, my classes attract a disproportionate number of underachievers looking for an easy A.*

"Oof," Drew says. "That hurts."

"She's so on to you," I tell him, laughing.

Mouse takes back the phone and types, *That's because they all want to take the hot teacher's class.*

"Holy shit," Drew says. "Mouse is a ladies' man on the down-low. Who knew you had it in you?"

"There's more to me than meets the eye," Mouse says seriously, pushing his glasses up on his nose.

Bailey sends another blushing emoji and I double over with laughter. "You guys are ridiculous," I wheeze out. "And I want to stay all night and see how this pans out, but I actually have to go soon."

Mouse's eyebrows knit together. "What should we do with the phone when we're not together? Who's going to hang on to it?"

Drew takes the phone from him. "I say we take turns. I'll have the first night."

Mouse looks at me and I shrug in response. "Doesn't matter to me. But I do think we should save the texting for when we're all together. I don't want to miss out on the fun."

"So, we just trust each other when we're not together?" Mouse asks.

"Trust each other about what?" Drew asks. "What's the worst that can happen?"

Mouse shrugs but looks unconvinced.

"You know what? I'll do you a solid," Drew tells him, handing him back the phone. "I'll give you the first night, and Jenna can take the second. I won't even touch the phone until night three. What do you say?"

I look at Mouse. "You'll just hold the phone for the night, right? No cheating and texting without us?"

"Of course," Mouse says, checking the screen. Bailey has texted back, asking if Tom's still here. Mouse types, *I'm on shift tonight and have to run. Text tomorrow?*

Bailey sends back a thumbs-up emoji and Mouse powers off the phone. "I'll keep it off till tomorrow," he promises. "You can trust me."

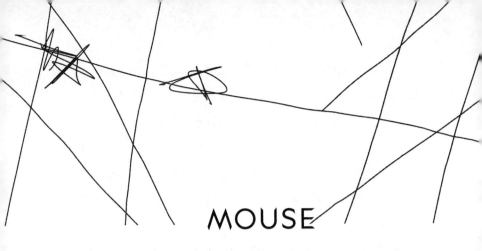

MOUSE

THE LIGHT IS STILL ON IN MY DAD'S OFFICE WHEN I GET HOME, SO I DROP MY STUFF IN MY ROOM AND GATHER MY COURAGE.

"Dad?" I ask, tapping on the open door. "Can we talk for a minute?"

He startles and swivels in his desk chair. "I didn't hear you come in," he says gruffly. He takes off his glasses and motions me into the room.

I clutch the printout of my MIT acceptance in my hands and take a deep breath. Something about spending time with Jenna and Drew lately has been pumping me up and giving me courage. I feel like they've started to look at me with new eyes—like they see a different side of me. Maybe it's time for my father to see me with new eyes, as well.

"What can I do for you, son?" he asks, sounding tired. I'm momentarily taken aback, surprised by the lack of sharp edges in his voice. I'm so used to his contempt and anger that it's unsettling to hear his voice without any traces of it.

"I . . . I wanted to tell you about something. But if I'm interrupting . . ." I gesture at his laptop open on the desk behind him. I can see that he's working on the accounting for his construction company.

He gets up and grabs a chair from a corner of the room and sets it down beside the desk. "I'm happy for the distraction, to tell you the truth. What's on your mind?"

I perch on the edge of the chair and look down at the printout in my hands. "I did something I'm afraid is going to make you . . . upset. But there's good news at the end of it. It's just . . . here." I thrust the page toward him and close my eyes as he takes it.

I hear him pick up his glasses off the desk, and I wait without breathing for his reaction. When he says nothing, I ease my eyes open to find him looking at me, his expression unreadable.

"I don't understand," he says in a flat voice, laying the printout on the desk. "I thought you weren't going to apply to MIT. We discussed this."

He's not yelling, which I take as a good sign. "Yes, sir."

"Where did you get the money for this?"

I hesitate, unsure how to answer. His face creases into a frown and I start to panic. "Troy," I say, without thinking. "Troy helped me." My dad loves Troy. Troy can do no wrong.

"Troy lent you money?" A hard edge creeps into his voice.

"Troy's family can't afford to do that. What were you thinking? Why would you trouble them with this when we'd already agreed on a plan?" I can see his anger and frustration building, and I scramble to make amends.

"He didn't lend it to me, sir. I earned the money. Troy had me design some apps—computer programs, I mean—for his friends on the team. They bought my programs."

My palms are sweating, and I pray he's not going to ask me for specifics.

"You designed computer programs?" he asks.

"Yes, sir."

His eyes bore into mine. "And you're telling me that Troy helped you with this. So, if I ask him about this, he'll corroborate your story?"

"Yes, sir." I can feel the sweat beading on my forehead, but I'm afraid to wipe it away. "Troy wanted to help," I say, stretching the truth. "He believes in me."

Dad grunts and picks up the printout again. "This is . . ." His voice trails off and he rubs his chin absently. "I'm not at all happy about the way you went about this," he says sharply. "I want to be clear about that. You lied and went behind my back, and I have my doubts as to how ethical it was for you to take money from your classmates for these *programs* you're describing."

My heart sinks in my chest. I look down at my lap, readying myself for the lecture and inevitable punishment.

"But . . . this is something, son. This is really something." His voice cracks, and I look up in surprise.

"I didn't know you had this in you." He takes off his glasses and swipes at his eyes, and I nearly fall out of my chair with the realization that he's emotional.

"I'm hard on you, Matthew. I know that. You've always been different. Ever since you were small . . ." He shakes his head. "You were so quiet and sensitive, and I've always been afraid that life would chew you up and spit you out if you didn't toughen up . . ."

He clears his throat and rests the letter in his lap. "But this . . . this took courage. And a faith in yourself that I didn't think you had. I guess what I'm trying to say is that I'm proud of you, son. I'm really proud."

I want to say something. *Thank you* or *I appreciate that*. But there's a lump in my throat that I can't force words past. I nod my head and try to smile.

"Can I keep this?" he asks, motioning to the letter.

I nod again and clear my throat. "MIT has very generous financial aid," I tell him, my words thick with emotion. "I've researched everything. There will be a package of forms coming . . . I just . . . I really think this could work."

Dad glances at his laptop and my heart beats faster. I don't even know how his business is doing. I don't know how this will affect him.

"Bring me the forms when they come," he says, turning back to his laptop. "I can't promise it will all work out, but I can promise to look them over and do my best."

I get up and head for the door, then hesitate and double back. I feel like I should hug him or shake his hand or show some form of affection, but my father and I have never had that kind of relationship. "Thank you, Dad," I say, fidgeting awkwardly.

"You're welcome, son." He nods at me and turns back to his work, and I slip out of his office.

Back in my room, I close and lock the door before giving in to the tears that have been building since the moment my dad said the words *I'm proud of you, son.*

I press my back to the door and then slide down so I'm sitting on the floor. I'd gotten so used to my father's disapproval that I thought I didn't care about his opinion. I'd convinced myself that it didn't bother me that he was ashamed of me. I had no idea how much of a lie that was. I had no idea how much his approval mattered until he told me he was proud of me.

I swipe the tears from my cheeks and close my eyes, reliving the moment.

I'm proud of you, son. I'm really proud. And he kept the letter. It meant something to him. He wanted to keep it.

I get up and grab my phone from my bag, then climb into bed to text Jenna. I have to share this with someone. I'm too happy to keep this all bottled up inside.

You there? I write.

Long minutes pass, and I get antsy, desperate to tell someone the story. After what seems like forever, three little dots appear, and she writes, *I'm here. What's up?*

Told my dad about MIT.

What?!? And you're still alive?

He told me he was PROUD, Jen. This might all work out.

She goes quiet for a full minute, and I stare at the phone in confusion. There should be emojis and all-caps and a lot of exclamation marks happening. But there's nothing.

Finally, she types, *That's incredible! I'm so excited for you. Congrats!*

Congrats?

Thanks, I type back and then wait for another response. When none comes, I set my phone aside, feeling disappointed and dissatisfied.

Jenna's not the type to gush, I tell myself. She said she was excited for me, and I believe her. But more than anyone, Jenna should know what a big deal tonight was. She knows how difficult things have been with my father.

I lie back on my bed and stare at the ceiling. There have been a handful of times in my high school years when I wished I had a close group of friends like other people have. Tonight is one of them. I wish I had people to meet up with. Friends who would drop everything to listen to me tell the story of tonight. I'm craving connection. I want to share this feeling.

An idea starts to take shape in my mind, and I get up and grab the Tom Anderson phone from my bag. I power it on and open the messaging app, debating.

Finally, I type, *You still up?*

Bailey responds right away. *I am! You still working?*

Yes. Just on a break. But I wanted to share some good news with you.

I'm all ears!

I got a promotion tonight, I type. *I applied for it months ago and kept it a secret because it was such a long shot and no one thought I could do it.*

She starts typing immediately. *Tom!!! I'm so happy for you! You must be so proud.*

I smile to myself. *I really am. It feels so good to show people what I'm capable of.*

That's fantastic.

I hesitate for a moment and then type, *Have you ever felt like people underestimate you?*

All the time . . .

I feel like people judge me by the way I look and then dismiss me. It's so unfair.

She sends back an eye-rolling emoji, with the message, *Oh please! You're gorgeous. Do you really think people dismiss you for being good-looking?*

I startle. For a moment, I forgot that I was supposed to be Tom

Anderson. *Sure,* I say, scrambling to cover my error. *People always assume that I'll be stupid just because I look like I do.* I wonder for a moment if that's how Drew feels and then push away the thought. Tonight is about me.

I apologize. I shouldn't have made light of the situation. To be honest, you inspire me.

Really?

The three dots appear for a long time while she composes her reply. *I can relate to keeping your ambitions secret out of fear of not being successful. It takes courage to go after what you want.*

What do you want? I ask her. *If you weren't afraid, what would you do?*

Oh gosh, she types. *I don't even want to write it.*

You can tell me. I want to hear.

My face is red just admitting this . . . but I would audition for a play. I've always wanted to be an actress, but my parents discouraged it when I was younger. Too unstable, no job security, a long shot . . . you know the drill.

You should do it! I tell her. *Who cares what other people say? If you want to pursue it, you should go for it.*

You really think so?

Yes. Absolutely. Trust me when I tell you that no one believed I could achieve what I have. If I'd listened to them and given up, I wouldn't be celebrating tonight with you.

I'm so happy you shared your good news with me.

Me too, I tell her. *My break's almost over, but I'm glad you were awake to share my happiness.*

Good night, she tells me.

Good night.

I read back over our messages, smiling to myself. Then I delete them all.

Jenna and Drew never need to know.

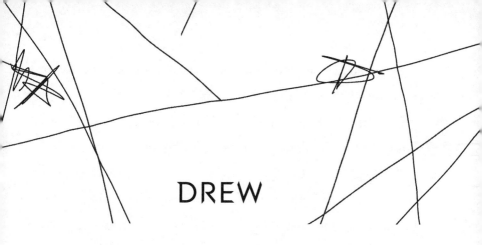

DREW

I THROW MY JORDANS INTO MY GYM LOCKER AND
GLARE AT THE CROWD GATHERING AROUND THE
SOPHOMORE WHO'S RUINING MY SENIOR YEAR.

"It sucks," Kev says, approaching me cautiously. "Coach got this
one wrong."

I nod, never taking my eyes off the kid.

"What'd Troy say about it?"

I shake my head and sit on the bench in front of my locker. "He
told me to get out there and earn my spot back."

"Solid advice," Kev says.

"Yeah." Troy is always full of solid advice. I wish he could stop
being the team captain for a second and be my friend instead,
ranting against the injustice of this situation just to make me feel
better.

Coach dropped me from the starting lineup. I'll now be
warming the bench on Friday while a fifteen-year-old *kid* takes
my spot.

Troy catches sight of me and motions for me and Kevin to come join the rest of the team.

"Oh shit," I tell Kev. "We've been busted by our fearless leader. I sense a lecture on team dynamics coming on."

"Every player on the team should be proud to wear the uniform," Kev deadpans, in a perfect imitation of Troy. "It's not about who's on the court at game time. It's what you leave on the court in practice."

I raise my hand in a salute to Troy, who's now frowning at me from across the room. "Don't forget: *It's not about us as individuals. It's about us as a team.*"

Kevin cracks up, and Troy makes his way over to join us.

"You're not still licking your wounds, are you, D?" he asks me, fist-bumping Kev. "'Cause this is a minor setback, not the end of your basketball career."

"The kid's a sophomore, T." I clench my teeth so hard that my jaw aches. "Coach benched me for a *sophomore*. That kid shouldn't even be on varsity."

"No one said you were out for the rest of the season," Troy says. "Coach is giving the kid a *chance* at Friday's game. And he's too good to waste on JV. He's ready."

I press my lips together and nod, just to get him off my back. It's easy for Troy to play Mr. Generosity when it's not his position on the team that's up for grabs.

"This is important for the team. You and I are outta here at the end of the year, and the new talent has to come up."

I paste a smile onto my face. "You're absolutely right," I tell him. "Let's go congratulate the little fucker."

Kevin whoops out a laugh and then tries to get himself under control when Troy shoots him a murderous look.

"Lighten up, man," I say. "I'm just joking around." I head over to the rest of the team, Troy and Kevin trailing behind me.

I find the kid's face in the crowd and step forward to shake his hand. "No hard feelings, MacDonald," I tell him.

He shakes my hand and then looks around nervously. "It's Milligan," he mutters.

"What's that?"

"His name, douchebag," Devaughn sneers. "It's Alex *Milligan*. You've only been playing on the same team as him for months."

"OK, then," I say stiffly. "No hard feelings, *Milligan*." I never bother paying much attention to the second stringers. No seniors knew my name when I was a sophomore, I can tell you that much. The young ones are there to watch and learn, not to take our spots.

"Appreciate that," Milligan says. "I'm really looking forward to the chance to play."

I nod and force another smile.

"Looks like you're not better than the rest of us after all, rich boy," Devaughn taunts me.

"Knock it off, Devo," Troy warns.

"Nah," I say, meeting the challenge in Devaughn's eyes. There's no way I'm gonna let a second-rate player like Devaughn think he's got anything on me. "It's OK. I'm all about the *team*, man. And Troy's right—the new talent has to come up. I'm willing to sacrifice my spot on the court for the future of the team."

"Yeah, right."

"I'm sure if you'd ever made it off the bench, you'd do the same, big man," I say, clapping him on the back.

"Burn!" Kevin shouts, laughing along with the rest of the team. I feel their support start to shift to me, and it's like a drug. "Besides," I say, unable to resist bringing them all in closer. "I have something major on the back burner, and this gives me more time to focus on it." Mouse had Tom Anderson's phone last night and Jenna has it tonight. But tomorrow . . . tomorrow I might be able to score some serious dirt on Bailey.

"You're full of shit," Devaughn says at the same time Milligan asks, "What's the something major?"

"You guys remember our little contest from last year, right?" Everyone but Milligan nods. "Well . . . think of that, but more epic. Infinitely more epic."

"You've got more photos?" Kevin asks. "Whose?"

"I don't have them yet . . . but I'm close. And you guys are gonna *die* when you see them."

The guys press in closer, hungry for information.

"You got Keisha Clarke, I know it," Kev says bitterly. "I've been trying to get in there for months. How'd you do it, man?"

"Keisha Clarke is small-time compared to the photos I'm gonna score."

"Who, then?" Troy asks, unable to resist getting in on the action. "Is it somebody's mom?"

"Better."

"A teacher?"

"I'm not saying anything yet."

"You're full of shit." Devaughn smirks.

"I'll have them within the week. That's a guarantee." I meet Troy's eyes and decide I don't care about the sophomore. It's not like I planned on playing ball after high school anyways. My talents extend far beyond the basketball court.

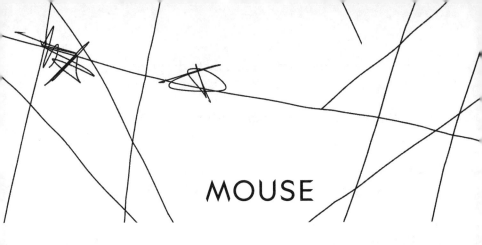

MOUSE

I GET TO MISS BAILEY'S CLASS EARLY AND WAIT ANXIOUSLY FOR JENNA TO ARRIVE. She had Tom Anderson's phone last night, and I've been worried nonstop that Miss Bailey might text and say something that would give away the conversation we had the night before.

Drew is already in class, slumped in his seat. He nods a greeting to me, and I feel myself start to sweat. Does he look irritable today, or am I just reading into things?

Jenna slips into class a few minutes before the bell and catches Drew's eye. *I have it*, she mouths to him, jiggling her backpack. My spine stiffens and I look around, making sure no one else is watching.

Drew motions her over, and I check to see that Miss Bailey isn't approaching the door before getting up and joining them at Drew's desk.

"Any developments?" Drew asks, as Jenna slips him the phone.

"I have no idea," she says. "I kept the phone off as per our agreement."

Drew powers on the phone and I start to panic as notifications start popping up. "Whoa," he says, swiping his thumb across the screen. "Someone was lonely last night."

Drew taps on the messaging app, and I freak out and grab the phone.

"What the . . ."

I angle the screen away from them and skim through Miss Bailey's messages from last night. I don't see anything about Tom's new job or their conversation about her acting, so I turn the phone to face them. "She must have sent thirty messages last night," I say, with forced enthusiasm. "Can you believe that?"

Jenna shushes me and looks pointedly around the room.

"Jesus, Mouse," Drew hisses, looking at me like I've lost my mind.

"What exactly were you looking for?" Jenna whispers suspiciously.

"N—nothing," I stammer, feeling my face growing hot. I check to make sure no one is looking and then murmur, "I'm sorry. I just . . . It was fun the other night when we were all texting and I got excited to check the phone." That's not a lie, technically, and I hope they'll let it go.

Drew plucks the phone from my hands and skims through the messages. "This is good," he says, before typing a reply. Jenna and I both lean in and read his message. *Can't stop thinking about you.*

Jenna smiles. "Add a blushing emoji and hit Send," she says, right as Miss Bailey walks in the room.

"Take your seats, everyone," Miss Bailey calls out. "We have a lot to cover today."

I scurry to my desk and watch as Miss Bailey unpacks her books from her bag. She looks up at the class and then slips something that looks suspiciously like a cell phone into her top desk drawer.

"We're going to start with a review of environmental protection laws this morning," she says, grabbing a set of handouts off her desk. "You have twenty minutes to fill this out to the best of your ability, and then we'll go over the answers before moving on."

She passes out the handouts and then slides her desk drawer open, peeking inside. I sneak a look at Jenna, who's eyeing Miss Bailey just as suspiciously as I am.

When I look back to Miss Bailey, she's blushing bright red and looking around the class furtively. "Eyes on your papers," she says, catching me watching her.

I look down and try to focus on the assignment. I must be wrong. Miss Bailey has a strict policy about cell phones in her class. She wouldn't dare check hers right in front of us all . . .

I peek over at Drew and see that he's got Tom Anderson's phone sitting in his lap. *Holy shit.* We're going to get caught for sure.

I try to catch Drew's eye but attract Miss Bailey's attention instead. "Is something wrong, Mr. Maguire?" she asks sharply.

"No . . . s-sorry. I just . . . I lent my environmental protection notes to Drew. Can I get them back?"

She narrows her eyes at me, then nods and looks down at her lap. She's texting for sure.

I scurry over to Drew's desk to find him shooting daggers at me with his eyes. He pulls some random papers out of his binder and then scrawls something across the top of one before thrusting them at me.

I slide back into my seat to find he's written, *Chill the fuck out.*

Easy for him to say.

I slide my own cell phone out of my bag and hide it under the notes Drew gave me. When I'm sure Miss Bailey isn't looking, I send a text to Drew: *Tell me you're not messaging Miss Bailey . . .*

He sends back a devil emoji.

I drop my head into my hands and stifle a groan. If Miss Bailey confiscates that cell phone, we're doomed. It doesn't even have a passcode on it.

Long minutes tick by while I try to console myself with the fact that Miss Bailey seems far too engrossed in her own texting to notice that Drew has a phone out. I even try to complete some of the handout to distract myself. But then Miss Bailey suddenly gasps softly at the front of the room and then clears her throat and coughs loudly to cover it up. She looks around the room to find us all staring at her. "Sorry," she says, coughing again. "I have a tickle in my throat."

I hear Drew snicker, and sweat starts to bead on my forehead.

Miss Bailey takes another look around the room and seems to come to a decision. "I'm feeling generous today," she says cheerfully. "We have less than a week until your major assignments are due, so rather than moving on to the next topic today, I've decided to allow you to use class time to work in your groups."

We all stare at her, stunned.

"Go on," she says, waving a hand at us. "Rearrange your seats into your assigned groups and get to work before I change my mind."

I pick up my books and move to the desk beside Drew's. "Put that away before you get caught," I hiss.

Jenna drops her books onto a desk on the other side of Drew and takes note of the phone in his lap. "I knew it."

"Miss Bailey?" Drew calls out, waving his hand in the air.

"Yes, Andrew?"

"Would it be OK if we used our devices today? For research?"

She smiles at him from her desk. "That's a great idea, Andrew. Thank you."

Drew flashes her a smile and then places Tom Anderson's phone on top of his desk, giving me a heart attack.

"I found some great resources," he says, loud enough to be heard by the groups around us. "Check it out."

Jenna and I pull our chairs closer and read the texts Drew's been exchanging with Miss Bailey all period:

Drew: *I can't stop thinking about you.*

Miss Bailey: *I know. Me too. I hardly slept last night, hoping you'd text.*

Drew: *Sorry. Night shift again. I have some days off coming up soon, though.*

Miss Bailey: *I'd love to see you.*

Drew: *God, me too. I've been going crazy imagining you.*

Miss Bailey: *Really?*

Drew: *Really. Send me a pic of you right now.*

Miss Bailey: *I can't! I'm in class!*

Drew: *Just one shot. Just so I can see your beautiful face.*

"You're crazy," Jenna says, laughing. "There's no way she's going to take a photo of herself in class."

Drew inclines his head toward the front of the room, and we both look up to see Miss Bailey walking casually toward the door, the outline of a cell phone visible in her back pocket.

"Holy shit," I say, "is she actually going to walk right out of class?"

Miss Bailey checks in with a few groups on her way to the door, then slips outside the classroom. Almost immediately, three dots appear on Tom Anderson's phone.

Just one photo, Miss Bailey writes.

We all hold our breath waiting for it.

"She's chickening out," Jenna declares when no photo comes after three minutes.

"No way," Drew says. "She's taking a bunch of photos, trying to get the best one."

Sure enough, a photo pops up on the screen seconds later. It's an extreme close-up of Miss Bailey's face against the wall outside the classroom.

"That's the best she could do?" Jenna whispers, recoiling from the phone.

"Her selfie game is *not* strong," Drew agrees.

Miss Bailey bursts back into the classroom, coughing loudly. "Sorry," she says, flustered. "I just needed a drink of water. This cough . . ."

I look down into my lap to hide my smile.

Drew waits for Miss Bailey to return to her desk before typing: *You're so beautiful. You must drive your students wild.*

Jenna laughs out loud, earning a stern look from Miss Bailey. "Please stay on topic, everyone," she says. "Don't make me regret giving you this time to work."

Jenna nods and ducks her head, then opens a binder so it looks like we're working.

You're ridiculous, Bailey responds.

I sneak a look at her to see that she's blushing so red that even her ears are glowing.

I want to see more, Drew types.

Jenna narrows her eyes at him. "Stepping things up a bit, are we?"

Drew shifts in his seat. "I'm just trying to get her riled up."

"Yeah, right. You're trying to score nudes," she accuses him.

My heart leaps in my chest. "She's not going to send nudes from the hallway," I protest.

Drew and Jenna both crack up. "He's hoping she'll send them later," Jenna explains to me, before turning back to Drew. "But I say, *dream on*. There's no way you'll score nudes from Bailey."

"Are you doubting my abilities?" he counters.

"Hang on, guys," I interrupt, struggling to keep my voice down to a whisper. "Do you hear yourselves right now?"

"I'll bet you a hundred dollars you can't get the photos before this project is due," Jenna challenges him.

"What?" I squeak out. "You can't be serious." I feel like I don't even know Jenna right now. This is the girl who had her life turned upside down by topless photos. She can't possibly be conspiring to put another woman's pictures into Drew's hands. That makes no sense.

She shrugs. "Why not?"

"Doesn't this offend you? As a girl?"

She raises an eyebrow at me. "Does it offend you?"

"Yes!"

"Then raise your own objections. Don't make it my responsibility just because I'm a girl."

273

She must be able to see the disappointment on my face, because she rolls her eyes and then looks back and forth between me and Drew. "Listen, I'll be honest here," she says, leaning in closer and dropping her voice to a whisper. "I'm actually thinking about your little *thought experiment* comment from the other day, Mouse, and I think it's time to put you boys to the test. I don't believe for one minute that the two of you could have photos of Bailey and not share them around or post them . . . so this is your big chance to prove me wrong." She looks me dead in the eyes. "Prove to me you're not a couple of Aaron Ducets."

"So, you want us to get photos of her and not say anything?" I ask, confused.

"You got it. And as a matter of fact, my hundred dollars will go to whichever of you manages to get the photos first." Drew looks up in surprise. "You saw Mouse the other day," she says, teasing him. "He's got as much game as you do. You can alternate nights and take your best shot at convincing her to send you photos. Whoever gets them first, wins."

"And when I win?" Drew asks.

"*Whoever* wins is then responsible for deleting them without making any copies. You both see the photos and let them go without sharing them in any way. Agreed?"

"Agreed," Drew says. "But how do you make sure the winner doesn't make copies?"

She sizes us both up. "The honor system won't do. We'll have to be together when you message. You each get one night, starting tonight. After we break for the night, I take the phone home with me to keep you both honest. Then I'll pass it off to the next person the next time we meet."

"Who goes first?" I ask, starting to get into this despite myself. The hundred dollars would be nice, but even more than that, I want to beat Drew. I think back to my conversation with Miss Bailey the other night, and I know that I can do this. Drew relies on his good looks to get girls, but that won't help him here. We'll be on an equal playing field, relying on our personalities alone to differentiate between us.

Jenna takes a coin out of her bag. "You can flip for it," she says. "Mouse, you call."

She turns so her back is facing Miss Bailey and tosses the coin in the air. "Heads," I murmur, crossing my fingers under the desk.

"Tails," Jenna says. "Drew will go first."

I swallow down my disappointment. "I'm still in," I say.

Drew nods his head and turns to Jenna. "I'm in, too. But not for the hundred dollars. I don't want your money. I want to show you that I've changed." His face is more serious than I've ever seen it, and my stomach sours at his words. "I really have changed these past few weeks, Jen. And it's important to me to prove that to you."

Jenna looks shaken but then pastes a grim smile on her face. "I guess we'll see, won't we?" she asks, gesturing at the phone.

Bailey has responded: *What kind of photos?*

Drew smiles and types, *Let's talk about it tonight.*

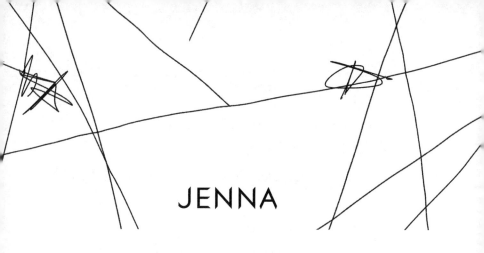

JENNA

BY THE TIME MOUSE PICKS ME UP TO HEAD TO DREW'S
HOUSE, I'M IN A FOUL MOOD.

"I've been thinking about the contest all day," he tells me
before I can even sit down in the car. "And I'm not even bothered
that Drew gets to go first. I really think that when you remove
Drew's looks from the equation, he's no better than I am, don't
you think?"

"Don't care," I snap, slamming the car door and slumping back
in the seat.

He startles and turns the key in the ignition, even though the
car's already running. "Oh God," he says, as the engine grinds in
protest. "My mother's going to kill me."

I close my eyes and lean my head back against the seat. I can't
take Mouse's neuroses tonight.

He unbuckles his seat belt and starts to get out of the car.

"What are you doing? Let's go," I tell him.

"Just checking the car . . . in case I damaged it."

I groan. "What exactly are you going to check, Mouse? You know nothing about cars."

His shoulders slump. "Do you think I broke it?"

"The car's fine. Just drive."

He refastens his seat belt. "My mom will kill me if I wreck her car."

"I'll kill you if you don't start driving."

He presses his lips into a line and shifts the car into reverse. "What's the matter with you tonight, anyways?"

"I quit my job after school."

Mouse sneaks a look at me. "And?"

"As usual, your empathy staggers me. Did you even hear what I said?"

"Yes. You quit your job. Though I can't fathom why that would be an issue. You hate that job."

"Forget it," I tell him. I don't feel like explaining that somehow Fran found out that I'm *that* Jenna. The one who sent the town's star athlete naked photos and then tried to destroy his life by accusing him of posting them online. When I stopped by to pick up my paycheck after school, she got out the words "questionable morals" and "poor judgment" before I ripped up the check and tossed it at her feet.

"Let me guess," he says. "You don't want to talk about it."

"Bingo."

The worst part of it is, I feel like I'm letting my mother down.

My mom is queen of the 24-Hour Rule. She's the woman who picked herself up and carved a new life from the wreckage of her old one without ever letting the past hold her back. I should be more like her. I should be able to leave the past in the past, and I should *definitely* be over this whole topless photo thing by now—it happened more than a year ago. But I feel like I'll never be free from the shadow of it. Even now, when I'm taking steps to move on, it comes back like a punch in the gut at the most unexpected times. I want so badly to be like my mother—to power forward without ever looking back. But, as it turns out, all it takes to knock me off my feet is a small-minded old lady in a frozen yogurt shop.

I take a deep breath and try to refocus.

"Jenna?"

"Yes," I say, turning to Mouse and forcing a smile onto my face. "I heard you. You're excited to beat Drew at his own game."

"I am, kinda," he says sheepishly. "But I also want to make sure you're OK with all of this."

I feel a flash of annoyance but push it down. Mouse is just trying to be nice. "*I'm* fine," I tell him. "The real question is, are you guys going to be OK with deleting Bailey's photos when the time comes?"

"I don't know about Drew, but it'll be a piece of cake for me," he assures me. "Seriously, Jen. You've got it all wrong if you think I'd even be tempted to post those pictures."

"We'll see," I say, smiling at the frown that creases his face.

I turn and look out the window, pushing away the memory of Franny's contempt this afternoon. Instead, to make myself feel better, I focus on listing everything I hated about that job. I manage to get to item number twenty-three before we pull into Drew's driveway.

Up in Drew's room, I pull out Tom Anderson's phone and hold it out to him. "Here you go, Romeo. Give it your best shot."

He tosses his Xbox controller aside and grabs hold of the phone, breaking into a wide grin. "Care to watch the magic happen?" he asks.

"Gross," I tell him, setting up my laptop on his desk. "Unlike you two perverts, *I* have work to do."

Mouse looks crushed, but Drew just laughs at me. "Yeah, right," he scoffs. "Wasn't this all your idea in the first place?"

"Testing your morals was my idea. Watching you put the moves on Miss Bailey? I'll sit that one out."

"I get it," he teases me. "You're jealous, right? Don't worry, Jen. I won't even need to bust out my best moves to make this happen. I'll save those for you." He waggles his eyebrows at me, and Mouse watches us intently.

"Go do your thing," I tell him, opening my laptop. "Let me know if you get anywhere."

Mouse hesitates, looking between us, and then comes over to

join me at the desk. "Are you done with your half of the project yet?" he asks, in a fake casual voice.

"Almost," I say, angling my computer screen away from him.

"Can I read it tonight?"

"Nope."

"But Drew and I are basically done, and I have time to help you."

I wave my hand at him. "Nice try, control freak. This is *my* part, and you don't get to comment. If you're bored, go help Drew scam Bailey. I've got work to do."

There's no way Mouse is going to get his hands on my write-up. I don't want him seeing it until Monday night, when it'll be too late for him to rewrite it. He and Drew might be fine with letting Aaron Ducet off the hook for what happened to Heather Morningside, but there's no way I'm going to.

Mouse turns to Drew. "I don't suppose you want to spend some time going over our part?"

"Nice try," Drew tells him, tapping away on the cell phone. "I'm not letting you distract me on my one night with Bailey."

Mouse flops into a chair beside Drew's bed. "By all means. Why worry about our futures when there are illicit photos on the line."

"If you're bored, you can go home," Drew tells him, winking at me. He knows there's no way Mouse would leave the two of us unsupervised together.

"N-no . . . that's ok. I need to . . . I'll just supervise your texts. Keep you honest."

"Of course you will," Drew mutters.

I put my head down and tune them out. The next few days are going to be busy ones, and I want to get my write-up finished before leaving today. Plus, with Mouse distracted by Drew's texting, I can work without interruptions.

By the time I look up from my laptop, more than an hour has passed. Mouse has fallen asleep in Drew's desk chair, Drew is still texting Bailey, and my part of the project is done.

"Any luck?" I ask Drew, stretching my arms above my head and yawning.

"Not yet," he mutters. "But the night is still young."

"It might be time to admit defeat," I tell him, knowing he never will. "Mind if I grab some water from the kitchen?"

He waves a hand at me without looking up from the phone. "Help yourself. Bring some chips and sodas up, too, if you want."

I shake my head at him and slip out of the room. Guys are so pathetic.

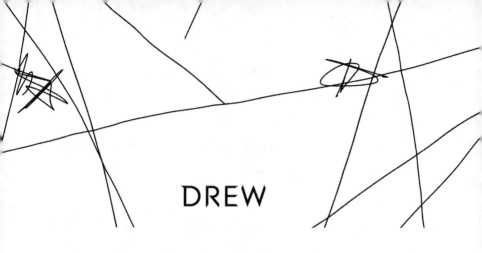

DREW

THE SECOND JEN LEAVES THE ROOM, I'M ALL OVER MOUSE.

"The database. What'd you do with it?" I ask, smacking him awake.

"Wh-what?" he asks, blinking his eyes in confusion. "What time is it? Where's Jen?"

"Downstairs. We only have a few minutes. Where's the database?"

"We destroyed it, remember?" Mouse says. "Troy made me delete everything."

"Yes, yes. You deleted our team database. But you're a genius who's in love with his creations. No way you deleted the actual program for the database."

"Well . . . no. I still have the program. Why?"

"Because we need it now." I flash the phone at Mouse, open to one of the shots Bailey sent.

"Oh, my God." Mouse jumps out of the chair and grabs the

phone from me. "I can't believe you . . . oh, my God." His eyes are bugging out of his face and he starts toward the door and then doubles back to me. "Oh, my God."

"Calm down," I command. "You need to save them. Right now. In your database." I leap off my bed to watch the door.

"No."

"Mouse! Don't be a fuckup. Jenna's gonna make us delete those pictures the second she comes in here. Either you save them, or I'll send them to myself. If you save them in the database, we both have access and we can discuss what to do when we have more time. If I send them to myself, you have no input."

"This is crazy! We *promised* Jen we wouldn't save these."

"I know. But this is some epic shit and we don't have time to think about this properly right now. I'm just buying us some more time, that's all. If you and I discuss it later and decide to delete them, we'll delete them."

Mouse rubs his eyes under his glasses and debates.

"She's on the stairs," I hiss at him.

He takes the phone and races into my en suite bathroom, closing the door just as Jenna comes stumbling into my room, balancing two bags of chips and three Cokes.

"Where's Mouse?"

"Bathroom."

She nods and lays everything down on my bed. "I have to be

home in an hour. I say we eat and then split. That gives you a full sixty minutes to make progress before calling it a night."

"No need," Mouse says, coming out of the bathroom with the phone in his hand. "You officially owe Drew one hundred dollars." He flashes the screen at Jenna, whose eyes widen in shock.

"She sent that? Just now?"

"She sent more than just that one," Mouse says, handing her the phone. I try to meet his eyes to see if he saved the photos, but he ignores me.

Jenna scrolls through the pictures. There are seven in total, ranging from some negligee photos to a full-frontal shot that I couldn't tear my eyes from. That shot's the reason I reconsidered our promise to delete the photos. I could have parted with the underwear shots . . . and even the topless ones. But the full frontal? I'll be a fucking legend with that photo.

"This is insane," Jenna says. "We need to delete these right now."

Mouse shoots me a look and I raise my eyebrows at him questioningly. He gives the tiniest nod, and I breathe out a sigh of relief. "I agree," I tell her. "Party's over."

She narrows her eyes at me in suspicion. "Just like that?" she asks, looking between me and Mouse. "You're both agreeing to delete these photos right now with no argument?"

Mouse starts to fidget, so I step in to distract her. "Of course," I say smoothly. "Even I didn't expect to win the bet quite this . . . *thoroughly,* and it's kind of freaking me out."

She turns the phone over in her hands. "And you're not tempted to hang on to these at all?"

"No!" Mouse shouts. "This is so, so wrong. This is the kind of thing that gets people expelled. The kind of thing that makes schools like MIT rescind their offers of admission." Mouse looks so shaken that I start to doubt whether he saved the photos at all.

Jen raises an eyebrow at me, directing the question my way. "I won't lie," I tell her, "the old me would have done anything to keep these pictures . . . but this is too much. Bailey's a *teacher*, and Mouse is right. We'd be in huge trouble if we got caught with those photos."

She nods her head and walks over to sit on my bed. Mouse and I exchange another look while she taps away on the phone, and I pray that Mouse didn't leave any traces on there that he saved the photos.

"OK," she says, after a minute. "They're deleted." She walks over to my desk and fishes a paper clip out of my top drawer. "This experiment is officially over, and Tom Anderson no longer exists." She bends the paper clip and inserts an end into the side of the phone, popping open the tray containing the SIM card. She holds it up and then sticks it in her front pocket, before sliding the phone itself into her back pocket.

"W-wait," Mouse says. "Shouldn't we destroy that SIM card?"

Jenna looks at me and I nod at her.

"You're right. That's a better idea," she says, retrieving the card. "How can we be sure it's destroyed?"

I take the card from her and grab a pair of scissors off my desk. "See ya later, Bailey," I say, as the scissors snap through the card.

Mouse picks up the pieces and takes them into the bathroom. "Just to be sure . . ." he says, dropping them into the toilet and flushing. "We can't have anything tying us to Bailey."

I nod at him and at Jenna. "Now what do we do with the phone?"

"I'll hang on to it for now," Jenna says. "The photos are gone, but I don't know . . . I don't want this phone going back into circulation for your business."

Mouse nods. "That's fair."

"Paranoid," I point out. "But fair."

"What about the dating site," Mouse says. "Shouldn't we delete Tom's profile?"

"Good idea," I tell him, retrieving my laptop and logging in as Tom.

Mouse comes around behind me and gestures at the screen. "Go in to Profile Settings," he instructs. "There! Click Delete Profile."

A confirmation message appears, asking if we're sure we want to delete our profile. I look up at Jenna and she nods her head. I click Yes to confirm the deletion, and we watch as Tom's profile disappears from the site.

"OK," Jenna says, rubbing her hands together. "I don't know about you guys, but I'm officially scarred for life after looking at those pictures. I say we get the hell out of here and meet back Monday night."

Mouse gives a nervous laugh. "Yeah . . . Monday night." He starts packing up his stuff, avoiding making eye contact with me.

I give Mouse twenty minutes to drop off Jenna before texting him: *Send me link & password.*

Three little dots appear, indicating that he's typing. Then they disappear and reappear several times. I roll my eyes and wait for him to compose a message he's happy with. When it finally comes in, though, it's not one that I'm happy with: *I need time to think first.*

Don't be a dick, I respond. *We either both have access or neither of us.*

Fine. Password is Bailey. He sends a link, and I click on it to verify he saved all the photos.

Thanks, Mouse.

What are you going to do with them?

Probably nothing, I respond. *We should decide together. Sleep on it tonight. If you want to delete them tomorrow, I'm OK with that.*

Good idea, he replies.

I navigate to my main messages screen and find the text from Tom Anderson, containing all seven images Bailey sent us. My insurance policy in case Mouse pussied out.

I scroll through the pictures, reliving the adrenaline rush of watching Bailey give in and send increasingly hot pictures. It took forever to break down her defenses, which made the victory even sweeter. I move the photos over to my password-protected folder and delete Tom's text. I'll be the hero of the team with these pictures.

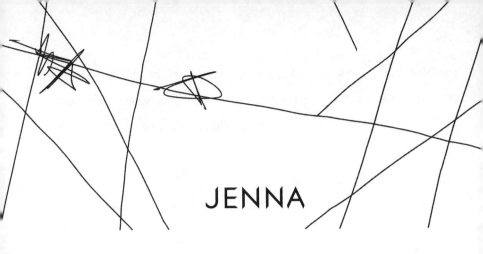

JENNA

"I CAN'T STAY LONG," I ANNOUNCE AS SOON AS I WALK INTO DREW'S ROOM.

Mouse groans. It's the night before our project is due, and I knew he'd be freaking out. "Fifteen percent of our grade, Jenna," he says. "I think you can stay until we format and print everything."

I brandish a thumb drive with my part of the project on it. "Already formatted and ready to go. You just need to print my section and attach it to yours. Done."

He takes the drive from me grudgingly. "We'll need some kind of write-up explaining why we chose to approach the case from two different perspectives," he says.

"I trust you with that. But I don't trust you with my half of the project. I want it included *exactly* as is. Don't touch anything—not even to correct any typos you find. Got it?"

He presses his lips into a straight line. "Got it. But what's on here? You didn't do anything crazy, did you?"

I roll my eyes. "Of course I didn't. But I did write a scathing indictment of Aaron Ducet, the press, and every guy who's ever felt entitled to violate a girl's privacy." I flash him a wide smile and point a finger at him. "Don't change a word, remember?"

I hike my bag up on my shoulder and glance at the door.

"Where are you going, anyway?" Drew asks.

"I have to babysit my brother tonight," I lie. "My parents are going out." In reality, I have an appointment that I don't want to be late for, but Mouse would never accept that. He'd lecture me until the end of time about not having my priorities straight.

I check the time on my phone. "Actually," I tell them, moving to sit down beside Mouse on Drew's couch. "I have a few minutes until I need to be home, and there's something I wanted to talk to you both about."

Mouse looks queasy, but nods his head and puts his laptop down on the coffee table. Drew sits beside him and looks at me expectantly.

I wring my hands, suddenly nervous. "Working on this project with you guys has really meant something to me," I start. "I'm impressed that you both agreed to delete Bailey's photos. And I appreciate you both allowing me to have free rein with my section of the project so that I can say the things I need to say. I feel like . . . like I'm getting some closure. Like maybe I can start moving on."

"That's great, Jen," Drew says, like he means it.

"I just . . . I consider you guys my friends. And I need something from you. Now. Tonight. I need you to answer a question for me so I can finally let go."

"Anything," Mouse says, his voice cracking.

"There's still so much I don't understand about the night Troy posted my photos. So many things that don't make any sense to me. And I'm kind of hoping that you guys can fill in some blanks for me. So, if there's anything at all that you know about that night, *please* tell me. No matter how small the detail. I just . . . I need to understand. I think it would help me let go and stop questioning things."

They look at each other, and my heart leaps in anticipation. But then . . .

"I'm so sorry, Jen," Drew says. "I wish I could help you, but I don't know anything that you don't already know. Mouse?"

Mouse shakes his head and offers me an apologetic smile. "Troy never talked about it to anyone," he says. "I wish there was something I could tell you that would help."

I sigh. "That's what I thought," I say. "I figured if you knew anything, you'd have told me by now." I pick up my bag and offer them a shaky smile. "I'll see you guys tomorrow when we hand in our project."

"Jen—" Drew calls when I reach the door. "I hope you know

that if Troy had said *anything* to me, I'd tell you. Honestly."

"Me, too," Mouse jumps in. "Honestly."

I nod, my heart heavy with disappointment. "Can't blame a girl for trying."

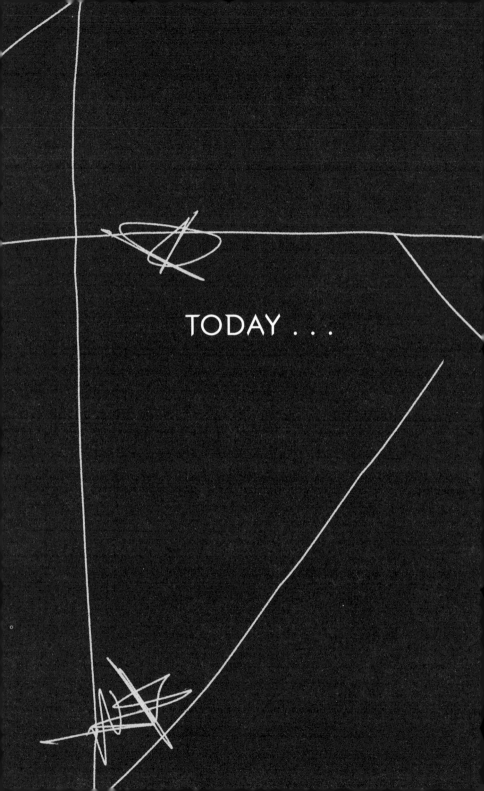

TODAY . . .

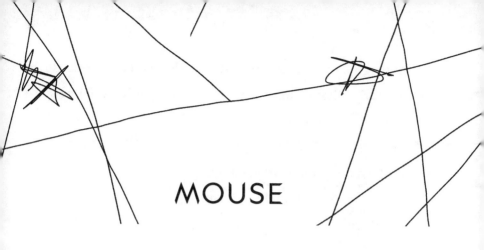

MOUSE

I HUG MY BACKPACK TO MY CHEST AND WATCH MY VICE PRINCIPAL, MR. JAIN, FLIP THROUGH A THICK BOOK OF HANDWRITTEN NOTES.

When Jenna texted earlier that she was in the office, I'd dismissed the jolt of fear it gave me. Jenna gets called to the office more than anyone else I know. I, on the other hand, never get in trouble. So, it feels like an awfully big coincidence that we've both been called down here at the same time. Especially today.

I feel a bead of sweat track down my back, and I struggle to concentrate.

"Matthew Maguire," Mr. Jain says, looking up from his notes. "We've met a few times before, haven't we?"

"Y-yes, sir. You gave me an award earlier this year."

"Indeed, I did." He swivels to face his computer screen and taps on his keyboard. "I'm impressed with what I see here. Perfect attendance, and top marks in nearly all of your courses."

"Thank you, sir."

"Your guidance counselor tells me that you've turned down several early offers of admission to Canadian universities because you plan to attend an American school."

"Yes. MIT."

"And what do you plan on studying?"

"Computer Science and Engineering."

A smile tugs at the corner of his mouth. "That certainly makes sense."

"Sir?"

"You have rather ambitious plans for the future, Matthew, and you're a smart young man. I'm sure you recognize that it would be incredibly foolish to be involved in anything that might jeopardize those plans."

It's about a thousand degrees in this office, but I resist the urge to wipe the beads of sweat from my forehead. *Think like Drew,* I tell myself. *Be cool.*

"I've been working for this for years, Mr. Jain. I assure you I wouldn't do anything to jeopardize my plans."

"Excellent!" He beams a toothy smile at me. "Then let's talk about who posted the photos of Miss Bailey last night."

I fight hard to keep my face blank. "I honestly have no idea."

"But you've seen the photos."

I consider lying but realize that would be pointless. "Of course. Everyone has seen the photos."

He nods his head slowly. "How are things going in law class?"

"Law class? Fine."

His eyebrows shoot up. "Really? I'm surprised to hear that. I've been looking over your notes, and I see that you filed official complaints with the office five times in the first three weeks of the semester. That doesn't sound fine to me at all."

"Oh, that. Yeah. I think . . . I had some trouble adjusting to her teaching style."

"That seems to be an understatement." He picks up his notebook and slides on a pair of glasses. "Let's see. *Verbally abusive, incompetent, inconsistent, doesn't know anything about the law.* I'm reading directly from your statements here. Those are your words, are they not, Mr. Maguire?"

"I may have been a little upset when I wrote those things."

"Clearly. All five times. So, what's changed in the last month or so?"

"I suppose I started to adjust," I say, shifting uncomfortably in my chair. I don't like where this is going.

"And yet, your grade in Miss Bailey's class remains one of the lowest grades you've ever received at Edgewood."

"Yes, but I hope to bring it up with the project we just completed," I tell him eagerly.

"I see. Still, for clarity, would you say that you've not been a fan of Miss Bailey's class this semester?"

I swallow down my panic. "Yes, I guess that's true. But that doesn't mean I posted naked pictures of her on the Internet."

"Whoa!" Mr. Jain says, holding his hands up in protest. "No one accused you of anything."

I set my backpack down beneath my chair and wipe my sweaty palms on my pants. "I feel like you're accusing me of something. Otherwise, why would I be here?"

Mr. Jain takes off his glasses and tosses them onto his desk. "Do I think you're the mastermind behind this little stunt? Obviously not. But do I think you might have sat by and watched it happen without stopping it? Yes, I think that's a possibility. And if my hunch is correct, I think you *want* to tell me what you know." He looks over my shoulder suddenly and nods to someone at the door. "Why don't you take a seat outside, Matthew, while I confer with our IT specialist. We'll talk again afterward."

I reach for my backpack and stand on wobbly legs. I'm irrationally offended that Mr. Jain doesn't see me as a mastermind, and I'm more than a little nervous about the presence of the IT specialist.

"So, I just . . . sit out there?" I ask.

"That's correct. I shouldn't be long."

I open the door and start to edge past the excited-looking IT guy.

"And Matthew?"

I turn around. "Yes?"

"While you're out there, think about sharing what you know. It would save us both a lot of time if you stopped playing games and just came out with it."

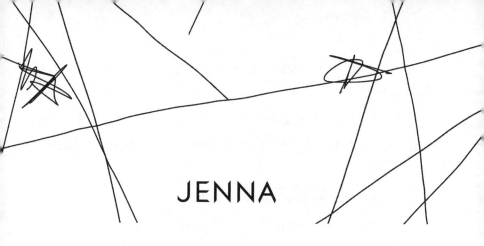

JENNA

I LOOK UP AS THE DOOR TO MR. JAIN'S OFFICE OPENS AND MOUSE STUMBLES PAST A MAN WAITING TO GO IN. He turns when Mr. Jain calls his name, but I can't hear what the VP says. I can see its effect on Mouse, though, and my heart starts racing.

Mouse catches sight of me and gives me a look that's equal parts relief and dread. He slides into the seat beside me and wipes the sweat off his forehead. "Tell me you're not here about Miss Bailey, too."

I let my head fall back against the wall and groan. "Have you heard anything from Drew?"

He shakes his head and leans forward to look at the door to Mr. Barnes's office. "Do you think he's in there?"

I shoot him a look. "Do you really think they pegged the two of us but figured Drew was too squeaky clean to be involved?"

"This is impossible," he says, turning toward me. "There is absolutely *no way* they could have guessed it was us. Not in a million years."

"What do you mean *guessed it was us*? Mouse—what did you do?"

"No! God, no! I mean, there's no way they could have guessed that we had the photos, not that we posted them. Because we didn't. Post them, I mean."

"You are not making me feel confident here."

He rubs his forehead. "Let's think about this logically. Photos get posted from an anonymous Twitter account, linking to an anonymous blog. Drew and I checked the blog out thoroughly— there was no personal information provided by the owner at all. Unless the office has some other information, there's no way they could have come up with our names as being related to this in any way. Which means we have to ask: What else do they know?"

"What else *is* there to know?"

"It had to be Drew, Jen."

"What? What happened to all the speeches this morning in the parking lot about us sticking together? You spend ten minutes with a VP and you're willing to sell Drew out?"

"I'm not selling anyone out. But we have to consider that one of us must have messed up somehow. I know it wasn't me, and I seriously doubt it was you. Think: Out of the three of us, who's the dumb jock?"

I take a deep breath and think about what he's suggesting. "Are you saying that you think he posted the photos? Or that he somehow gave us away?"

"Does it matter? If they find out we're Tom Anderson, it won't matter who posted the photos. They'll have all the information they need to destroy us."

I shake my head. "No. I don't buy it. Drew might be what you call a dumb jock, but he's savvier than the both of us combined when it comes to covering his tracks. I don't think he screwed up, and I really don't think he posted the photos. You heard him the other day: He was completely in favor of deleting the pictures."

A shadow passes over Mouse's face. "And yet the pictures still exist."

My jaw drops. "You think he saved them?"

Mouse looks like he's in pain. "I don't know *what* happened, Jen. I just think we need to—"

The door to Mr. Jain's office opens, and Mouse clamps his mouth shut. Mr. Jain strides out carrying a file folder, trailed by the man who went in earlier.

"He's an IT specialist," Mouse whispers.

Mr. Jain walks into Isaacs's office without knocking and closes the door behind them.

"An IT specialist? Like, a computer specialist?"

"Yes."

I turn to face him and drop my voice low. "Do we have anything to worry about, Mouse?"

Before he can answer, the door to Isaacs's office swings open, and all three of them walk to Mr. Barnes's office. I can feel Mouse shrinking lower and lower in his chair beside me.

Isaacs looks over at us and presses her lips together. I know she's not happy we've been talking. She says something to Mr. Jain and then knocks on Mr. Barnes's door.

"Enter!" a voice shouts from within the office.

"Sorry for interrupting," Isaacs says in a voice that sounds anything but sorry. "But Rakesh and I would like the three of us to confer a bit before continuing. Would you mind taking a seat outside, Andrew?"

My stomach flips over. Drew *is* in there.

Drew steps out of the office and nods at me with a look I can't decipher.

"Take a seat over there," Isaacs says, pointing to a chair just outside her office. "And Matthew, please move over here."

They shuffle over to their seats as Mr. Barnes emerges from his office. "And no talking!" he shouts. "Miss Singh, please ensure they don't talk."

"Of course, Mr. Barnes," Miss Singh replies.

"Anyone says a word, I want to hear about it."

They all disappear into Mr. Barnes's office and I search Drew's face for signs of worry. He's been the most confident all along, so I'm eager to know whether whatever happened in Barnes's office freaked him out.

Drew leans over and lifts the leg of his jeans, then pulls his cell phone out of his sock. He holds it up to the two of us and then starts tapping on the screen.

I pull my own phone out of the waistband of my jeans and wait for his message.

What the hell happened? How are we all here?

I look up and shake my head, letting him know that I have no idea. We both turn to face Mouse, who's staring at us blankly.

Check your phone, Drew mouths, waving his cell at Mouse.

Mouse shifts in his seat, looking uncomfortable.

Drew types something else into his phone and we hear a faint ping from a basket on the desk outside of Barnes's office.

"Are you fucking kidding me?" Drew says out loud, startling both Mouse and Miss Singh.

"Andrew!" Miss Singh exclaims. "You heard Mr. Barnes."

Drew lets his head drop back to thud against the wall. *You handed in your phone? Your actual phone?* he mouths.

Mouse squirms in his seat. "There's nothing on there," he whispers, while Drew holds his head in his hands.

"Go get it," Drew says quietly.

Mouse looks to me, fear in his eyes, and I shake my head at him. "No way," I whisper to Drew. "It's right outside Barnes's office. He'll get caught for sure."

"That's enough!" Miss Singh hisses. "If you keep talking, you're going to get *me* in trouble, too."

Drew sighs and closes his eyes slowly, then leans forward in his chair. "How are we supposed to communicate if we don't all have phones?" he asks, as low as he can.

"We're not," Mouse whispers grimly as the door to Barnes's office opens. "I think that's the whole point."

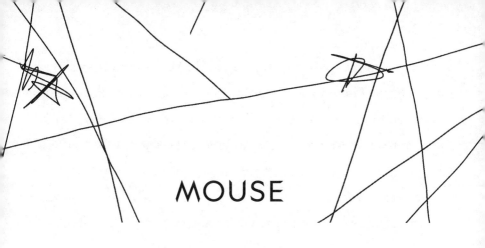

MOUSE

"COME IN, MATTHEW," MR. JAIN SAYS, WITH A SMILE THAT MAKES MY STOMACH HURT.

He turns to the IT specialist. "Thank you, Mr. Campbell. You've been most helpful."

Mr. Campbell nods his head and looks at me pityingly before heading out of the office. My mind stumbles over itself trying to figure out what he might have found.

Mr. Jain shuts the door behind me and motions for me to sit down. He sits and places the file folder he's been holding in the middle of his desk, lining up its edges so that it's perfectly centered.

"There are two ways we can go about this, Matthew. I can go over the evidence I have in here," he says, resting his fingertips on the folder. "Or you can be straight with me. The first option will take more time and effort and will not put me in a very forgiving mood. The second option will show me that you have remorse about what happened and that you're willing to work with us. Which will it be?"

I close my eyes and try to think. What could possibly be in there? There's no way anything on the dating site could be traced to us, and the cell phone was a burner phone with a SIM card that doesn't even exist anymore. He's got to be bluffing. I open my eyes and take in the impatient look on his face. If he had real evidence, he'd have shown me already. Mr. Jain doesn't strike me as the kind of guy who'd pass up the chance to show off.

Still, they've somehow managed to track down the three of us in record time, so there must be *something* out there. If I give him nothing, then I'll look as guilty as everyone else if they have something on us. But what can I give him? Anything I say will implicate me, too. And if we admit to being Tom Anderson, this little incident will blow up into something huge.

"I'm sorry, sir," I say, with genuine regret. "I wish I had some information for you. I'd love to help you catch whoever posted those pictures of Miss Bailey, but I truly don't know anything."

Mr. Jain presses his lips into a tight line and sighs. "I was afraid you'd say that. All right, then. Let's begin."

He opens the file folder, and I lean forward to see its contents.

"Miss Bailey was kind enough to give us access to all her correspondences over the last month. Emails, private messages, texts . . . everything."

I squirm in my seat but keep my expression neutral.

"As you're already aware, an email was sent to Mr. Fischer, our principal, at six o'clock this morning."

"I wasn't—"

"Does this email look familiar?" He hands me a printout and I scan it quickly.

Dear Mr. Fischer:

Later today, you will find that compromising photographs of one of your teachers, Miss Bailey, have been posted online. If you'd like to see them, you can find them by clicking the link at the end of this email. I have information about the person responsible for this, but I can't give it to you directly without causing a lot of trouble for myself. If you want to find out what happened, start with Jenna Bradley and Andrew Wilson. They know everything you need to know to catch the culprit.

"I-I'm not even mentioned in this email," I say, lowering it onto my lap to hide that my hands are shaking. "How would I know anything about it?"

"When we received the email, we took it to Miss Bailey to look for connections between Jenna and Andrew. She confirmed that they've been working together on a group project and that you are the third member of that group. Which got me thinking. If this email referred to the members of your group, why would your name be left out? Unless you were the one who sent it . . ."

"I'm not an idiot, Mr. Jain. How stupid would I have to be to point to the other members of my group but leave my own name off? Have you considered that maybe I'm being framed? That whoever . . ." I check the name of the sender. " . . . *anonymouslyyours536@gmail.com* is, maybe they wanted you to *think* I was involved?"

"Of course, Matthew. I'm not an idiot, either." He pulls another sheet of paper out of the folder. "This is the email you sent to Miss Bailey the night before the group project was assigned. I had our IT specialist take a look at both messages. Did you know that there's all kinds of information embedded in the header of an email? Including the IP address of the sender."

"But I didn't . . ." I take the sheet of paper he's offering me and see an email sent from my account.

Miss Bailey:

According to the course schedule, you will be assigning the group projects tomorrow. I know from fellow students who've taken your class in the past that you will assign the groups and group leaders.

I know we didn't get off to a very good start, but I really want the opportunity to prove to you how seriously I take your course. Please do me the honor of allowing me to be a group leader.

I would also very much like to work with Andrew Wilson and Jenna Bradley. Our friendships have been strained in the last year, and I would like the opportunity to work with them and repair those relationships.

I know I'm asking a lot, but I'm hoping you will put your trust in me. I'm a very conscientious student, and I think that together the three of us could produce a truly great assignment that will make you proud.

Sincerely,
Matthew Maguire

"I didn't send this, Mr. Jain," I say, panic making my voice break. "This email wasn't from me."

"I assumed you might say that, given that you're smart enough to have put the pieces together already. The email to the principal is from the same IP address as the email you sent Miss Bailey. Which means you *have* information for us but you're afraid of sharing it."

"No!" I tell him. "I can prove it. I didn't even have my laptop the night before the project was assigned! I lent it to Jenna. Ask her."

"That would be quite the alibi, Mr. Maguire . . . *if* your laptop was the only way for you to send an email. As I said, I'm not an idiot."

I crumple the sheets in my hands. "You have to believe me. I didn't send either of these emails. I think someone is trying to set me up."

Mr. Jain shakes his head at me. "I'm very disappointed to hear you say that, Matthew. I'd hoped you would be more willing to assist in the investigation. You have to know that your lies do not help your situation at all."

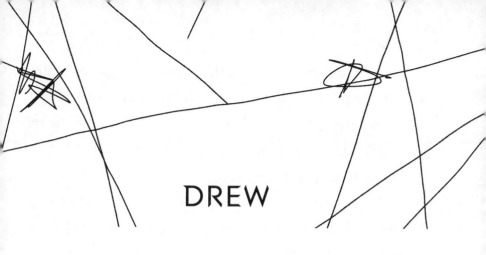

DREW

"LISTEN, WILSON, IT'S PRETTY OBVIOUS WHAT'S HAP-PENING HERE. You kids got carried away. It happens. I'm not out to crucify you. I'm trying to *help* you. I was a kid once, too. But I can't help you if I don't know what we're dealing with. So why don't you start at the beginning and tell me exactly what happened?"

Barnes has his pen gripped in his sausage fingers, eyebrows knit together in anticipation. This joker seriously thinks I'll hand him the scoop. He actually thinks I'd be stupid enough to trust him.

"The beginning?" I ask, fucking with him. "Like, when this all started?"

"Exactly. When it all started." His eyes flash with excitement, and I can tell that he's all pumped up, imagining himself as the one to crack the case. What a loser.

"Well," I say quietly, looking behind me at the door like I'm afraid someone will overhear. "When I woke up this morning, there were about twenty new notifications on my phone telling me that something went down on Twitter during the night."

Barnes's eyes go hazy, and I can tell that he's trying to figure out why I'm starting with the ending.

"So I opened up Twitter and saw that someone who goes by @yrwrstnitemare tweeted out the link everyone's talking about. I checked out the photos, texted a few friends, and then came to school."

"And . . ."

"And that's it. That's how it started. For me, at least."

Realization dawns in his beady little eyes. "And at what point did you create the Twitter account?"

"My Twitter account? I've had it for years."

"No. The @yrwrstnitemare account."

"That's not mine."

"I think it is."

I shrug. "What can I say? You think wrong."

"Well, then, why don't you tell me whose it is?"

I laugh. "That's the million-dollar question today, Mr. Barnes. Everyone wants to know that—teachers and students. And I really wish I knew, because I'd like to buy that guy a beer, if you know what I mean."

"You'd have to buy him that beer in jail, Mr. Wilson. This is no laughing matter."

"I don't think they let you buy beer in jail, Mr. Barnes," I deadpan. "Not that I've ever been in jail. But from what I've seen on TV, it's not really something they sell there."

Mr. Barnes's left eye starts to twitch, and I have to cough into my hand to hide my smile.

"You think you're so slick, Wilson, but we know a lot more than you think we do."

"Is that so?"

"The name Tom Anderson mean anything to you?" he asks, sneering at me.

"Nope."

"So, you didn't impersonate him to convince Miss Bailey to send you pictures of herself."

"Nope."

"Of course not. Tell me, do you think Matthew and Jenna are your friends?"

I shrug and sit back in my chair. "More like acquaintances."

"Then you won't feel betrayed when you find out that they've turned on you?"

I give him a wide smile that I know will frustrate the hell out of him. Barnes thinks he's so smart, but he's just a third-rate former gym teacher who couldn't handle working with kids and so became a VP. His bad-cop routine is embarrassing. "I guess I'd be worried *if* there was anything for them to reveal about me. But since I'm innocent, I'm not even a little bit worried."

Barnes's eyes light up. "God, I was hoping you'd say that,

'cause I'm going to enjoy taking you down a peg or two." He waves a sheet of paper in my face. "Want to see the email that your pal Matthew sent the principal this morning? Your name is in it and everything."

I snatch the page out of his hand and read it. *What the hell?* "Mouse didn't send this."

"No? What makes you so sure?"

"It's a fake email address and probably a fake email. Did you whip this up on your computer while we were sitting outside?"

Barnes's face goes red. "That guy who was in here with us before? Computer specialist. Matched this email to others your buddy has sent. It was from Matthew, all right. And it seems he's pretty eager to pin things on you. What do you want to bet he's in Mr. Jain's office right now, singing like a canary?"

"He's got nothing to sing about," I say, with more confidence than I feel. "So again, I'm not worried."

"And what about Jenna? You don't think she wants to see you nailed for posting naked pictures of someone? She went through something similar last year and I'll bet she'd just love to see justice served."

"I'm positive she wants the person responsible caught. But since I'm not that person—"

"Let me guess . . . you're not worried."

"That's right."

"And would you be worried if I told you that Jenna has confirmed that you were the one to get the photos from Miss Bailey?"

"I'd be extremely worried—because it would mean she was lying."

"Well now, this is some coincidence. It seems *everyone* is lying but you. Good thing we can move forward based on the information they've already given us."

He's bluffing. I know he's bluffing.

"So, before I start writing all this up, are you sure there's nothing you want to tell me? Because the more you cooperate now, the less likely Mr. Fischer will be inclined to involve the police."

I bite my lip and look out the window, faking like I'm taking his advice seriously. Barnes is a fool. There's no way I'm gonna be outsmarted by a balding loser who lives off donuts and coffee.

"Gee, Mr. Barnes . . . since you put it that way . . ."

He leans forward in his chair, practically drooling all over his desk.

"I'd have to say . . . nope."

"You're an idiot, Wilson," he tells me. "Your friends are hanging you out to dry and you're stupid enough to believe that they'll stay loyal to you. You're a high-profile student athlete involved in a case of online harassment of a teacher. You think the police won't make an example of you? Not only will you go down for this, but you'll go down hard, and you'll go down publicly. Your face will be in all the papers, son. And this will be the legacy you leave here. Think about that."

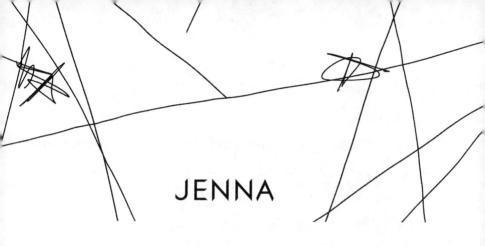

JENNA

I GET UP TO PACE AGAIN, EARNING ANOTHER PLEAD-ING LOOK FROM MISS SINGH. I can tell I'm making her nervous, but I have too much pent-up energy to just sit here and do nothing.

Both Mouse and Drew got called back into their VPs' offices more than twenty minutes ago, but I've been left out here by myself, with no word from Isaacs at all. I'm dying to know what's happening in there.

The door to Barnes's office opens and I fling myself back into my chair. The last thing I need is Barnes freaking out over me wandering around. It's Drew who emerges, though, and the dark look on his face makes my heart beat faster.

I pull out my phone and text him: *What's happening?*

He sits outside of Barnes's office and scowls at the screen of his phone before responding. *What did you tell them?*

I flick my eyes up to him, surprised to see the distrust on his face. *Nothing. I've been sitting here this whole time.*

He puts his phone in his lap and rubs his forehead. When he looks up again, he's focused on a spot over my head, a faraway look in his eyes.

I check to make sure Miss Singh isn't looking and then scoot over to a chair closer to him. "What's wrong?" I whisper.

"Barnes says you told them that I was the one who got the photos of Bailey," he says quietly.

My eyes widen in surprise. "I absolutely did not. I told Isaacs that I don't know anything about the photos."

A muscle in his jaw jumps and he blows out an exasperated breath. "They know things they couldn't possibly know, Jen. And if you didn't say anything, then there's only one other explanation." He looks pointedly toward Mr. Jain's office.

"Mouse? No. No way," I say firmly, catching Miss Singh's attention. She clears her throat and glances at the chair I'm supposed to be sitting in.

I move back and smile sweetly at her, waiting for her to turn back to her computer screen before texting Drew. *He'd be implicating himself by saying anything about you getting the photos.*

He frowns at his phone screen and then responds, *Think about it. He's a genius, right? He's smart enough to know that the office is onto us and that the best way for him to weasel out of any responsibility is to turn the blame onto me. And you.*

Me?

There's an email. Barnes showed me. Mouse emailed the principal early this morning and mentioned your name and mine. I think he's setting us up.

I look up and meet his eyes. "That doesn't make sense," I whisper, stifling a groan as Miss Singh looks over at us. She starts to say something, but is interrupted by the office phone ringing. I sneak a peek at Drew while she answers it and see that he's slipped his cell phone back into his sock.

" . . . Yes, I have them right here," Miss Singh says, glancing at a stack of papers on her desk. "But I can't really leave the office right now." She presses her lips together and looks at Mr. Barnes's door. " . . . Yes." Her shoulders slump. "Five minutes. I'll be right there."

She hangs up the phone and shoots a worried look at me. "I have to run to the Guidance office for just a moment," she says sternly. "I'm going to be *right back*. No talking. Please." She snatches up the papers from her desk and hurries out the door.

I don't even wait for the office door to swing shut before sliding into the chair next to Drew. "It can't be true," I say. "If that email was sent early this morning, then that's what tipped off the office. That wouldn't be Mouse panicking and covering his tracks . . . that would be him turning us in, and that doesn't make any sense."

"Unless he posted the pictures and then framed us for it."

"This is *Mouse* we're talking about. He's afraid of his own shadow, and he has his dream-college admission on the line. Why would he take a risk like that? And he would never implicate me." I tilt my head at him. "You, maybe. But not me."

"You think Barnes is making up the email?" he asks me. "Because I thought that, too. But then, how else would they know to come after us? And how would they know that *I'm* the one who asked Bailey for the photos?"

"I don't know," I concede. I bite my thumbnail and think about how Mouse hinted that Drew might have saved copies of Bailey's photos. "I also don't know how any of this is even possible. I deleted those photos myself. How is it that they're up on the Internet right now?"

I hold my breath and wait for his answer.

"Shit," he mutters, scuffing the toe of his shoe against the floor. "I didn't want to tell you this, but Mouse saved them to his database."

"His what?"

"His database. He designed a database for storing pictures . . . last year. And he saved Bailey's photos on there."

"How do you know that?"

He grimaces and gives me a guilty look. "Because I told him to."

"You guys are *idiots*," I hiss. "So, it could be either one of you, really."

"No. It wasn't me."

"Let's look at this logically for a minute. Who does it make more sense posted the photos . . . you, who has a history of soliciting naked pictures of girls, or Mouse, who's never done anything wrong in his life?"

"First, what makes you think I have a history of *soliciting naked pictures*, and secondly, you're wrong about Mouse."

"He told me about the competition," I say, making him suck in a sharp breath. "I know all about how the team collected photos of our classmates."

"And I suppose he neglected to tell you that he designed and managed the database that stored those photos?"

Now it's my turn to look shocked. "No!"

"Yep. The team paid him five hundred dollars for his efforts."

I slump down in my chair. "I feel like I don't know either one of you."

"It's him, Jen. I'm telling you, we can't trust him."

"But why would he post the photos? That's what I can't wrap my mind around."

Drew looks out the window while he thinks. "What does Mouse want more than anything else right now? Money and grades. Maybe he was blackmailing Bailey for one or both of those things."

I roll my eyes at him. "Then he'd be shooting himself in the foot by posting the photos online, wouldn't he? Blackmailing involves *threatening* to do something like that unless the other person pays up. What would he have to hold over her if he'd already posted all of the pictures?"

Drew shrugs. "Maybe she refused to pay. Or maybe he posted them to show her he was serious and then demanded money before taking them down. Who knows what's going on in that twisted little brain of his."

I drag my hands through my hair and think about what Drew's saying. He makes a compelling case, but then, he's an experienced player and has a vested interest in bringing me onto his side.

I jump as the door to Isaacs's office whips open.

"Jenna," Isaacs says sharply, looking between me and Drew. "I thought Mr. Barnes instructed you not to talk to one another."

I lift one of my shoulders in a shrug and meet her eyes.

"Come in, please," she tells me. "We have a lot to discuss."

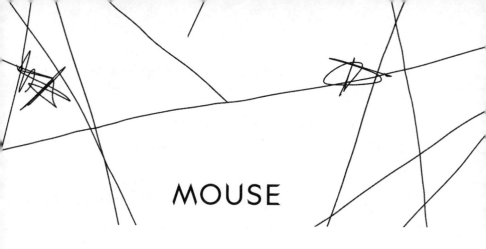

MOUSE

"LET'S GO OVER THIS AGAIN," MR. JAIN SAYS, TAKING A LONG SIP FROM A GLASS OF WATER ON HIS DESK. I lick my dry lips and try to focus.

"May I go get a drink?" I ask.

"When we're finished here," he says, not even bothering to look up from the file folder in front of him.

I sigh and sit back in my chair. "We've been over and over this," I say, unable to hide my irritation. "How many different ways do you want me to say that I didn't write the emails and I don't know anything about the photos."

"Let's try a different approach, then," he says calmly, looking up at me. "Why don't you tell me what you know about Tom Anderson."

Before I can stop myself, I feel my eyes widen and my mouth drop open.

"I see you recognize the name."

"N-no. I was just surprised by the change in topic," I say weakly. "Who's Tom Anderson? Does he go to school here?"

The corner of Mr. Jain's mouth turns up in a smirk. "In a manner of speaking."

"I . . . I don't understand what you mean."

"That's not what your friends say," he challenges.

"What friends?"

"Indeed. I'd hardly call them friends myself. Let's say acquaintances, then. The acquaintances you've managed to get yourself into trouble with."

I shake my head. "I've never heard of anyone named Tom Anderson."

Mr. Jain nods his head slowly and closes the file folder. "I don't think you fully appreciate the seriousness of what's happening here."

I keep my face blank and will myself not to break eye contact. A bead of sweat tracks down my back, but I refuse to let him see how nervous he's making me.

"You mentioned earlier that you hope to attend MIT in the fall, correct?"

"I *will* be attending MIT," I tell him. "I've already been accepted."

"I see. Congratulations."

I shift in my seat.

"You do understand that MIT is located in the United States, right?"

"Yes . . ."

"And do you realize that you can be turned away at the border if you have a criminal record?"

"What?"

"You can be denied entry to the United States if you have a criminal record." He turns his computer monitor to face me and reads from the screen. "A Canadian citizen can be denied entry if they have a conviction for a crime of moral turpitude." He leans forward and rests his elbows on his desk. "Now, I'm not a lawyer, but I'm guessing that creating a fake online identity, soliciting salacious pictures of a teacher, and then posting those pictures online *might* qualify as a crime of moral turpitude. What do you think?"

I think I'm going to be sick, that's what I think. I read through the text on his computer screen and struggle for breath. I haven't worked this hard to get turned away at the border for something stupid. I hear my dad's voice telling me how proud he is, and I have to swallow down the vomit rising in my throat. My life will be over if this gets out.

"And that's if MIT doesn't just revoke your acceptance preemptively, given your legal troubles." Mr. Jain takes in my panic-stricken face and softens his tone. "As I said before, I don't think this was all you. But I do think you have information. You tell us what you know, and we can work to protect you."

I sit back in my chair, thinking hard. "Can I talk to Jenna for a minute?"

"Absolutely not." Mr. Jain turns his monitor back to face him. "Don't take this for a joke, Matthew. This is a serious investigation, and you'll not be permitted to coordinate your statement with the others'."

"That's not . . ."

"Listen. The clock is ticking on this offer. If one of your friends provides information before you do, then all deals are off." He looks at his watch. "I have some work to attend to. Why don't you take ten minutes to think about my offer and then we'll talk again."

I get up to leave the office.

"Sit down. You can stay right there and think things through." He starts typing on his computer. "I'll let you know when your ten minutes are up."

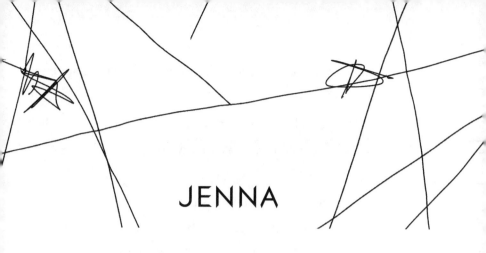

JENNA

"THIS IS QUITE THE MESS, JENNA," MRS. ISAACS SAYS
GRIMLY. "I'm not in the mood to play games with you today, so
I'm just going to come out and tell you—it's become clear that
either Matthew Maguire or Andrew Wilson, or both of them
together, posted Miss Bailey's photos online, and I'd like you to
help us prove it."

I bite my lip and consider Isaacs. She's looking me right in the
eye, and her normally fidgety hands are resting in her lap. She's
not bluffing.

"How do you know?"

She leans back in her chair. "There's a trail of evidence that
points to it. I'd rather not go into all the specifics right now."

"If you have a trail of evidence, then you don't need me. I
don't have anything. You're much more convinced it was them
than I am."

Isaacs places her hands on her desk and leans toward me. "Are
you really so sure? Do you honestly think that they're incapable of

this? I should think you'd be more skeptical, given what happened to you last year."

There's a tiny spark of the old anger, but it doesn't ignite. She's right, of course. Anyone is capable of anything.

"I just can't see either one of them doing this," I say.

Isaacs purses her lips. "And why is that?"

I shrug and choose my words carefully. "This isn't their style. I mean, I guess I could see them sharing pictures like that with their friends or whatever. But on Twitter? Anonymously? That doesn't sound like either one of them to me." I don't tell her that Drew's an egomaniac who'd want credit for posting pictures like that, or that Mouse is too scared of his own shadow . . . and his dad's wrath.

"People can surprise you, Jenna. I'd think you'd have learned that by now."

I clench my jaw at her tone.

"I guess that's true," I force out. "But you asked for my opinion and I gave it to you."

"I didn't ask for your opinion. I asked for information. There's a difference." She looks past me and motions for someone to come into her office.

I sit back in my chair, expecting one of the other VPs to interrupt us. So, when I hear Miss Bailey's voice, my heart seizes.

"I'm sorry to interrupt," Bailey says hesitantly. "You wanted to see me?"

"Yes, please come in," Isaacs says gently. "Jenna and I were just discussing what happened last night, and I'm hoping she might have some information that will help us."

I look down at my feet as Miss Bailey passes. I don't want to see her. Just the sound of her voice is making it hard to breathe.

"I know you have no reason to want to help me," Bailey says in a hollow voice. "But it would—" Her voice catches and I feel my face flame red.

I'm not prepared for this.

"It would mean the world to me," she finishes, a little sob escaping her. I look up for a fleeting second and the expression on her face undoes me. In that instant, she's not Miss Bailey, the teacher—she's me. My heart stutters and my vision goes hazy. I grab my bag and run, unable to see through the tears in my eyes.

The next thing I know, I'm at the front of the school, gulping air. Last year crashes over me like a wave, and I drop onto my knees. The look in Bailey's eyes. The resignation and the shame and the crushing humiliation.

I rake my hands through my hair and squeeze my eyes shut. I need to *focus*.

"Jenna?"

I look up to find Isaacs approaching cautiously. "I'm so sorry. Are you all right?"

I sit back against the wall of the school, too drained to respond.

Isaacs sits down beside me, her black dress pants getting marked up with the salt the custodians use to melt the ice on the walkway. "I shouldn't have brought Miss Bailey in. I didn't think about how difficult that would be for you." She shakes her head and looks up at the sky. "I'm messing this whole thing up. Don't think I don't know that."

I swallow hard and wipe any remnants of tears off my face.

Isaacs leans forward and stares at my arm. "What is that?"

I startle and look down at where the sleeve of my sweater has ridden up to expose the bandage on my forearm. "It's nothing."

"Raise your sleeve, please," Isaacs says, emotion making her voice hitch.

I ease my sleeve up over the bandage. "It's not what you think."

"What I think," she says sadly, "is that this is all too much for you. Have you been cutting?"

"No! Of course not." I pull my sleeve back down and glare at her. "I'm not self-destructive."

She searches my face and then sighs. "You know, I took this job because I wanted to *help* people. Not hurt them." She looks back at my arm. "Things are so much harder than I thought they'd be. So much more complicated . . ."

I look at her, sitting on the ground with me, and I can almost see the person she must have been when she started out. Someone who wanted to change the lives of kids like me, before she got mired down in all the crap that goes on in a school and got distracted from her goals.

I give my head a shake. *I'm* not going to get distracted. Not by Isaacs and her regrets, or by Bailey and her humiliation.

"I'm ready," I say, standing up and dusting off my jeans.

Isaacs looks up at me, confused. "Ready for what?"

"To finish this," I say, as she scrambles to her feet. "I can give you what you need."

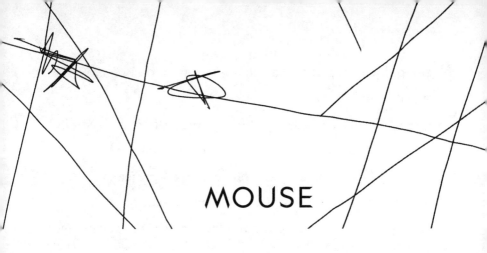

MOUSE

MY THOUGHTS ARE INTERRUPTED BY A KNOCK ON THE
DOOR.

"Come in," Mr. Jain calls, waving in an excited-looking Mrs.
Isaacs. She purses her lips at the sight of me but can't hold back
her smile when she looks at Mr. Jain. "We have what we need," she
says. "We can meet in my office and then call the two gentlemen
in shortly."

The two gentlemen?

"What about Jenna?" I ask, before I can stop myself.

Mrs. Isaacs raises her eyebrows at me but ignores my question.
"Would you prefer to have Matthew wait in here? Or outside your
office?"

Mr. Jain sizes me up. "Outside, I think." He stands and motions
for me to leave the room. "We'll let you know when we're ready
for you."

I stagger to a chair outside his office, wondering what *we have
what we need* could possibly mean. I look up to see Drew scowl-

ing at me from outside of Mr. Barnes's office, and I regret all over again that I gave my cell phone to Miss Singh.

"What's going on?" I whisper to him.

"I'd better not say anything," he snaps at me. "Wouldn't want you emailing the principal about it."

"But I didn't—"

The door to Mrs. Isaacs's office opens, and Jenna emerges, trailed closely by her VP. "Thank you, Jenna," Mrs. Isaacs says, giving her a quick hug. "Now promise me you'll get that arm looked at."

"Sure," Jenna says, pretending like we're not even there.

What did she do?

"Jen," Drew says. "What's—"

"Leave her be," Mrs. Isaacs snaps. "I need the two of you in my office now." She walks Jenna as far as Miss Singh's desk and then watches her leave the office before turning back to us. "Now."

We both get up and file into her office, where we find our stern-looking vice principals and a visibly upset Miss Bailey.

"Gentlemen. I assume you know why we've called you in here together," Mr. Jain says.

I can't even think, I'm so nervous. Why did Jenna leave? And why are Drew and I both in the office? If it was Drew who posted the pictures, then I should get to leave, too . . .

"Do you need more information from me?" I ask, wiping my forehead with the back of my hand. "I can answer any questions you have, but I don't think it's appropriate for Drew and me to be in here together."

"A bit late to suddenly have answers," Mr. Jain says, resting a hand on Miss Bailey's shoulder. Miss Bailey, whose bloodshot eyes are narrowed at me.

"If we could just have a moment alone, Mr. Jain . . ."

"To do what?" Drew asks. "To try and blame all this on me? No way. It wasn't me, and it obviously wasn't Jenna, so that pretty much leaves you."

"Gentlemen," Mrs. Isaacs interrupts. "If you'll answer a few more questions, I'm quite certain we can conclude our investigation. I'm sure you'll both be cooperative and honest with us, correct?"

"Of course," Drew says, knocking his shoe against mine. "We have nothing to hide, do we, Mouse?"

"Good," says Mrs. Isaacs. "Then let's proceed. Which of the two of you was the one to find Miss Bailey's profile on the dating site and come up with the idea to create a fake profile to contact her?"

"That was Jenna!" Drew says excitedly, looking over at Miss Bailey. "Jenna saw you checking the site the day she asked you for the presentation outline after school."

Miss Bailey shakes her head at the VPs.

"That's what happened, right, Mouse?"

I nod. "That's exactly how it happened."

"And that might sound convincing, except Miss Bailey was

quite open with us about the fact that she occasionally checked her profile at school *last year*, but after Troy Maguire caught her looking at it one day, she stopped accessing it at school," Mrs. Isaacs says.

"No offense, Miss Bailey," Drew says, "but I don't think you were being quite honest about that."

Mr. Barnes points his finger at Drew menacingly. "Enough. We had the IT tech check it out, and it's true. Miss Bailey hasn't visited that site on a school computer this year."

Drew shrugs, looking surprisingly calm. "So what? So Troy saw the site and told his girlfriend about it. Still doesn't mean Jenna wasn't the one to show us."

"Except that Jenna and Troy were no longer speaking at that time," Mrs. Isaacs points out. "So, which is more likely: that Troy called up his ex-girlfriend to tell her he saw Miss Bailey on a dating site or that he told his best friend?"

Drew shakes his head, and I look back and forth between them. This doesn't make any *sense*. I was sitting right there that day. I remember Jenna telling us what happened.

"Let's move along," Mrs. Isaacs says, pulling a laptop out of the top drawer of her desk. "Do either of you recognize this laptop?" She opens the screen and turns the computer toward us.

"That's mine," Drew says in surprise. "Where did you get that?"

"That's unimportant at this time," Mr. Jain says. "Please log in for us."

Drew looks at the laptop and then at the door.

"Log in, Wilson!" Mr. Barnes says. "Quit stalling."

Drew gives his head a little shake and regains his composure. "I'm not stalling. Just confused." He reaches over and types in his password. "I have nothing to hide."

I let out the breath I didn't realize I was holding. Of course, Drew wouldn't have saved anything incriminating on his laptop. He's smarter than that.

Mrs. Isaacs turns the computer back around and we can hear the click of the track pad as she explores the contents of his computer.

"This is an invasion of privacy, isn't it?" Drew asks casually. "I didn't give you permission to go through all my files."

Mr. Jain leans over the computer and points at something. After a few more clicks, Mrs. Isaacs exchanges a look with him and then types something on the keyboard.

"What are you doing?" Drew asks, standing up to get a better look.

"We'll discuss that in a moment," Mr. Jain says. "But first we have another device that needs identifying." He pulls a familiar-looking cell phone out of his jacket pocket. "Miss Singh identifies this as the cell phone you turned in when you came into the office, Matthew. Is that correct?"

"I . . . I think so."

He hands the phone to me. "Please take a look and make sure it's yours."

I unlock the phone and open my photos and notes. "Yes. This is mine."

I'm not sure what he's getting at. I've never saved anything related to Miss Bailey on this phone, and there's nothing at all that could get me in trouble with the office.

"Where did you get this phone?" Mr. Jain asks.

I can feel Drew shift in the chair beside me, sending me a silent warning not to mention his cell-phone business. "My parents gave it to me."

"Is that so?" Mr. Jain asks. "Because we spoke with your father earlier today, asking about this phone, and he told us that you don't currently have a cell phone because he confiscated it weeks ago. Is that true?"

My stomach plummets, and I look to Drew for help.

"Y-yes, that's true. I bought this phone from someone here at school."

"And who would that be?"

"It's not important," I rush out. "I just . . . I needed a cell phone. You know how it is."

"An untraceable cell phone," Mrs. Isaacs says, making it sound like I'm a criminal.

"No! It wasn't like that. I just needed a phone, that's all."

"Miss Bailey," Mr. Jain says. "Do you have your cell phone on you?"

"Yes."

"And do you have the contact information saved for the person you sent your photos to?"

Her face reddens, and she nods her head.

"Please call that number now."

She taps at the screen of her phone and then looks up as my cell phone starts to ring.

"But that's . . . that's impossible," I say, staring at the phone. The SIM card for Tom Anderson's phone got destroyed. Cut in two and then flushed down the toilet. Unless . . .

"She swapped the SIM cards," I tell Drew, remembering how Jenna slipped the card into her pocket and then fished it back out, so we could destroy it. "She must have had a spare one. That's the one we destroyed."

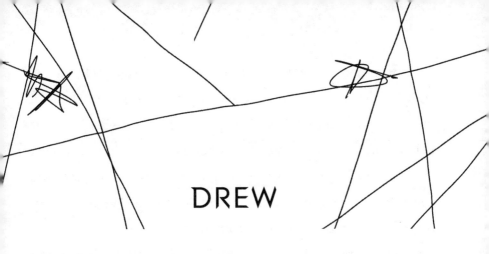

DREW

I BLINK STUPIDLY AT MOUSE, UNABLE TO MAKE SENSE OF WHAT'S HAPPENING. "What do you mean, she swapped the SIM cards?" For the first time all day, I feel panic climbing up my spine.

"Think about it. My phone was out there in that basket this whole time. She must have snuck Tom Anderson's SIM card into it while we were talking to our VPs."

"That's enough of that talk," Mrs. Isaacs says. "You'll have a hard time convincing us there's a conspiracy against the two of you. Especially given the emails we just forwarded from your account, Andrew."

"Emails?" I ask, my stomach roiling. My laptop was in my locker and now it's here. And Jenna swapped the SIM cards and made it look like . . .

Isaacs turns to Miss Bailey. "Thank you for assisting us," she says gently. "There's no reason for you to have to sit through any more of this."

The minute Miss Bailey leaves, Isaacs turns back to me. "Emails. From the Gmail account in your mail folder. Detailed messages exchanged between the two of you, discussing your plans to save Miss Bailey's photos behind Jenna's back and post them online." She swivels the computer screen toward me, and there in my email program is a Gmail account I've never seen before, registered to *andrewwilsonxxx@gmail.com*.

"She created a whole account," I tell Mouse, clicking on a message. "And one for you, too. She must have imported the account into my mail sometime this morning."

"Quit blaming the girl and accept that you've been caught," Barnes barks at me.

Mouse and I exchange a look. If she faked a SIM card *and* an email conversation, how long was she planning this? I think back to how she talked Mouse into taking Bailey's course. "How did she know we'd end up in the same group?" I ask him.

"The email," he says, his face turning a shade of green I didn't think was possible. "She impersonated me and requested that we all work together."

Mr. Jain claps his hands slowly, startling us out of our conversation. "This is a fine performance, gentlemen, but we're not buying it. You're both looking at some very serious consequences. The principal is on the phone with the police at the moment, and we'll be calling your parents soon, too. Is there anything either of you would like to say before we meet with Mr. Fischer to discuss next steps?"

Mouse looks at me, but I shake my head at him. Anything we say now will just make things worse.

The VPs get up to leave. "Stay in here, please, gentlemen," Mr. Jain says, closing the door behind him.

"We have to *do* something," Mouse hisses, the minute the door clicks shut. "She can't get away with this."

I look out Mrs. Isaacs's window and see Jenna walking across the front of the school toward a familiar-looking car. A beat-up Ford Focus that my best friend bought with the insurance money he got after his girlfriend lit his truck on fire.

Troy.

Troy, who knows my locker combination and my computer passwords. Troy, who supposedly hasn't spoken to Jenna in more than a year.

Jenna climbs into the passenger seat of the car, and the last of my hope vanishes.

"You were right all along, Mouse," I tell him. "She knew it was us. And so did Troy."

Mouse drops his head into his hands as my phone starts to vibrate against my leg. I pull it out of my sock and see an unfamiliar number.

"Hello?" I answer.

"You were right," Jenna's voice says. "These burner phones are a great idea."

"Who is this?" I ask, just to make her say it.

"I'm *your worst nightmare*, Drew. I'm a girl who fights back."

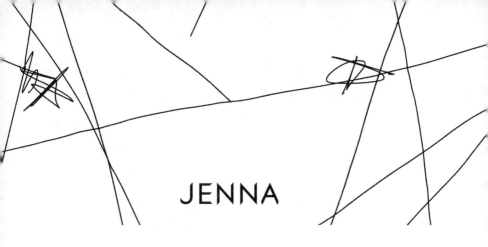

JENNA

"EVERYTHING GO ACCORDING TO PLAN?" TROY ASKS AS I HANG UP THE PHONE.

"Perfectly," I tell him. "They're calling the police right now."

"So, we're not a secret anymore?"

"Not even a little bit," I say, leaning in for a kiss. "Thank you for letting me handle this my way."

I feel his smile against my lips. "Like I had a choice," he murmurs.

I pull back, laughing, and give him a little shove. "I'm being serious here. I know you would have dealt with this differently, and I appreciate you stepping back and trusting me."

He shrugs and pulls out of the school parking lot. "You're right about that—I'd have beat the shit out of both of them. But it was your battle to fight." He reaches for my hand as he merges into traffic. "You sure you're OK? No regrets?"

"No regrets," I tell him, pushing away the memories that threaten to undo my resolve—Miss Bailey's tearstained face, Mouse's shock, and Drew's hurt. Instead, I fortify myself with other memories: Miss Bailey shaming me for making the exact same decision she'd make a year later, Mouse and Drew lying to my face about not posting my photos, and Mrs. Isaacs telling me there was no way to decisively uncover who was responsible.

If there's one thing I've learned in the last year, it's that there are different rules for different people. I tried to get justice the straightforward way, but no one would listen to me. Everyone gave up. So, I found a way to make sure that justice was served. Instead of drowning in the shame and frustration I felt, I used my mother's strategy of rising up and taking control. The system failed me, so I found a way of taking what was broken about the system and making it work to my advantage.

Of course, it sucks that along the way, Miss Bailey had to experience a taste of what I went through. But she'll get justice for what happened to her. She'll get the closure that comes with seeing someone held accountable for wronging her. And, by proxy, I'll finally get the same thing.

Troy pulls up to a stoplight and turns to face me. "So, are you finally going to show me this now?" he asks, resting his hand lightly over the bandage on my arm.

I pull up my sleeve and ease the tape off the bottom edge of the bandage, peering underneath. It's just as incredible as I remember. "Are you ready?"

I rip off the bandage in one quick and painful motion and watch as his eyes widen in amazement.

"J.J.," he says. "It's beautiful."

"My mom did it," I tell him, inspecting it closely. It's a tattoo of a butterfly that looks as though it's perched on my inner forearm, ready to take flight.

"I'm surprised," he says as the light goes green. "I thought you hated butterflies."

"I used to." I run my fingers over the still-tender skin and think about Mouse and Drew back in the office. "But that was before I learned more about them. Did you know that monarch butterflies are toxic to anything that tries to prey on them?"

ACKNOWLEDGMENTS

I'd first like to thank Mackenzie Brady Watson, literary agent extraordinaire. Mackenzie has championed this project since the day I first described it to her in a confusing rush over the phone, and her guidance and editorial feedback were instrumental in helping me craft a story out of those first excited ramblings. Mackenzie is a tireless advocate for her clients, and I can never thank her enough for how hard she worked to find the perfect home for this story.

I'd also like to thank Maggie Lehrman, Executive Editor at ABRAMS and Amulet Books. From my first conversation with Maggie, I was desperate to work with her. Her enthusiasm for *Easy Prey* bowled me over, and her insights and expertise brought this novel to a whole new level. From day one, I felt confident that *Easy Prey* was in the very best hands, and I am beyond grateful for the chance to work with, and learn from, such a talented editor.

Thank you to the entire team at ABRAMS and Amulet Books. I have felt welcomed and supported at every step of the way, and I appreciate all the hard work that has gone into transforming *Easy Prey* from a manuscript to a finished novel. Thank you to Penelope Cray, who copyedited the book, and to Erin Slonaker, who proofread it. Your attention to detail and expertise saved me many an embarrassing error, and your insightful comments improved the text immeasurably. Thank you also to Evangelos Vasilakis, the managing editor for *Easy Prey*, for overseeing this project and bringing everything together.

I am head over heels in love with the art design of this book. Thank you to art director Alyssa Nassner, to June Park, who designed the extraordinary cover, and to Siobhan Gallagher, who designed the interior. I am so grateful for all your hard work.

On the personal front, I owe thanks to the many people in my life who support my writing and who help me carve out the space and time needed to do this work that I love.

Thank you to my husband, Ernest Lo, who supports me in all things and celebrates my writing like no other. And to my children, Ethan and Mackenzie, who show enormous patience when I'm sequestered away with my computer, when I'm wandering through the house distracted by edits, and when I'm in grumpy deadline mode.

Thank you to my parents and to my sister and brother, Brianne and Chris. My love of books traces back to my childhood and the example our parents set, being avid readers themselves.

Thank you to my circle of friends who make me laugh, keep me sane, and answer all my neurotic texts. Andrea, Claire, Suzette, and Heather: I appreciate your friendship more than you know.

Thank you to all the students who have let me into their lives and shared their stories with me over the years. A special shout-out to the lunchtime crew in room 104—you know who you are! Keep reading, keep asking questions, and keep demanding more out of life. I believe in you, and I cannot wait to see the incredible things you will do in the future.

Thank you to my fellow authors in the Kidlit community. I have grown as an author and as a person through my friendships with all of you. The support and generosity of our community is unparalleled, and I am forever grateful for the advice and guidance you have so generously given me. The list is far too long to name every person I am thankful for, but I'd be remiss if I didn't single out the following people for their ongoing support: Laurie Elizabeth Flynn, Janet Taylor, Marisa Reichardt, Shannon Parker, Jennie K. Brown, Darcy Woods, Heidi Heilig, Jeff Zentner, Ashley Herring Blake, Sarah Glenn Marsh, Lindsay Eagar, and Brie Spangler, among others.

A huge thank you to the book bloggers and librarians who champion YA fiction and connect young readers with books. Thank you for the work you do.

And last but definitely not least, thank you, dear reader, for choosing this book and giving it the honor of your time and attention. I made this for you.